Praise for *The Bourbaki Gambit*

"A svelte tale, a fable of elite scientists nudged through mandatory retirement from a life of privilege into a modicum of self-examination." —*The New York Times Book Review*

"A scientist whose work has changed the very nature of modern society, Carl Djerassi is now making his mark on literature. *The Bourbaki Gambit*, though a work of fiction, may very well be compared to Watson's classic *The Double Helix*. The author reveals, as only an insider can do, how much of scientific research is fueled by human passions."
—Arthur C. Clarke

"In *The Bourbaki Gambit*, Carl Djerassi again demonstrates his unique ability to make modern science both comprehensible and the stuff of absorbing fiction."
—David Lodge

"Very funny. Mr. Djerassi bounds about cheerfully among the current gender and other social issues. Bang up-to-date . . . plenty to enjoy . . . suspense to spare."
—*The Washington Times*

"Absorbing, eminently readable fiction."
—*Library Journal*

What the scientists think

"Probably the quintessential science novel of the past year"
—*Science*

"Lively, well-crafted . . . There is delight in finding the world with which one is familiar rendered real as art."
—*Chemical & Engineering News*

"The dialogue fairly sizzled."
—*Scientific American*

"A lovely book . . . a triumph."
—*Chemistry in Britain*

PENGUIN BOOKS

THE BOURBAKI GAMBIT

Carl Djerassi, professor of chemistry at Stanford University, is an internationally renowned scientist, best known for his synthesis of the first steroid oral contraceptive, "The Pill," for which he won numerous awards, including the National Medal of Science (1973). In 1991, he received the National Medal of Technology (for novel approaches to insect control) and in 1992 the Priestley Medal, the highest award of the American Chemical Society. He is the recipient of fifteen honorary doctorates, and a member of the U.S. National Academy of Sciences and the American Academy of Arts and Sciences. He also founded the Djerassi Resident Arts Program near San Francisco which supports working artists in various disciplines.

His books include two other novels, *Cantor's Dilemma* and *Marx, Deceased*; the autobiography, *The Pill, Pygmy Chimps, and Degas's Horse*; and essay, poetry, and short story collections, including *The Futurist and Other Stories*.

There is a Web site about Carl Djerassi's writing located at http://www.djerassi.com.

By the Same Author

THE
Bourbaki
GAMBIT

A NOVEL BY
Carl Djerassi

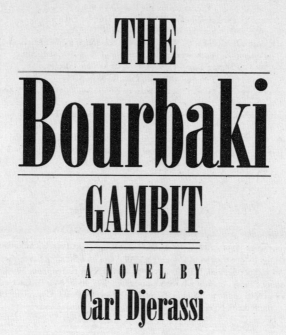

PENGUIN BOOKS

PENGUIN BOOKS
Published by the Penguin Group
Penguin Books USA Inc., 375 Hudson Street,
New York, New York 10014, U.S.A.
Penguin Books Ltd, 27 Wrights Lane, London W8 5TZ, England
Penguin Books Australia Ltd, Ringwood, Victoria, Australia
Penguin Books Canada Ltd, 10 Alcorn Avenue,
Toronto, Ontario, Canada M4V 3B2
Penguin Books (N.Z.) Ltd, 182–190 Wairau Road, Auckland 10, New Zealand

Penguin Books Ltd, Registered Offices: Harmondsworth, Middlesex, England

First published in the United States of America
by the University of Georgia Press 1994
Published in Penguin Books 1996

3   5   7   9   10   8   6   4

Excerpt from "Live or Die," by Anne Sexton, copyright 1966 by Anne Sexton.
Reprinted by permission of Houghton Mifflin Co. and Sterling Lord Literistic,
Inc. All rights reserved. "Haiku No. 796 [Spring]" reprinted from *Traditional
Japanese Poetry*, translated, with an introduction, by Steven D. Carter, with
the permission of the publishers, Stanford University Press. Copyright 1991 by
the Board of Trustees of the Leland Stanford Junior University.

PUBLISHER'S NOTE
This is a work of fiction. Names, characters, places, and incidents either are
the product of the author's imagination or are used fictitiously, and any
resemblance to actual persons, living or dead, events, or locales
is entirely coincidental.

THE LIBRARY OF CONGRESS HAS CATALOGUED THE HARDCOVER AS FOLLOWS:
Djerassi, Carl.
The Bourbaki gambit: a novel/by Carl Djerassi.
p.   cm.
ISBN 0-8203-1652-0 (hc.)
ISBN 0 14 02.5485 4 (pbk.)
1. Intellectuals—United States—Fiction.   2. Polymerase chain reaction—
Fiction.   3. Scientists—United States—Fiction.   4. Aged—
United States—Fiction.   I. Title.
PS3554.J47B68   1994
813´.54—dc20   93–44392

Printed in the United States of America
Set in 11 on 15 Bodoni Book
Designed by Richard Hendel

FOR

GILBERT,

KOJI,

KURT,

AND

DIANE

Foreword

The Bourbaki Gambit is the second volume in a projected tetralogy that concentrates the unforgivingly bright light of contemporary life on today's scientists. Science is conducted within a close-knit culture whose members are generally reluctant to disclose their tribal secrets. This may be one reason why so few novels, plays, or films use ordinary scientists as main characters.

I call my genre "science-in-fiction" to distinguish it from science fiction. As a tribesman, I demand of myself a degree of accuracy and plausibility that impart to my storytelling a high ratio of fact to fiction. In the preceding volume, *Cantor's Dilemma*, I wrote about trust (without which the scientific enterprise cannot function), about ambition (the research scientist's indispensable fuel, but often also a contaminant), about the mentor-protégé relationship (a sine qua non of the culture of science), and about women (who as scientists must cope with the barriers of a male-dominated field). Throughout that "veri-fiction" I selected dozens of real scientists for supporting roles. In *The Bourbaki Gambit*, I focus on three issues: scientists' passionate desire for recognition by their peers, science's inherent collegiality, and the graying of Western science.

With one exception, my main characters have either passed or are approaching the biblical age of three score and ten years. The reason for favoring that age group is more compelling than the personal identification I acknowledge freely. In Japan, North America, and Western Europe, where most of the frontier research in biomedical science is currently conducted, we are witnessing the emergence of geriatric societies: not too far into the twenty-first century, a quarter of the population of these regions will be beyond the age of sixty. We read all the time about the social problems associated with such a skewed age distribution—problems of medicine, politics, economics, and even recreation.

Some other implications of the aging of our culture are discussed much less frequently; among these is the rapidly increasing size of the geriatric element of the intellectual elite. *The Bourbaki Gambit* examines in a semifictional context some of the challenges these demographic changes raise in such circles.

The title addresses the twin issues of collegiality and the desire for fame, pointing to the tension between the collaborative effort at the heart of modern science and the desire for individual recognition in the hearts of most scientists. It refers to Nicolas Bourbaki, whose career marks one of the rare instances in which scientists have seemingly managed to rise above that tension. It is notable, however, that this triumph was achieved only by the most extraordinary means: despite a flourishing reputation bolstered by a massive bibliography, Nicolas Bourbaki does not exist. He is in a sense himself a work of fiction, the nom de plume of a group of leading mathematicians, mostly French, who have taken that name in a collaborative effort that has lasted for decades. Yet name recognition remains the most powerful component of any research scientist's ambition. In writing *The Bourbaki Gambit*, I have attempted to answer a question: How many scientists would be satisfied with making a sensational discovery and then launching it into the world unattached to their own balloon?

This is also, of course, a novel about science itself. In 1989 the prestigious multidisciplinary journal *Science* designated PCR—an acronym standing for polymerase chain reaction—"Molecule of the Year" and "one of the most powerful tools of modern biology." The acronym was not even coined until 1986, but within three years of its invention PCR had swept the biomedical field to become the most frequently cited technology in the life sciences. Even the *Jurassic Park* fantasy would have lost whatever plausibility it may possess without the existence of PCR. Yet how many laypersons have heard of PCR? And of those who have, how many can explain the concept behind it? Part of my purpose in telling this story is to make this revolutionary development and some of its applications intelligible in everyday language.

Aside from some unavoidable fictional compromises, *The Bourbaki Gambit* maintains a high standard of verisimilitude, thanks to the help of numerous advisers on subjects as diverse as Japanese scientific culture and ancien régime French feminism. My Japanese informant on the former topic shall remain anonymous, but it is not for lack of gratitude or affection that I omit his name. Felicity Baker (University College, London), Nina L. Gelbart (Occidental College), and Guy Ourisson (University of Strasbourg) offered valuable references to the semifictional eighteenth-century French research field I chose for my heroine, Diana Doyle-Ditmus, including a rare copy of *La Spectatrice*, the first feminist journal, published in 1728. Hyman Bass (Columbia University) was generous in allowing me to introduce him by name as a character who functions in my novel (as he did in real life) as one of my sources of information on the original Bourbaki group; Liliane Beaulieu (University of Quebec), a prospective biographer of Nicolas Bourbaki, offered additional details. The field of catalytic antibodies, considered by my fictitious scientists as a potential research objective, is real, cutting-edge science pioneered by Stephen J. Benkovic (Pennsylvania State University), Richard A. Lerner (Scripps Clinic), and Peter G. Schultz (University of California). As already noted, PCR, the scientific discovery made by my fictitious heroes, is not fiction but glorious fact. In real life, this discovery was made by a group of scientists at Cetus Corporation, notably Kary B. Mullis, who received the 1993 Nobel Prize in Chemistry for his invention. While my novel pays tribute to their science, in no way should the actions or behavior of my Max Weiss, Hiroshi Nishimura, Charlea C. Conway, and Sepp Krzilska be attributed to any living person.

Lastly, it is my pleasure to acknowledge two outstanding debts. The ultimate meeting of my scientists in *The Bourbaki Gambit* occurs in a setting of dazzling beauty: the Villa Malaparte in Capri. I owe Rosanna Chiessi the privilege of access to this private retreat. But there is another Italian connection in my novel. The last eleven chapters were written while I was a guest at the Rockefeller Foundation's sumptuous Villa Serbelloni in Bellagio on the shores of Lake Como, an environment that even my fictional characters in Capri might have envied.

The Bourbaki Gambit

O

"A visionary is a person capable of seeing with closed eyes."

My eyes were closed; Sam was trimming my eyebrows. I was thinking of Virgin Gorda, trying to remember what she had said. It had been something like that. And something else—what was it?

"Easy, Professor," Sam said, bringing me out of my reverie. "I'll be done in a minute. Let me brush you off. White hair is so easily seen on a blue suit."

White hair, I thought. Since meeting her, I'd started to see myself as silver haired. Fine, pale hairs floated around me, settling gently to the floor. "It's my biography," I wanted to say, but didn't. Looking down, all I saw was biographies. An unread library was lying on the floor: volumes of *Who's Who*, medical histories, hidden sins.

It's gotten almost so I can't bear to see the stuff swept away. Who would have thought two years ago that we would now be negotiating for one strand—a *portion* of a strand—of those precious two locks from Abraham Lincoln, consisting of 183 strands, none of them longer than five centimeters? How could the curator begrudge us a few millimeters of hair when it could provide the answer to a question that has intrigued historians for decades: Did Lincoln suffer from Marfan's Syndrome? Would he have died anyway in the 1860s, even if Booth hadn't assassinated him?

It was odd, I thought, as my own hairs fluttered in the air around me, how so many of these questions came down to the matter of dying: odd to find in the source of life so much information about death. But that was how it all started. With a question about death.

So much has been swept away: biographies, it seems. I'd never known they were so fragile. Or so easily forged. But I had foreseen even less how many other lives might be altered in the process.

All the time I had been constructing my vision of revenge, I had been blind to what it would involve. None of us would ever be the same.

But she had seen it from the beginning. I still remember what she said when I confessed it all, long after she'd called the four of us visionaries. It had pleased me at the time: tickled my vanity in a way I doubt she had intended. She barely knew me then. But even then she had had questions. Questions I would have done well to listen to.

"You say that scientists have the conceit of authorship?"

I interrupted. "I said 'pride.'"

"Pride, conceit. It's all the same." She waved the objection away. "Both are incompatible with Bourbaki."

"Finished," said the barber, and then, when he caught my look, "Something wrong?"

"No, of course not," I replied quickly. What else could I tell him?

As I passed out the door into the streets of Manhattan, which still surprise me each morning with their vitality, their energy—their youth—I had to admit to myself that, although I had spoken out of habit, I had not lied. Nothing was wrong. For the first time in years, not a thing was wrong.

It was a glorious day to be old.

1

"What would *you* use to commit suicide?"

That's the first sentence I remember her uttering. At least, that's what I tell her now, although we both know it isn't completely true. Still: *se no è vero, è ben trovato.* What she actually said first was, "You *must* be Professor Weiss from Princeton," and

then she sat down on the sand.

I was about to retort that I was past the age when I *must* be anything, but my second look at her convinced me that flippancy was unlikely to turn her off. At the time, I doubt I could have said why. It might have been the seigneurial air with which she placed herself upon the sand, the complete matter-of-factness with which she seemed to assume that I was going to pay attention to *her* and not the journal I had been reading. Or perhaps it was her attire, which invited my second look, to which she seemed not so much oblivious as indifferent. She wore a wide-brimmed straw hat to protect her face from the fierce sun. The hat, dark glasses, and pale orange shift with long sleeves hid most of her slim body. (Of course, I didn't know yet about her oncophobia; in her view, anything that could metastasize—breast, cervix, colon, lips—might, if given the opportunity.) I didn't guess her to be a day older than sixty.

"Why *must* I be Professor Weiss from Princeton?" I asked. It was obvious she was not going to let me read—not the way she was looking up at me, her arms clasped tightly around her covered knees, like a schoolgirl at the feet of her teacher.

She stared at me levelly from under the broad-brimmed hat, and then added directly, "Joss claims you changed her life."

"Joss?"

"Jocelyn, my granddaughter. You had her in class last semester."

"Ah . . ." I said and reached for the suntan lotion. It gave me something to do while trying my usual system: Jocelyn A., Jocelyn B., Jocelyn C., Jocelyn D. . . . Jocelyn P.—Powers . . . Jocelyn Powers. "Mrs. Powers?" I murmured, trying to sound diffident.

"No, Doyle-Ditmus. She is my daughter's daughter."

"Of course," I said stupidly. There was nothing "of course" about it, of course, but it served to hide my confusion. "Changed her life," the woman had said. Only the young could be so eager to have their lives changed.

A change in the woman's tone alerted me to an incoming question. My ears switched back to her wavelength: ". . . with all that, why are you retiring? You hardly look seventy."

3

Hardly seventy! Women usually tell me I look five years *younger* than my age. At that time I didn't know her real age, or I would've realized she was paying me a compliment.

"It's best to retire when people ask Why are you retiring?" I replied, "and before they ask When are you retiring?"

I might have spared myself the effort of a retort: she had already switched to weightier matters. "Tell me," she said slowly, aiming her sunglasses point-blank at me. "What would *you* use to commit suicide?"

It occurred to me suddenly that I might be dealing with a lunatic, a potential suicide—or worse. I decided to play it cool and answer as if it were something I'm asked every day. "Cyanide," I said judiciously.

"Hm," she nodded, "I suppose so. But where would I *get* cyanide?"

"You asked me how *I* would commit suicide. I've got plenty of cyanide in the lab."

"Would you give me some?" she asked. She might have been asking me to pass the salt.

"Of course not," I broke out laughing. "That would make me an accessory." I squinted to get her into better focus. "But you aren't serious, are you?"

"About wanting some cyanide? Dead serious. But not about committing suicide. I only want some—just in case."

I raised my eyebrows and waited for some elaboration on "just in case," but she got up from the sand.

"Will you have dinner with me tonight?" She pointed in the direction of the thatched roof of the dining pavilion. "Shall we say eight o'clock?"

Naturally I accepted. I wanted to put to rest the doubt she'd raised with this bizarrely practical talk about suicide. It didn't seem likely, but—just in case—I wanted to know if I'd been responsible for putting an idea in her head. We exchanged a perfunctory "Till eight, then," and she walked off across the sand, shrouded in shimmering orange.

Doyle-Ditmus. But what was her full name? I had the man at the reception desk write it down for me, and I sporadically tested myself during the remainder of the day: after a lifetime of teaching, I seem to have exhausted my capacity for retaining names. For Diana Doyle-Ditmus I coined a private mnemonic: D_3. The subscript gave it a comfortable chemical ring.

Only that evening, when she appeared for dinner half an hour late—this time in a sleeveless mauve silk gown with a Paisley shawl draped around her—and I helped her into the chair, did I notice the tea doily design of the wrinkles on her hands. That's when I added a half dozen years to my earlier guess of her age. Weeks were to pass before I discovered that I was still off the mark.

The hovering maître d' and the swarm of waiters made it obvious that I wasn't at the Faculty Club back home, or even the Princeton Club in Manhattan—two locales I've been frequenting a great deal since Nedra's death. I don't usually go to places like Little Dix Bay.

I was still deciding what to order when I realized that D_3 was reading the elaborately printed and tasseled menu, I swear, through a lorgnette. I had never before seen anyone with a lorgnette—not outside of the movies, at least—but the matter-of-factness with which she clutched the long silver handle redeemed the gesture of any taint of the theatrical. She turned from the menu to the hovering maître d'. "Vichyssoise. A small salad of endive with hearts of palm. And the tournedos. Rare." She didn't say please, but the omission seemed neither offensive nor supercilious. Perhaps it was the way she and the maître d' exchanged looks, a sense of easy familiarity flowing between them. "In that case, Madame will want the Pètrus," he murmured and turned to me.

Now, I don't have a large cellar at Princeton, not in the place I moved to since becoming a widower, but I do know something about wine. Not that I would ever order a $150 bottle, but I'm always curious about what restaurants carry. And I could have sworn that there was no Pètrus among the many Bordeaux on the wine list I'd studied here the night before. It was a wine I had never tasted—although I had come close once, in Paris, at the last Biochemistry Congress. The price had dissuaded my colleagues; but now, wearing an open-necked shirt and seersucker jacket, the trade wind ruffling my hair and the sound of the surf hitting the sand at my back, it seemed I was about to be offered a glass of this most fabled of Bordeaux, courtesy of a woman who only a few hours ago had asked me how to commit suicide. Maybe I should have said "cyanide-laced Pètrus." I was beginning to realize that my life had taken a turn into the unexpected.

"And what will you have, Professor Weiss?" she asked as she placed her lorgnette into the beaded clutch bag by her side.

Instead of answering her, which would have been the polite thing to do, I turned to the towering maître d'. "Did you say 'Pètrus'?"

The man must have known what I was about to ask. "Madame," he nodded in the direction of D_3, "brought a bottle; 1970," he added.

"Oh," I said and swallowed hard. "I see." I knew I sounded, and possibly looked, like an oaf, but suddenly the Pètrus had taken over the entire meal. And what a vintage she had picked! I tried to look at the menu, but now saw nothing except *Pètrus '70* written all over it. I glanced up in desperation and found my guest-turned-host studying me. She smiled but said nothing. Quickly, I turned to the waiter. "I'll have the same as . . ." I began, and then turned red as total blankness descended over me.

". . . Madame." He finished the sentence for me and took the menu out of my hand.

2

Two glasses of the Bordeaux restored my equanimity. I kept swirling the glass and sniffing the wine as if I wanted to inhale it all that way. "Divine bouquet," I said dreamily. "Maybe it's just my imagination, but you can actually taste the flavor of truffles. Tell me . . ." I stopped again, my mnemonic completely forgotten.

She raised her glass. "You may call me Diana."

Of course: D_3. In the glow of the Pètrus I reflected that "Diana" was much simpler than "Doyle-Ditmus." "Call me Max," I said, and then we clinked glasses.

"You were going to ask me something, Max?"

"What I wanted to ask was simply, how and why the Pètrus?"

"The *how* is simple: I bought two bottles to toast winning a jackpot. But we were abstemious and consumed only one bottle. So I decided to bring the other one with me." She seemed to think I knew about her jackpot, because she continued without interruption. "The *why* is a bit more complicated. You may not have guessed," she made a deprecating gesture with the hand holding her knife, "but I'm a feminist. That's why."

I thought more was coming, but instead she pierced a small piece of meat and put it daintily in her mouth.

"I've probably missed something," I said hesitantly.

If an elderly woman can look kittenish, D_3 did. "I was just testing you, Max," she said mischievously. Before I had a chance to figure out just what the test had been and whether I had passed, the subject seemed to have changed again. I was having trouble keeping up. "You mentioned the taste of truffles in the wine. Did you know that that's characteristic of Pètrus?"

I nodded (I hoped) offhandedly and tried to regain my grasp of the conversation. "So what grade do I get? B+? A—?" It seemed a mistake to hope for more.

Diana shook her head. "At guessing why? At best a C; maybe   7 even a C—, but then I don't want to discourage you too much. I'm a tough grader, Max, not like you Princeton professors. According to Jocelyn, once you get into Princeton, it's difficult to flunk out."

"Is that why your granddaughter liked my class? Because I'm an easy grader?" When it came to ruffling my self-regard, this woman seemed to have an endless repertoire.

"No, Max." She reached over and patted my hand. I found myself abruptly aware that it was our first physical contact.

"So why?" I asked.

"Because you changed her entire outlook on science."

I blushed, feeling transparent. "I didn't mean that," I lied. "Why the Pètrus?"

"Oh, that." She took a swallow and nodded. "Pètrus—the winery—was owned by one of the grandes dames of the wine world, Madame Loubat. Her successor was also a woman—her niece, Madame Lacoste. All things being equal—in fact, even if they are not quite equal—I always prefer an operation run by an efficient woman. Besides, I got to know her when I visited Pomerol with my second husband."

Somehow the number attached to the husband seemed of a piece with D_3's interest in efficiency: everything by the numbers, I mused. But behind my amusement I was aware of a growing need for biographical information. "How often *have* you been married?" I asked.

"So far, twice," she said coolly. "And you?"

It was her point again, and I no longer liked the game. "Once. My wife died two years ago. But Diana, you said 'so far.' Is your husband not alive anymore?"

"I'm a widow," she said noncommittally. " 'So far' simply means that theoretically I might get married again." She sipped her wine, at the same time examining me across the brim of her glass. Under her gaze, I started to squirm. Perhaps she noticed my discomfort, because suddenly she continued. "But that's unlikely. At my age, a man would have to be very unusual to interest me. By the way, when Joss raved about you, she said she was lucky to have taken the course because it was your last. Why does such a gifted teacher retire? That's what I asked her. And you know what she said? 'Gran, why don't you ask him yourself. He's going to your place.' By 'your,'" she added helpfully, "Joss meant *this* place." A bantering tone accompanied the casually regal gesture of her right hand. "So I thought, why *not* ask the man? So. Why retire, Max?"

It wasn't simply the Pètrus, I suddenly understood, that had been making the whole scene just a bit unreal. A total stranger heads straight for me on the beach as if I had a mark on my forehead; she sweeps me up and pours Pètrus down my throat—all, it seems, simply as a preliminary to asking the one question I had come here to avoid.

I tried to avoid it a little longer. "How did you know I was here?"

"I told you. From my granddaughter."

"But how did she know?"

"You must have told her, Max."

Had I? The idea baffled me for a moment; could I have been that upset by McLeod's letter, to go around discussing my travel plans with students? What had I been trying to prove? That I at least had the money to begin my forced retirement at an expensive resort?

"But how did you know—"

"How to find you on the beach? Elementary, my dear Max. First of all, there were not many people on the beach, and only a couple of men by themselves."

"How did you know . . ."

". . . you were alone at Little Dix Bay? I asked about you at the front desk. I also knew something about your approximate age. And *you* helped by looking so much like a professor: glasses, a slight potbelly . . ." She saw me flinch but just waved her hand good-naturedly. "Don't mind about that. It's here where all the action is." She tapped her head. "If your belly is all that important, watch your diet. Like me, for example. But that doesn't have anything to do with making a man interesting. Or *productive*." She took a sip of wine, the raised glass scattering the candlelight in **9** spectral glints on our table. "And in addition to your professorial shape," she concluded, "you had an academic journal lying by your side."

"*Biochimica et Biophysica Acta*." I was reduced to mouthing Latin at her, I confess it.

"Or something like that. So now tell me: Why are you retiring? To cultivate your garden?"

"Who said I was going to cultivate my garden?" I retorted. "Or any garden, for that matter."

"Max," she said soothingly, and for the second time she placed her ringed hand on my ringless one. This time she kept it there. "Don't be so literal. Why are you retiring? Why don't you teach more young people like Joss?"

"It's complicated," I said and drained the remnants of the bottle into my glass. At the very first twirl I regretted the gesture: only murky ink sloshed back and forth in my glass. Instead of savoring the last sip of the velvety, deep red Pètrus, I was left with the tannins of the years.

"Why can't you continue?"

Look at what I just poured into my glass, I wanted to say, but that was not what D_3 had been asking.

"Is it a question of money?"

Was it the dregs of the Pètrus or her question that had suddenly put me into a bitter humor? "Isn't it always?" I shot back. Then, more calmly, I tried to explain. For the splendid wine, if nothing else, I owed her at least civility. "Well, yes and no. Or really no and yes. To continue my research, I need money. But so does everyone, and we all get it from the same sources: the government and the foundations: Rockefeller, Hughes, MacArthur—"

"I didn't know one could *apply* to MacArthur."

The nature of her interruption should have told me something, but I was too focused on my own problem to pay attention to nuances.

"Then forget about them," I snapped. "There are lots of others." With one grand gesture I waved away the MacArthur Foundation—and promptly knocked over the narrow-stemmed vase with

10   its single yellow rose.

Before I could even right it, our waiter was there. A starched napkin whisked the puddle away. "I'm sorry," I said, "it's my irritation. Retirement incentives are metastasizing all over academia."

"Metastasizing! What a horrible word!" Diana shuddered. "The body academic getting cancer. I suppose it would be in the brain."

"No," I said, shaking my head at D_3, "not the brain. If we have to pursue this metaphor . . ."

"I'd just as soon we didn't," she interjected, but I was too enamored with the comparison to let it go.

"I'd pick the liver and gallbladder. The liver detoxifies, the gallbladder adds the bile. And why do I pick these two organs? Because the universities are so damned eager these days to get rid of the older professors—irrespective of how wide-awake and productive they still may be—that they bribe them with all kinds of financial incentives to head them out to pasture."

"And why the gallbladder?"

"Because even though you accept the money, you feel bilious."

Her questioning had started me thinking—for the first time, it seemed, since that insufferable letter had appeared on my desk. Why had I let the administration convince me to take early retirement? Legally, they couldn't have forced me to become an emeritus for another five years. Instead, they had blackmailed me, plain and simple: retire now and live well with laboratory privileges; wait and become a labless emeritus.

I hadn't realized it at the time, but the seed was planted somewhat earlier, when I went to see the dean about the departmental chairmanship, which rotates every three years. I had never pushed for that post: my research was too important to me to sacrifice it for the thankless task of administration. But somebody has to do the job, so a couple of years ago, when the position opened up again, I decided my time had arrived. When the dean finally called me to his office, I took it to be the regular anointment process. As I walked down the hall, I'd even made up my mind to hold out for one extra perk: a reserved parking place.

"You realize that the chairman's mantle is about to fall on you, **11**

Max." He eyed me craftily. "After all these years, you must be dying to be chairman."

"Well, I'm not *dying* to become chairman," I replied. No researcher will ever admit to being interested in an administrative position. "But . . ." I was about to add that nevertheless I was willing to do it pro bono publico, when the dean performed the fastest rug-pulling act in my experience.

"In that case, Max, whom would you suggest?"

It wasn't meant as a question; he didn't even give me the chance to respond once I'd fallen into his trap. It was simply a preamble to announcing a decision he'd obviously made some time ago. "What about Seymour? I think he'd work out very well: good fiscal disciplinarian, yet diplomatic; still in his prime . . ."

So I'm a wastrel, tactless, and approaching senility? He didn't say that—in fact, he complimented me on my wisdom, which supposedly was the reason he was soliciting my advice—but I knew damn well how to read between the lines. After Seymour became chairman of our department, I didn't cross the dean's path until three years later, when he called me again to his office.

"Max," he said with a lupine smirk, "I am appealing to your insight. You've been here for . . ." he turned a page in the folder on his desk and quickly scanned it, "over thirty-three years." This time, he did not catch me unprepared. I leaned back, crossed my legs, and never took my eyes off his perspiring face. I didn't say a word. To this day, I recall some of the key phrases: ". . . distinguished service . . . twice elected to the academic senate . . . admiration of your peers . . . credit to the institution . . . National Medal of Science . . . skewed age distribution . . . new blood . . . deserved incentive."

"How much?" was all I said.

"How much?" he echoed, suspicion dawning as his eyes narrowed. I know what made me interrupt him: I wanted to catch him the way he had caught me earlier about the chairmanship. And I had: the coldbloodedness of my question disconcerted him, and I enjoyed that. So I drove a hard bargain, pushing at him recklessly until, in the end, I couldn't afford to turn down his offer. I knew that five years down the line, with all the cards in his hands and no advantage of surprise, I wouldn't do half as well. But even as I thought I had him on the ropes, I did make one mistake.

"Of course you can continue your research, Max. How could you even ask? Our star in the biochemical firmament," he'd said on the day we signed the generous agreement. "You do understand that university rules preclude making long-term contractual commitments with emeritus professors. But you can trust me, Max. I'll get you something in writing." So I trusted him, and eventually I did get something in writing: that infamous one-sentence letter from the secretary of the Board of Trustees—a missive that still makes my blood boil.

"*Dear Sir:*" McLeod had written. Not *Dear Professor Weiss* or even *Dear Weiss*. My thirty-four years at Princeton—twenty-seven of them as Donohue Professor of Biochemistry—apparently counted for nothing. Just "*Dear Sir: I have the honor to inform you that at a meeting of the Trustees of Princeton University held today, you were appointed Senior Research Biochemist in your department, without stipend, for the period June 1, 1988, to May 31, 1989. Respectfully yours, Seth T. McLeod.*" It isn't often one remembers an entire letter verbatim, but this one, in its insolent brevity, was one for my permanent mental files. It wasn't so much the "without stipend" caveat, although it could have been done with a dash of grace. But one year at a time?

Despite the bitter taste it left each time I inwardly recited this single sentence, I wasn't sure I wanted to forget it: now that I had been cut adrift, my resentment, at least, was something to hold onto.

I was so irritated by the trustees' missive that I couldn't even decide whether to look for a place other than Princeton to continue my research. That isn't so simple. The entire scientific establishment—not just the universities but the foundations as well—is sold on youth. When you are pushing seventy—which was what I was doing, having just passed my sixty-eighth birthday—all but your contemporaries stop taking you seriously. Why isn't that true in politics? Why are politicians in their late sixties just "mature"? Why are Supreme Court justices appointed for life?

The arrival of dessert brought me out of my sour memories.

"What's this?" I demanded. I hadn't recalled ordering dessert.

"Mango sorbet with lichees," D_3 replied. Her tongue licked daintily at a spoonful. "It's delicious. And low calorie."

Despite the queer name, I had to agree with her description. But I could no longer keep my mind on present pleasures: her question about my retirement had set my thoughts running down a well-worn path. I could no longer keep myself from it, despite the distractions of the moment. But perhaps because of those distractions, I could no longer keep it to myself.

"Have you ever heard of Bourbaki?" I asked her.

"Yes, of course," she answered matter-of-factly, and ran her spoon around the side of the bowl. "Why do you ask?"

D_3's spoon was still traveling around the inside of her cut-glass dish. "How do you know Bourbaki?" I sputtered.

The way she smiled at me, an innocent smile, but framed in hard metal—probably platinum—should have warned me. "I read," she said. "In fact, I read a great deal. And, if I may say so, I forget very little."

"Yes. Of course." I was doing it again: there was nothing "of course" about the matter. "But where did you read about Nicolas Bourbaki?"

"Not Nicolas. Charles."

"It's Nicolas!" I realized I was behaving like a pedant, but this was absurd. All fifty-odd of his publications bear the name "Nicolas Bourbaki."

"Charles! If you want the full name, it's Charles Denis Sauter Bourbaki." She punctuated this pronouncement with a now-shut-up look, but I was not going to put up with such nonsense, not even from the woman who had wined me with Pètrus.

"Diana," I said in the same tone that used to drive Nedra up the wall, "I'm sorry, but I *know* it's Nicolas."

"Max," she purred, the way a tigress might as the adrenaline enters her bloodstream, "for your information, Charles Denis Sauter Bourbaki was a French general who established his reputation in the middle of the nineteenth century in battles in the Crimea and in Italy, then lost it as commander in chief of the French forces during the Franco-German War in 1871. In case you don't remember, the Germans won that war. *Charles* Bourbaki then ran for parliament, but he never made it. When I told you I read, I omitted to mention that French history is my métier." She drew the shawl around her and straightened up as if she were ready to leave. "I understand there are some lovely beaches around here with hardly a soul. Why don't you join me on a trip to Mountain Trunk Beach tomorrow morning? We could take a picnic and continue our conversation. After all, you haven't told me yet what General Charles Bourbaki has to do with your retirement plans."

I was flabbergasted. Of course Bourbaki is called Nicolas. But were there two of them? Was mine the second? I still remember the first time I told Nedra about Bourbaki. Her response? "You could never do that. I know you and your confrères too well." Nedra was always clever with words, like *confrères*, that had a faintly censorious touch about them. At the time, I thought she was right. But three years had passed, and Nicolas Bourbaki had not left my mind. And in all that time I hadn't stopped wondering if I couldn't find some confrères to help me pull it off.

3

There wasn't a guest in sight when I arrived at the dock a few minutes before ten the next morning. By 10:15, I wondered whether I'd missed her. At 10:25, I headed down the beach toward an unoccupied deck chair. I must have been a few hundred feet from the dock when I heard a distant "Max!" I turned and saw D_3, wearing some sort of visored captain's cap on her head. She was waving.

"Good morning, Max," she said when I reached her. "I'm sorry I'm late, but the kitchen took their time." She pointed to the insulated chest. "I should have ordered the picnic last night. I hope you didn't think I'd forgotten you." A sly smile stole over her mouth. "You do look slightly peevish, though."

I didn't recall anyone lately having called me peevish. "I didn't sleep well," I said peevishly. My mind was still in Princeton. Besides, I don't usually take a holiday before Christmas—I feel guilty about it. It will take more than a couple of days at Virgin Gorda to get accustomed to a new regimen, I consoled myself.

The boat shot forward, pitching me toward a seat.

"Having trouble adjusting?" Diana asked sympathetically.

"He started too soon." I pointed accusingly at the boatman, but she shook her head.

"I meant retirement, Max." She inclined her captain's cap at the coastline rushing past us; for a long minute we both looked at the lush vegetation that lay beyond a thin belt of white sand, an occasional house visible among the trees and bougainvillea. It was moving by at a surprisingly rapid pace. "It's lovely here, and very relaxing. But I can't take it longer than a week. And it's not just the sun either. You wouldn't believe what I have waiting for me . . ." she trailed off.

I couldn't think of an appropriate response other than to nod. During most of my married life, virtually the same words used to be my standard pronouncement. According to Nedra, I said them within five days of the start of any vacation. We remained quiet until the boat started to head for the shore. "Over there," D$_3$ pointed. "See those huge boulders? And the small beach next to it? That's Mountain Trunk Beach. There won't be a person around." She looked at her watch. "It's almost eleven. What do you say about having them pick us up at three?"

The boatman had brought us so close to the beach that the bow jutted over the sand. One could jump down without even getting wet. I went first, ignoring the boatman's proffered muscular arm. I wanted to show I wasn't helpless, paunch and all. The boatman cleared the rail like an acrobat on a bar, legs straight and close together. Reaching back, he offered one arm to D$_3$ and, as in a pas de deux, swung her onto the sand. It was quite a sight—her white shift billowing in the breeze as she landed gracefully by my side. Mentally, I deducted all the years I had added to her age last evening.

"Over there," she called back at her dancing partner, then set out up the slightly sloping beach. As we ambled along, the man passed us and, as resolutely as an explorer claiming this island for his sovereign, planted two red-striped parasols in the sand. He spread out two beach towels, *Little Dix Bay* embroidered in their centers, and then returned with the cooler, a white wicker basket, and two more towels. "Anything else, Madame?" he asked.

"Just pick us up at three," she said, dropping into the shade of the umbrella. As it had been yesterday, her body was covered completely, this time in white. There was something regally bridal about her as she pointed to the towel by her side. "Make yourself comfortable, and then let's talk."

I stripped down to my bathing trunks, held in my stomach until I was nearly breathless, and stretched out in the sun. "Max," she called out sharply, "for heaven's sake, get under the umbrella and put on some sunscreen." As if by sleight of hand she produced a bottle. "You don't want to get skin cancer!"

"No," I said, trying to mollify her, "just a tan. We academics— or at least this one—don't get much sun."

"You'll get enough under the umbrella."

I humored her and moved partly under the shade. "What shall we talk about?"

"Bourbaki, of course. You're the first American I've ever met who's even heard the name. Even if you did get his *prénom* wrong. But what does Charles Bourbaki have to do with your retirement?"

"Your Charles Bourbaki? Nothing. But my Nicolas? Now that's another question." And then I poured it all out to her—the first person, man or woman, since Nedra to get the whole tale. First, I told her the amusing part: how in 1934 a group of French mathematicians—said to have included Weil, Chevalley, Dieudonné, and the son of the world-renowned Cartan—decided to compose a logically rigorous and conceptually coherent account of the fundamental structures of mathematics, and to do it under the collective nom de plume of "Nicolas Bourbaki." By now around a dozen volumes and more than forty booklets had appeared under that name. Rumors had it that the composition of Bourbaki fluctuated over the years; but as the books became more famous and decades passed, relatively few mathematicians, and hardly anyone from other scientific disciplines, worried anymore about the identity of Bourbaki. Now most people refer to *him*, not *them*.

Diana listened with rapt concentration, her arms encircling her legs in the same schoolgirl position she had assumed when we first met yesterday afternoon, her eyes fixed on my face. God, I thought, wouldn't it be fantastic to have an entire class of such attentive students? That's precisely when she interrupted me.

"But Max, weren't you curious to find out why they picked that name? And who they are?"

"Not really," I confessed. "I'm not a historian."

"Then assume I'm one." D_3 sounded annoyed, as if I'd cheated her. "So why did you bring them up in the first place?"

It was my turn to show some irritation. "Because I'm not interested in Nicolas Bourbaki, the person or group of persons, him- or themselves. I'm interested in the Bourbaki concept."

"I'm sorry I interrupted you, Max. Go on."

"Have you known many scientists?"

"Known personally? Quite a number, but none very well. And I'm not sure I actually *know* you yet."

In retrospect, I wonder why I didn't ask her where and how she'd met "quite a number" of scientists. Perhaps Nedra was right: I've never really listened to the answers I get to my leading questions. I went on. "The public image of a scientist, especially an academic one, is of an egghead, someone who works long hours with mysterious apparatus to make incomprehensible discoveries. And, except for the Drs. Frankenstein, Strangelove, and that lot, most scientists are generally viewed as harmless."

Diana's eyebrows were slightly raised above her sunglasses. I could see she was not impressed. I'm talking down to her, I realized. And worse, she knew it. But a lifetime of lecturing had given me habits I couldn't break. "There is one character trait," I continued, "which is an intrinsic part of a scientist's culture, and which the public image doesn't often include: his extreme egocentricity, expressed chiefly in his overmastering desire for recognition by his peers. No other recognition matters. And that recognition comes in only one way. It doesn't really matter who you are or whom you know. You may not even know those other scientists personally, but *they* know *you*—through your publications."

"I would say that's typical of most academics doing research, not just scientists." D_3's eyebrows had dropped to their natural level. "Historians, for instance. But go on."

"That brings me to Bourbaki. Nicolas, that is. Given that egocentricity, that desire for *personal* recognition, why would—"

"Max, get to the point!" I was so startled by her peremptory tone that I rolled over to face her. Her dark sunglasses stared straight at me. "You already said you're not interested in those mathematicians, and neither am I. I want to know why *you* are interested in what you call 'the Bourbaki concept.' Aren't you an egocentric scientist?"

Christ, I thought, this woman doesn't even permit conversational foreplay. Yet, if Nedra had been here, she probably would have said the same thing. "All right," I said, thinking that if she wanted a succinct answer, I'd give her one. "The point is revenge."

Diana looked at me expectantly. "Go on," she said. "You can't stop now."

I thought it was time to reestablish equality between us. "At the risk of being rude," I said, "I don't think I can go on without some fortification. It's that kind of story."

"It sounds serious," she said drolly.

"It is," I replied. I sounded more serious than I had intended.

She smiled at me before opening the cooler. "Not so serious, I hope, that it requires something very substantial. Because we're *both* on a diet, Max; the choices are limited. But the quality is good. Here you are," she said, handing me a plate, cutlery, and napkin. "Crudités, Bath Olivers biscuits, *taramasalata*, and lots of fruit. What will you have to drink?"

I laughed. "Pètrus?"

She wagged her right index finger. Today, I noticed, she wore **19** no rings. "Not on a beach," she said. "That would be de trop. Besides, we finished the bottle last night. Today, it's Gewürztraminer or Perrier."

I had stretched out, this time completely under the shade of the umbrella. She was right: the midday sun was scorching. Even the reflection from the sand was more than sufficient for a tan.

"Max," she asked before I could manage to doze off, "will it spoil your digestion if we continue where we left off?"

Lazily, I shook my head. "Nothing could spoil my digestion today. But what's your hurry?"

"Revenge," she said, a mysterious smile on her face.

My momentary confusion must have shown. "Yours," she added. "Bourbaki and your revenge."

"Ah, yes," I replied and felt my eyelids getting lighter. I turned onto my side to face her. I had put it off as long as I could. It was time to put up or shut up. "I think it would be great," I began, "if a group of older scientists could take on the cult of youth and teach it a lesson. Scientists who still have a lot on the ball, like . . ."

I was trying to think of some names that would mean something to her, but she beat me to the draw.

"Like you?" she asked.

Well, of course like me. I had intended to be modest and mention someone like Linus Pauling, but since she brought up my name, why not? "Sure," I said, "for instance me. Now suppose some of us got together. Not many—half a dozen, maximum. We have already published a lot, received plenty of kudos" (though never enough of them, I thought), "so a few more papers under our own names won't make much difference. Suppose, however . . ."

"Yes," she broke in and grabbed my arm, "why not form a Bourbaki of old scientists?" Seeing me cringe, she quickly corrected herself. "You know what I mean, not really old, just . . ." She groped in vain for a word, and we both broke out laughing.

"Mature?" I offered. "Yes, I know what you mean. That's exactly the revenge I had in mind. If it doesn't turn out to be a panacea for my wounded pride, then it will at least serve as a placebo. I'll get a few such men together—"

"Just men? Why not some women?"

"No reason," I said quickly. "It's just that I don't know of any in that situation."

"Hmph. All right, forgiven. For now. Go on."

"We'll put our heads together and go to work on some real intellectual gambles. The kind of thing most younger scientists aren't willing to try because they may risk tenure or other advancement. If one of these works out, it will cause a sensation. Everyone will want to meet that new star, and then they'll find out . . ."

Always before, when I had told it to myself, my Walter Mitty tale had run out at this point, and I had found myself back in the world where "mature" professors find themselves so pointedly without stipend. I had grown used to this awakening, I suppose, because when Diana called out, "So why don't you do it?" I momentarily recoiled.

"Ah," I sighed, "because there are a few practical difficulties."

"You won't find enough revengeful *mature* scientists?"

"Oh, I don't know about that. I'm thinking of something much more mundane: like money. And an address."

"Money can't be all that difficult." She held up her hand to stop me from interrupting, a girlish grin on her face. "You said that with a good grant application you could still get research support from some public or private trough. Surely your *experienced* Bourbaki could come up with a sufficiently exciting application."

"You've obviously never seen such an application. One of the key components is a detailed curriculum vitae. *You* tell me how to do this with a Nicolas Bourbaki. And that ties in directly with the question of the address: you need an institution, such as a university, before you can apply for such grants. We are not artists. Research grants in science are never given to individuals."

"Hm," she murmured and gave me a long stare. "Is that so? What about MacArthur grants? They're *only* given to individuals."

It was the second time since we'd met that she'd brought up the MacArthur Foundation. I should have picked up on that, too.

"You mean the 'genius awards'?" I realized that there was something dismissive in the way I said "genius awards." If **21** pressed, I probably would have admitted that this was jealousy. After all, who wouldn't love to get $50,000 or more a year for five years with no strings attached? "Forget about MacArthur grantees," I said. "They are the exception that proves the rule."

Our conversation had petered out. I was lying on my back, wondering how it came about that I had told a virtual stranger about my dream of revenge.

"Do you know what time it is?" she suddenly asked. "I didn't bring my watch."

"Two," I said. We had another hour together on this Robinson Crusoe beach. Sufficient to learn something about her. "Diana. I think that after Bourbaki, it's my turn."

"To do what?" she asked lazily.

"Ask questions."

"Oh?"

I'm always amazed how much variation there exists in this simple sound.

"What about that cyanide question yesterday? Do you usually start conversations like that?"

"As a matter of fact, yes, I have talked about it with a couple of friends."

"Why?" I asked and raised myself on one elbow.

She seemed to have receded into her sunglasses. When she spoke, her voice appeared to come from within her voluminous shift. "Independence. I have already outlived two husbands; my friends are dropping like ducks at a shooting gallery."

"God! What an analogy."

"I know," she sighed, "but it's true. When this," she pointed to her head, "or that," she drew her hand over her body, "deteriorates beyond a certain point—say, Alzheimer's or incurable cancer—I want to be able to say enough! and end it there." She turned to me and lifted her glasses. The eyes that looked out searched mine. "Isn't that reasonable?"

"Fair enough," I conceded, trying to sound lighthearted.

"In that case, will you give me some cyanide?"

"Diana, be serious!"

22 "I am. Dead serious."

"You used that expression once before."

"I know. It's precisely the meaning I want to convey."

"All right," I said soothingly. "But I don't take cyanide with me on my vacations."

"The day might come when you do. By the way, when are you returning to Princeton?" she asked.

"In five days. Are you asking to find out when you can pick up the cyanide?"

"Not really." The sly smile appeared again. "At least not yet. But I'd like to stay in touch with you, all the same. What are you doing for New Year's Eve?"

"I haven't planned that far ahead."

"I have begun to lose my taste for big New Year's Eve parties. They're too puerile. How about a tête-à-tête at my apartment in New York?"

I was curious why she wanted to pick a date this far in advance, but she seemed to have read my mind. "I'm leaving tomorrow," she said, looking past me out to sea.

Neither of us said much on the boat ride back to Little Dix Bay. I was hoping she'd suggest that we meet again for dinner that evening—I was beginning to realize that I found her company stimulating. If it had taken me so long to realize this, perhaps it was because my original purpose in coming to Little Dix Bay had been just the opposite: I hadn't wanted company. I had come here to salve my wounded pride with daydreams of revenge—dreams that my professional life was not at an end. Now, having told that dream to Diana, I found the prospect of her departure depressing.

When we got off at the dock, she reached into her basket and produced a small handbag. After rifling through it for a moment, she handed me a card. "My apartment is on Central Park West near Seventy-first," she said with a slight apologetic chuckle. "Shall we say half past nine, then, on the thirty-first?"

4

My trip to the Virgin Islands and the social hustle of Christmas—
the one time widowers seem to be remembered by everybody—
had left me with a lot of end-of-the-year detritus. The unpostpon-
able items were the unpaid bills, especially those that could be
deducted from my income tax; I would have to get them to the
post office today. Before sitting down to that dreary task I had
wanted to brew some tea. But when I went to the cupboard, there
wasn't any left. It's little things like running out of tea—not just
the undefinable emptiness in crowded places, like eating alone at
a restaurant—that bring Nedra back all the time. As long as I had
to go out, I figured I might as well buy some other provisions for
tomorrow, when everything would be closed. Only when I stepped
out the front door did I see that at least a foot of snow had fallen
during the night, and it was still coming down steadily. I went
back for my boots and an airline bag to protect my purchases on
the walk back from Davidson's.

The unpaid bills were not my only chore. Nedra was a great
Christmas card sender, which I'm not. I had sorted this year's
avalanche into two piles. The much bigger one consisted of cards
whose senders would simply have to understand that I couldn't
be bothered anymore. The rest—still a great many—required
some reply: the few remaining relatives, some old friends, and—
I blush to admit—some people in whose good graces I wanted
to remain. All of these were getting a card featuring one of those
cleverly confusing M. C. Escher prints and a hand-written *"All
the best for the New Year, Max."* The fact that I used pen and ink
rather than just a printed message was supposed to prove that I
really meant it. Digging up the various addresses took an annoy-
ingly long time—another reminder of Nedra's efficiency—and it
was early afternoon before I started to think seriously of my New
Year's Eve date in New York. Clearly, I should bring a gift. But

what? Given the lousy weather, I was definitely not going to drive to Manhattan, and it would be a pain to take flowers on the train. Wine? What wine could I take to a person who travels to Virgin Gorda with Pètrus '70? Hand-made Belgian chocolates? We actually have a real chocolatier on Palmer Square—but I remembered D_3's reference to my belly and her diet. That left a book.

Buying books is not a problem in Princeton. It was still snowing strongly, so I put on my boots again and was about to grab my overcoat, when—in one of those series of flashes that sometimes create ideas out of memory—I heard and saw D_3 saying, "I read"; then, "I'm a feminist"; and I remembered that the only Princeton English professor I knew well enough to telephone was a woman.

Elaine Showalter answered the phone and within seconds came up with the right title for a feminist reader, assuring me that the U-Store, just a few blocks from my place, was bound to carry it. Forty-five minutes later, I was brushing the snow off my coat as I reentered my apartment. In its gift wrapping and waterproof bag, *The Madwoman in the Attic*, by Sandra Gilbert and Susan Gubar, weighed several pounds at least. At the university bookstore I had written on the flyleaf the words *For an eminently sane woman, from Max Bourbaki*.

I own one dark blue suit, and I thought that would be most appropriate for the occasion. White shirt, orange-and-black-striped tie (surely D_3 would know those are the Princeton colors), and black shoes almost chose themselves. It was still snowing, though now only lightly, and I took out my rubbers, which looked more urban than the galoshes I had worn on my errands. To keep my hair dry (it gets too curly when wet) I picked the Astrakhan hat I'd bought in Moscow three years ago but had hardly worn. Another reminder of Nedra. She had accompanied me to Moscow when I was invited to speak at the opening of the Shemyakin Institute and had picked out the hat for me at GUM, but it had been August in Moscow, and the last two winters in New Jersey hadn't seen much snow.

There was hardly a soul on the Dinky, the two-coach train to Princeton Junction, and very few passengers on the Amtrak to New York. When I exited Penn Station I discovered midtown Manhattan congealed in snow. There was not a cab to be had. Eighth Avenue was reduced to a two-lane track on which a trickle of traffic moved at glacial speed. After one look at the scene, I withdrew into the innards of the station and took the subway to Columbus Circle. When I got out at Central Park South, it was clear that I'd have to walk some ten blocks to D_3's digs.

With so little vehicular traffic, and despite the difficult footing, the city was quite beautiful—almost too perfect. As I toiled north through a shin-deep paste of trodden snow, the clouds lifted. Some stars were already visible—I could make out Orion, the Irish constellation according to some Princeton wag—and the lights of the high-rise buildings along Central Park sparkled on the snow. But it was cold, so cold that for the first time ever I pulled down the earflaps of my Russian hat and moved along as fast as the footing allowed. It took me fifteen minutes to reach the apartment house, by which time my feet were numb and my pant cuffs frozen solid. I wished I had been less concerned about my appearance and had brought my galoshes. After being examined by the imposing doorman, I was led to the elevator and the fifteenth-floor button was pressed for me.

The door to apartment 1501 was already open, but instead of my hostess, I found myself facing a young woman with startlingly green eyes and hair the color of crystallized honey. It took me a moment to recognize my former student and sometime matchmaker, Jocelyn Powers.

"Professor Weiss, happy New Year!" Jocelyn, bundled up in a long coat and scarf, vigorously shook my hand. "This is my friend Alan." She pointed to the young man behind her. "We're off to a big New Year's party and we're terribly late." She grinned self-consciously. "I would have loved to have heard from you how you met my grandmother. Maybe next time."

"Glad to have met you, sir," mumbled the young man as he pushed past me toward the elevator. "And thanks again for the drink, Dr. Ditmus," he called back into the apartment.

Before I could say anything, D_3 appeared behind him. "Max!" she exclaimed, arms outstretched, but then stopped and broke into laughter. "You look as if you've just stepped off the Trans-Siberian Railroad."

She started to help me take off my coat. As I slipped out of the sleeves, I turned sideways and saw my reflection in the full-length mirror. I did look silly: blue suit and a fur hat with the flaps still covering my ears. "It's wonderful to see.you again," D_3 said and kissed me on the cheek. "Oh! You're wet and cold! We seem to meet only in extremes: first the tropics, and now the Arctic." She stepped back and inspected me. "Take off those shoes," she commanded, "and sit next to the radiator."

I don't ordinarily take off my shoes at social functions, but here I meekly complied, then padded after my hostess as she led me into a huge, high-ceilinged living room. "Rent controlled," she said somewhat sheepishly.

She steered me to a wing chair near the softly gurgling radiator. "Let me get you something to warm yourself."

The heat from the radiator started to restore the circulation in my toes, but at the same time it thawed my icy pant cuffs, which commenced to drip on the Oriental carpet. "Max, some cognac?" Diana started to say, but then she stopped. "But you poor man," she exclaimed, "you must be soaked. You've got to take off your pants." Before I could protest, it became clear this was not a request but a virtual fait accompli: "Let me take you into the guest room, and you can put on a dressing gown and slippers. And let's do something about drying your shoes," she added, picking up my shoes and propelling me out of my chair.

When I came back, in leather slippers and a royal blue dressing gown that (to judge from the way it hung down to my ankles) must have come originally from the back of a basketball player, D_3 greeted me approvingly. "This *must* feel better," she exclaimed, guiding me once more to the chair by the radiator. Which, of course, was true, but I did feel silly as I sat back in my chair, barefoot and pantless, in a jacket and my underwear, about to greet the New Year. I drew the dressing gown around me. I didn't want her to see that I still had on my jacket.

"Cognac?" she asked again as she sat down beside me.

"Frankly, right now, I'd prefer some tea," I replied, remembering that I hadn't eaten for hours.

When I was on my second cup, I started to focus on D_3. She wore a high-necked, long black dress with white embroidery around the sleeves, a string of pearls and pearl earrings, and, except for light coloring on her thin lips, practically no makeup. Her hair seemed even blacker than I remembered from Little Dix Bay. Again I was struck by the remarkable absence of wrinkles on the face of a woman her age. But then, why should I have understood the reasons? Even though I know a lot about the chemical structure and biological function of collagen, I've never given a moment's thought to its cosmetic applications.

I had just finished getting comfortable when I remembered my gift. "Diana, I brought you something. I left it outside," I said and rose to fetch it from the side table in the entrance hall.

Diana had a charming, girlish way of unwrapping a package. "How thoughtful of you," she exclaimed after she'd finished reading the end flaps of the book jacket. "And what an apropos inscription! That reminds me of my own offering." She swept out, leaving me only a moment to take in the room before she reappeared, her smile grown both wider and mysterious. "Here, Max Bourbaki, is a New Year's gift for you." In her outspread hands she held a very thin, flat package wrapped in fine tissue paper. It held only two typed pages, bound in an exquisite Venetian manuscript folder: *The Genealogy of Nicolas Bourbaki.*

I was amused, at first, by what I read: In the seventeenth century, two Cretan brothers, Emanuel and Nicolas Skordylis, fought the invading Turks so bravely that in admiration the enemies referred to them as *vour bachi,* the Turkish expression for a "leader of hitmen." The brothers proudly accepted that appellation, which they passed on to their descendants in slightly modified Greek form as *Bourbaki.* Emanuel's great-grandson, Sauter Bourbaki, assisted Napoleon in his return from Egypt to France. In gratitude, the emperor provided for the education of Sauter's three sons. One became the father of General Charles Bourbaki, he of the French army in the 1870–71 war. The general's sister married a descendant of the original Nicolas Skordylis, and out of this branch of the Bourbaki clan came . . . my amusement had long since given way to astonishment: I had taken it at first for a joke, but this thing seemed persuasively real.

I looked up to meet D_3's triumphant gaze. "Where on earth did you dig this up?" I stammered. "And is it really true?"

She shrugged. "I have my sources. But is it true? As true as your mathematicians' Bourbaki. I think we should drink to that."

I was eyeing the last two slices of dill-sprinkled smoked salmon when my hostess announced that supper was ready.

While we were eating the sole, in a seemingly aimless way, I picked up the ball that Jocelyn's friend had thrown me as I entered D_3's apartment. "Tell me, *Doctor* Diana Doyle-Ditmus . . ."

"If you use that title, Max, then just 'Ditmus' me," she said mildly, "or we end up with too many D's."

"All right, Doctor *Ditmus*, why didn't you tell me you had a Ph.D.? Or is it an M.D.? Or perhaps you're a Doctor of Divinity?" I was about to slip on the dangerous slope of sarcasm when she stopped me.

"Ph.D."

"And why did I have to find that out from your granddaughter's boyfriend?"

"Not boyfriend. Alan is just her friend."

"All right, friend." I realized that she was just being playful, but I was too curious to play along. "Why did I have to learn from Jocelyn's *friend* that you have a Ph.D.?"

"Because you never asked me, Max."

"Couldn't you at least have dropped a hint?"

The look she gave me was no longer entirely playful. "How? Do you introduce yourself as *Doctor* Weiss?"

"Of course not."

"Well then? When we first argued about Bourbaki's name, should I have finished the discussion with, 'excuse me, but I *know* it's Charles because I have a *doctorate* in French history'?"

I shook my head helplessly. "Diana, you're really an amazing woman."

She reached over and gently tweaked my cheek. "So you've finally discovered that?"

In any experiment, once you discover a fact, you proceed from there. In this instance, the fact was that D_3 had a Ph.D.

"It's quite likely that I would never have gone for a Ph.D.— at least not in French history—if I hadn't met Philip Doyle at Swarthmore. Like Jocelyn with you, I didn't meet Philip until I was a senior."

And so I learned the first installment of Diana Doyle-Ditmus's biography.

Philip Doyle came from a wealthy family, "comfortably wealthy," she called it, "but not rich. Maybe that's why he was a scholar." He was a professor of history at Swarthmore, his specialty eighteenth-century France. He was in his late forties and the father of two teenage boys when Diana Ransome ended up in his class. Since the honors seminar she had really wanted to take had been oversubscribed, she picked Doyle's class—and not long thereafter became his wife. "I was bright," D_3 said between sips of coffee, "and had gone to a first-class girl's boarding school. I had no trouble getting into Swarthmore. But I didn't feel challenged. My family was reasonably well off, and in those days parents wanted their daughters to stay out of trouble and get married. There weren't any expectations in terms of performance. But then I took Philip's class, and I was never the same again. It's been . . . well, never mind the years—just call it decades—but I still remember his very first lecture. He didn't lead off with the usual characters—the men—but with the women of that period. He started with the salons run by—"

"Madame de Sévigné?" It was the only historical morsel I could think of in terms of French salons, so I offered it to Diana.

She looked up, surprised, but, I could tell, pleased. "Philip's lectures didn't go that far back; he started with Madame de Tencin. But let me tell you about Philip: he was my father's age, but that meant nothing to me. 'When I'm 101, you'll be 128. Who'll care then?' I said to him. From the very first I liked his sandy hair and those soft, penetrating eyes: he never needed glasses. He was an avid squash player, and his shoulders and thighs showed it. I found out about that later, of course.

"During the Easter break, he took a few of us on a tour of France. When we came back, he divorced his wife, and that summer, right after my graduation, he married me.

"As you can imagine, this was not the sort of marriage my parents had had in mind. Everybody was scandalized and predicted it wouldn't last: after all, his children were almost my contemporaries. But it did work for eleven years, most of them quite glorious, even though we had our problems."

I raised my eyebrows but said nothing.

"Max, do you have any children?"

I shook my head.

"Then you wouldn't understand . . . or maybe you would—you come from the same generation. Right after our marriage, I enrolled in graduate school—at Penn, which wasn't much of a commute. But in my third year, just as I'd started on my dissertation, I got pregnant." She shrugged her shoulders and grimaced. "Accidents happen. In most respects, Pamela's birth was a happy accident, but back then, motherhood was supposed to be a full-time occupation. Philip felt that way, and I was probably too conditioned to disagree. So I dropped out of school."

"That's too bad," I said, commiserating.

"That's how I felt at the time, but much later I discovered the silver lining: the experience had turned me into a feminist. When I went back to graduate school, I took up a very different dissertation topic, one that changed my life."

"What was that?"

Her hand waved the question away. "Enough of that, Max. Some other time."

"So what happened after the eleventh year?" I asked quietly.

"Philip had a heart attack and died. On the squash court. I was absolutely devastated. I was certain I'd never marry again. We had an eight-year-old daughter—Jocelyn's mother. She was the image of Philip. Pamela was tall for her age and rangy: a real tomboy. It was two years after the war, and I decided I'd go to France, where Philip and I had fallen in love. I had an excellent nanny, and my parents were living in Philadelphia, so I just took off for a couple of months."

"Sounds like something out of Hemingway," I interjected.

She nodded. "Almost too much so. Here was this youngish widow . . ."

Suddenly I started to calculate: if the war had been over for two years when she went to France, it must have been around 1947; if I subtract eleven from that, she had gotten married in June 1936, when she was in her senior year at Swarthmore. But that meant—

"What's the matter, Max? Why are you looking so strangely at me?"

What could I say? That I had suddenly realized she must be past seventy rather than in her early or middle sixties? "Oh, nothing," I stammered. "I was just thinking—"

"That I married again so quickly?"

I must have missed that part of the story, but I nodded anyway.

She seemed satisfied, however, because she continued with the story of her second husband, the forty-four-year-old former adjutant-general she'd met in Paris, also a recent widower. After their return to America, they moved into this huge apartment facing Central Park. From here her husband, Alexander J. Ditmus, commuted to his corporate law practice in lower Manhattan. He didn't mind that his bride retained her first husband's surname; Diana Doyle-Ditmus sounded quite *distingué*, rather British. For her fortieth birthday (my calculation, not her admission), Alexander Ditmus bought her a dilapidated château in the Dordogne. "You know the Dordogne," she said, giving me no chance to tell her that I didn't. "There must be hundreds of castles. This one, near Beynac-et-Cazenac, was quite small; we got it for a song. But I really fixed it up, and until the children—my Pamela and Alex's two kids—grew up, we went there every summer. Alex was very much a Francophile. That's where I learned about wines—from Alex, who started a magnificent cellar at the château. He died when he was eighty-two.

"I was lucky with my two husbands."

She was starting, I could tell, on yet another epoch in what I could see was a long life story. I was beginning to wonder how

I would find out why, where, and when she got her Ph.D., but at that point she looked at her watch. "My goodness," she exclaimed. "It's a quarter to midnight. Another year almost gone by." She rose from her chair and stretched out her hand. "Come, Max. Let's get some more champagne. We'll toast the New Year over by the window. It's a grand view."

If there was any New Year's celebration down on the street, it couldn't be heard on the fifteenth floor. Precisely at midnight, we touched glasses: the ring of crystal sounded through the room; in another part of the suite, bells were sweetly chiming twelve. "To your Bourbaki, Max," she said softly, then took a sip. "Let us do it."

Maybe all the champagne had dulled my responses, but for a second or two I'd lost her. "Let's do what?" I heard myself say. "Us?" I asked again.

"Don't be so dense, Max. Remember what you told me on the beach: that you wouldn't be able to pull it off?"

I remembered nothing of the sort.

"About needing money and an address?"

I could only goggle at her in amazement.

"Let that be my contribution. I've always wanted to start up a salon—you know, like the Mesdames de Sévigné and Tencin, or Mademoiselle de Lespinasse. I'd like your Bourbaki to be my own private, scientific salon."

A combination of surprise, confusion, and irritation turned me momentarily speechless. A salon was *not* what I had had in mind. Nicolas Bourbaki a salon?

"Have you any idea," I protested, "how much it costs to support the research of even one—"

"Max." It was amazing how many syllables D_3 managed to find in my name. "Whenever you scientists talk about a new project, you always start by complaining about how little money you have and how much you'll need. Instead, why don't you—"

"What would *you* know about scientists and their need for money—exaggerated or real?"

"Hadn't I told you that I've known a number of them in my days?"

Something registered in my brain. "What does 'in my days' mean?"

"When I was Dean." She pronounced the word with a capital *D*.

"Dean of what?" Was I croaking, or did it only seem that way to me?

"H and S at NYU. For six years—long enough to expose me to quite a number of chemists, physicists, biologists—"

"Diana, stop." I was pleading, not commanding. My head was swimming and I needed to digest this information. Dean of humanities and sciences at New York University? Was she pulling my leg? Why hadn't she told me that back at Virgin Gorda? My feelings must have been drawn on my face, because she leaned over and cupped my chin. It was certainly an effective way to maintain eye contact.

"Max, don't be annoyed. Why didn't I tell you when we first met?" She let go of my chin and sat back in her chair. "You know what professors want from deans: money or perks or both. A couple of weeks ago—and even more so tonight—I thought: here's an opportunity to really get to *know* a scientist. I hope you aren't sorry; because I'm not."

"No, not sorry."

She threw me a warm smile. "I don't think you will be, either. Your Bourbaki, Max: I think I can help."

"How?" I *was* croaking.

Her smile had gone mysterious again. "A good dean learns how to find money where there isn't much. And I was an exceptionally good dean."

She stood. "But all in good time. It's getting late. Come. Let me show you one more thing."

34   Diana took me by the hand and led me into her study. I fol-

lowed meekly enough. I was still reeling from the shock of what I'd learned—of realizing how much I had assumed about Diana, and how far those assumptions had been from the truth. What else didn't I know? I was willing to find out—and eager to know what she had in mind.

Although the bookshelves in her study reached to the ceiling, the books were piled chaotically everywhere—a sure sign of a functioning library. The desk was covered with journals and magazines; once again I was taken by surprise. This wasn't a lady's study designed by an interior decorator; this was lived-in working space. D_3 swept to the desk and rummaged through a stack of papers. "Here," she said proudly, "take a look at this one."

"*Nicolas Bourbaki und die heutige Mathematik,*" it said on the title page. I had no difficulty in scanning the German text, but what amazed me was its origin, from a journal so obscure that I had never heard of it: *Arbeitsgemeinschaft für Forschung des Landes Nordrhein-Westfalen.* It was the text of a talk given on January 8, 1958, by none other than Henri Cartan, the famous French mathematician who had been rumored to be one of the original Bourbakis. "I'll be damned," I finally murmured, which concession seemed to please D_3 no end.

"I wanted you to see that I took your Bourbaki idea seriously—at least as a historian. I haven't finished yet with my research, but I've learned enough to realize that you could pull it off without a new address and heaps of new money."

My head was really spinning now, and not just from too much champagne. This was simply too much for one evening. "Diana," I said, "look what time it is." I held out my wristwatch. "I've got to get home."

"And how will you do that?"

"The way I came, of course."

"Max," she said in that naughtily drawn-out manner of hers, "I haven't taken a train for a long time, at least in this country, but I can't imagine that at 2:00 A.M. on New Year's Day there are trains running to Princeton."

"God, I forgot. It's a holiday!"

"Max. How do impractical men like you do practical science?"

Her tone was playful, not sarcastic, and the hauteur with which I replied was equally so. "My science is not practical. It's important."

She laughed. "You're right. But you're fortunate that one of us *is* practical: I made up a bed for you and put out some pajamas. It's the room where you changed before. You'll find everything you need in the bathroom."

I spread out my hands and inclined my head. Of course it made sense to accept. "Diana, you're a paragon of hospitality."

"Not really," she said and rose from her chair. "Only when it pleases me. And you please me, Max. Happy New Year."

I had a terrible time falling asleep. It wasn't the unfamiliar surroundings, or the unaccustomed feeling of silk pajamas. Generally I'm not bothered by new places. I do a fair amount of traveling, mostly professional, and I've slept in much less luxurious, and certainly stranger, quarters than this bedroom on Central Park West. And two in the morning is way past my bedtime. It was D_3's "Let *us* do it." In the past, my speculations about a Bourbaki had been just that—speculation, a fantasy of vengeance, a fraternity (yes, my imagination had always assumed they would be men) of aging academics, men like me who would understand my hurt and share my determination to vindicate myself before a world that held me old, and therefore useless. But now that my cherished fantasy threatened to turn into reality, but a reality such as I had never imagined, realized by a woman who dreamed of French salons, I was getting cold feet. Somehow, the net effect was equivalent to incomplete catabolism of a double espresso.

I tried my usual trick: to focus on something pleasant and uncomplicated until sleep takes over. I thought about the Château d'Yquem that D_3 had produced for dessert, but instead of putting me to sleep it reminded me of last year's Biochemistry Congress in Paris. There had been a stag dinner at the Taillevent in the Rue Lamennais; an Yquem had been on the wine list, and I had tried as unsuccessfully as with the Pètrus to talk my companions into sharing the staggering price for a bottle so as to end the meal in a totally nonacademic style.

I lay there for some time, trying to remember who had finally put the hex on my proposal by making some witty comparison between the thinness of his wallet and his dean's generosity, until my synapses fired: Sepp Krzilska. His Christmas card, showing snow-covered Innsbruck, had included a few lines in his Germanic script: "I must tell you already now that we shall meet no more at Taillevent dinners. Our *verdammte* university administration has retired me at 65! So it's *Auf Wiedersehen zur Molekularbiologie.*" I hadn't known Sepp was that old. The thought of Sepp had a soothing effect on my nerves. I could feel myself relaxing, settling into the familiar dreams that Diana's intervention had made so strangely real. Sepp Krzilska would make a great Bourbaki member. If he was really so irritated with his administration, joining a new Bourbaki might be just the right balm for his bruised ego. As sleep finally fell, the name *Bruce Dego* hovered in the darkness before me. I wondered what D_3 would think of it as the name for our Bourbaki.

6

"Dee, ee, gee, oh?" She spelled it slowly, as if she were tasting it—like the grapefruit she was having for breakfast. "I'm not sure, Max. It's not just the resemblance to 'Dago.' There's something else not quite right about it. It's not as if this is a joke for you."

"You're right," I conceded, putting another dollop of lingonberry preserves on my toast. "Besides, 'Dego' is too short."

Diana had an amused look. "Aren't we being a bit premature? Worrying what to call the author when we haven't selected the people to do the work?"

There she was again: jolting me back to reality. " 'Premature' is a colossal understatement," I said. "There is no purpose in thinking of people unless we first address the question of money."

"Typical scientist's response."

I deferred to her with a mock bow. "Then enlighten me, Dean Ditmus."

"I will, provided you wipe the smug expression from your professorial face and pay attention."

"Yes, Dean." Until now, I had taken it all as play, but her sudden change of demeanor—the way she leaned forward, pointing her spoon at me—made me realize that she was serious.

"How large a group are you thinking of?"

"For a start? Four. No more than that."

"That shouldn't be too difficult to fund. What about support personnel? If your group is typical, you've long ago forgotten how to do research by yourself; you'll need pairs of hands—grad students and postdocs—to do the actual work for you."

I was about to object, but her spoon stopped me. "Unlike, I might add, those of us in the humanities. We do our *own* research to the day we retire. Some of us think it keeps us honest."

"Unfair, Diana. All you do is read and write."

"All?"

"I don't mean to say that's nothing," I added quickly, retreating from that spoon. "But it doesn't require much in the way of equipment. Beyond the library."

"And computers."

"All right, computers. Of a sort. But what are you driving at?"

"I'm trying to get some idea of the budget you'll need. Beyond personnel, I assume there will be laboratories, equipment."

"Actually," I said, "there won't."

"No labs?"

Using her momentary confusion to regain the floor, I matched her spoon with a monitory index finger, a gesture I had acquired from years of lecturing. "The original Bourbaki worked in mathematics; he, or they, focused on theory. We shall do the same. Not

only are equipment costs kept to a minimum that way, but very few people need to be in on the secret. There are several areas in theoretical biology where the same favorable conditions for anonymity exist, provided there is access to library resources *and* computers." There was something too declamatory in the way I came down on that final "*and* computers," as if I was actually pacing at the front of an auditorium. Embarrassed to find I'd been lecturing, I finished diffidently. "The only reason I mentioned theoretical biology is that it has a pretty wide scope; it even fits my latest research experience. That's all."

"In that case," she mused, "we'll have to fund only four people—"

"*We* only," I muttered. I was surprised to hear I'd said the words aloud.

"That's right, *only*, and, of course, free access to computers, which even a senior research biochemist without stipend can probably arrange. The libraries are similarly paid for. And since your Bourbakis will all be retired, all we need is some supplement to their pensions. That shouldn't be too difficult. Take MacArthur, for instance—"

The word registered a bright blip on my mental radar. Why always them?

"They give the biggest grants to older people—for five years at a time."

I remembered our earlier conversation. "But you can't apply for them, you've got to be nominated."

"So? If you got four very bright candidates, they might be nominated. And even if only one of them got a MacArthur, you could easily be talking about $350,000 over a five-year period." She threw me a QED look.

I have to admit that on occasion I have dreamed about those "genius awards"—usually while reading the annual list in the *Times*. But I didn't know the details of the selection process. "Do you know any MacArthur nominators?" I asked.

"Yes."

"And how they pick the candidates?"

"Yes."

I was getting intrigued. "And winners? Do you know any personally?"

"Yes."

I'll be damned, I thought. Did she pick this up as dean of H and S at NYU? "You mean you know them well?"

"Exceedingly well."

It was the word *exceedingly*, and the very faint, but nevertheless discernible, look of triumph in D₃'s eyes that finally gave me the clue.

"Tell me," I said slowly. "Did the two bottles of '70 Pètrus have anything to do with the MacArthur Foundation?"

"Uh-huh," was all she said.

"Congratulations. When did you get it?"

"Just a couple of months before going to Little Dix Bay."

I realized my curiosity might appear gross, but I couldn't help asking. "And what are you doing with all this money?"

She grinned. "Sipping good wine in interesting places and supporting my research."

"On?"

"Diane de Poitiers. I am writing a new biography of her. From a feminist perspective," she added.

"Oh."

"Her name doesn't mean anything to you, does it?"

My "oh" had given me away. I realized this was a familiar scene: the professor plumbing the depth of the student's knowledge (or lack thereof); the student doing his level best to disguise same. It's just that it had been awhile since I'd played the role of the student.

"The keeper of some French salon?" I offered cautiously.

"Too early. She was born in 1499. Eventually, she became the lover of Henri II."

"Oh," I acknowledged.

"She was nineteen years older."

"Oh." My unconscious frown must have given me away.

"I see you don't approve." Before I could object, she continued, **40** "And he loved her until his death. At age forty. His age, not hers."

"Oh," I said again before deciding to risk a multisyllabic response. "The age difference—is that what interested you?"

"Partly, but also the role of women in sixteenth-century France. You see, *my* century is the eighteenth, and after my retirement, I thought I might as well move back a couple of hundred years. How women establish financial independence is one topic feminists are interested in. And my Diane managed that very well."

"And that's what MacArthur decided to support?" The moment I said it, I realized my words sounded dismissive.

If she felt so, she didn't let on. "The beauty of the MacArthur grants is that they require nothing from you—they just let you do your own thing. With me, it's a feminist analysis of a sixteenth-century Frenchwoman, and with you—if you got a MacArthur [did my incipient blush show?]—it would be instigating a new Bourbaki in theoretical biology."

"So tell me about *your* century. Why the eighteenth?"

Her hand waved the entire century away. "Some other time. Let's return to your Bourbaki and money." In that gesture, she had reverted to dean.

"I'm not even sure whether any of your pensions need topping off. They may be generous or there may be some other independent income." She smiled. "I noticed you managed Little Dix Bay without a grant. But even though you said your Bourbaki would be a theoretician, I'm sure that some extra money is needed: travel to scientific conferences, to your own meetings—unless you all come from one institution—"

"Highly unlikely," I interrupted.

"I agree," she nodded. "And dangerous. Harder to keep the secret. Decentralization is safer. It will also simplify raising the necessary funds."

"Oh?" I found myself returning to my favorite monosyllable.

"Max, you can't possibly be naive in grantsmanship. One can always siphon off some portion of a grant for other purposes. You scientists do this all the time. *You* know it, your *dean* knows it, and even the grant-giving agency knows it. If you don't overdo it, they probably even approve. Bootlegged funds—at least among 41 academics—usually are used frugally and for interesting ventures."

"So?"

"So if there are four of you—far apart and probably already funded for ongoing research—you could each divert a bit for your Bourbaki project. Unless, of course, one of you should get a MacArthur."

"Forget MacArthur." I had a vague recollection that I had said that before. Besides, she was right: the budget we'd need could probably be funded by four emeritus professors who were still on the ball. "But what about our Bourbaki's address?"

"What about it? The original Nicolas Bourbaki solved that problem easily: he claimed to be working at the University of Nancago."

I frowned. "Nancago? I've never heard of it. Where is it?"

Diana beamed at me. "You wouldn't have. It's made up: a combination of Nancy and Chicago. I suppose you know that some of the early Bourbakis came from the University of Nancy, although some also were at Strasbourg and at Clermont-Ferrand; but at least one of them, André Weil, ended up at the University of Chicago. In 1949 the *Journal of Symbolic Logic* carried a paper by Nicolas Bourbaki of the University of Nancago."

"And where did you discover that piece of information?"

A prim, pleased smile creased her face. "I have my sources."

I had a feeling that I'd heard those words before, too, but I decided to let it pass.

"Let's drop the bureaucratic stuff and focus on the key question: The quality of a salon does not really depend on the furniture or the address, but on the quality," she tapped her head for emphasis, "of the participants. You said you wanted to start with no more than four. Only three more to go, then. How will you find them?"

"Perhaps we have only two to go." I told her enough about Sepp Krzilska for her to agree that he was a candidate worth considering. Sepp had always been among the avant-garde: he had been the first Austrian to attend one of the superexclusive Cold

Spring Harbor Symposia in Woods Hole—the Mecca of molecular biology. His English was quite fluent, though sprinkled with Germanicisms. Our first meeting had ended on a disarming note when Sepp asked whether I could lend him a "security needle," because he'd torn his pants. His literal translation of the German word, *Sicherheitsnadel*, for "safety pin" became a private joke. To this day, when we exchange reprints, I fasten them together with safety pins. I knew he was temperamentally right for our Bourbaki as well: he had the requisite bruised ego.

"What about the remaining two?"

I shrugged my shoulders. "I'll have to give that some thought. I ought to see first how Sepp responds to the idea. Frankly, Diana, I don't even know how to present it to him. What should I say? 'I met this remarkable woman on a beach, who—after getting some advice on suicide, but without volunteering that she was a Mac-Arthur genius—offered to encourage the intellectual outpourings of some superannuated academic *rentiers* . . .'"

Diana's laughter was infectious, but then she turned all business, as if she were checking off items on a list. "How long will it take you to find the other candidates?"

"Two or three months, I'd guess."

"That long?"

"Well, you know how long mail takes," I said, defensively. "I have to write to Austria, I may have to write to Japan. I'll have to study the literature a bit and look at some biographical compendia to check ages and present positions. I'll have to—"

"Max," she said pityingly, "surely you aren't going to do this by ordinary correspondence—using your quill pen, I don't doubt. Call them. Fax them—"

Her condescension, even if it was in fun, irritated me. "There are times when a fax is not the ideal vehicle for proposing a dramatic change in a person's lifestyle."

"Like a marriage proposal?"

Who's talking about marriage proposals? I wanted to say.

But I didn't.

7

Condensing, filtering, discarding, cleaning up—these are all common activities in the lab, a part of the routine you hardly notice. But when you do them in preparation for the move from your splendid office into the rather Spartan quarters reserved for a *"Senior Research Biochemist without stipend,"* then you notice, and the task is painful as well as time-consuming. It wasn't something I could easily delegate, because only I could decide which papers to discard and which ones to pack and store, leaving out only the most important ones to go into the three-drawer file cabinet in my new "office."

I had decided to spend two hours daily on this detritus sifting: it was the only way to get it done by the beginning of March. Yet my mood had lifted, and I had to admit that Diana was largely responsible for this change. My bitterness at the university, my sorrow at the mortal resonances associated with moving after some decades of comfortable solidity—these had begun to recede. As I searched my files for discardables, I found myself happily playing with names for my new Bourbaki. I was like a parent testing names for a new offspring—a pleasure I had heretofore not experienced.

"Professor Weiss. A student from last semester's class, a senior named Jocelyn Powers, wants to make an appointment. Do you want to see her?"

Jessica has been my secretary for more than a dozen years—thirteen to be precise—and she still calls me Professor, a gesture I appreciate. I've never been able to understand why some professors permit their secretaries and students to *tutoyer* them; it's like going to a formal party without a jacket and tie. Sure, it's chummy; but does it have style? Then why don't I address her as

Miss Szabo? Because the very first day she started working with me and I "Szaboed" her, she said, "Please call me Jessica."

There is little Jessica doesn't know about me. Since Nedra's death, she's even helped me with my personal affairs. I saw no reason why Jessica shouldn't know about Bourbaki, especially since she would be deeply involved in the affair if we could pull it off. Powers's call was precisely the opening I needed. I told Jessica to set up an appointment for tomorrow, then called her in. I pointed to the door. "Close it, Jessica, and sit down. I've got something to tell you." She didn't interrupt me once; even my transparently evasive references to Diana's role in the affair met only with raised eyebrows. But at the end, she surprised me. She looked at me dreamily and said, "I've always fancied leading a second life under another name." In all my years with Jessica, I don't recall her ever having said "fancied" before.

"I'm so glad my grandmother caught up with you at Little Dix Bay. You two seem to have had a marvelous time. I wasn't surprised, though."

I would have given a lot to find out how D_3 had described our meeting to her granddaughter, but instead I just nodded. "Yes," I said, "we did meet. Now, what can I do for you?" I leaned back, my chin in one hand, the fingers of the other drumming slowly on the side of the armchair: the studied posture of an academic adviser. The finger drumming was an ingrained habit—*get to the point*—except that this time I didn't mean it. I was curious and not in a hurry.

What I could do for her seemed to require a good deal of explanation. With very little prompting on my side, she volunteered her curriculum vitae. She'd been quite good in science and math at Andover, and when she got to Princeton—her father's alma mater—had started out as a chemistry major. She hadn't been "turned on" by anything in particular (I always shrink when students "turn on" or "off"—almost as much as when they tell me that some class or professor is "neat"), but when her grandmother, who had always been so concerned about cancer, had asked "why not medicine?" she'd followed the path of least resistance. It was an oddly apologetic story, although I couldn't quite see why. Was she apologizing to me? For what?

As she told me that story she lifted a lock of her glossy hair and twisted it slowly and rhythmically around her forefinger. The childish gesture called attention to her elegantly elongated face. Slowly, however, her finger fell still, and she turned her attention full on me. "Last fall, I'd finished all the premed requirements, so I decided to take some electives. I was thinking of art history when I heard about your comp biochem course."

"Rather different from art history," I observed.

"Not really, if you think about some of the molecular models you showed us. You know that Kenneth Snelson sculpture? The one in Procter Court, in the Graduate College?"

By God, she was right: the tubes, balls, and wires of that Snelson could almost be a weird molecular structure. But why is she telling me all this? I wondered. Is she buttering me up for a letter of recommendation?

"Halfway through your course, I was asking myself, Why go to medical school? To be treated like an undergrad for another four years? All along, I've wanted to do research. I don't need an M.D. for that."

I put up my hands to suggest that she consider carefully before leaving a house she'd barely entered. But she didn't give me a chance; with the enthusiasm I still find touching in the young, she was warming to her subject.

"I've decided to get a Ph.D.—either in biochemistry or molecular biology—and to do it right here at Princeton."

"Now wait a moment," I interrupted her. "Have you at least considered some of the other top institutions? The Whitehead at MIT? Or the West Coast: Paul Berg is building quite an empire at Stanford; or some of the University of California campuses, like Berkeley or San Francisco or San Diego? Why do all of your studies in one place?"

"Why not?"

46   "Inbreeding."

"But I like it here. I don't mean *right here,* but the proximity to New York, to my family, to . . . you know . . ." Her stream of words petered out.

"I know," I said quietly, although I wasn't sure I did. "But still: you do want to learn other viewpoints, other approaches. You know . . ." I caught myself mimicking her.

"Viewpoints?" She looked puzzled, vaguely offended. "But this is science! Besides, the professors in graduate school aren't the ones I had in my undergraduate courses, except for you, and even that was for only one semester. I can always do a postdoc somewhere else."

"All right," I yielded, trying to suppress a smile. Had I ever been so earnest? "So what advice do you want from me?"

As she calmed down, she started again to play with her hair. This time she stroked it for a long moment, as if it might produce a genie, or some other source of inspiration. Abruptly, she put her hand on my desk and leaned forward. "It isn't exactly advice. I came to ask whether you'd accept me into your group."

I'd seen it coming, of course, but even so I was pleased. In all my years as a professor, after all the graduate students who have done their doctoral research with me, I still get a flush of pleasure when a student comes and asks to join my research group. I've always thought that medieval priors must have felt the same way when a novice showed up at the door of the monastery. The abbot in me gave a benedictory smile. "I appreciate your asking, Jocelyn." There are several right moments to start using a student's first name. This was clearly one of them, even though I was going to disappoint her. "But I'm not accepting new students anymore."

She looked crestfallen. "You're not stopping your research too, are you?"

"Certainly not!" I straightened up in my armchair. "But taking on a graduate student is too long a commitment at this stage of my life. It wouldn't be fair to the student." Now why wasn't I telling Jocelyn Powers the whole truth—that a "Senior Research Biochemist" couldn't serve as a thesis supervisor?

"You couldn't make an exception?" She looked at me earnestly, with that wholeheartedly pleading expression only the young let others see.

"An exception?" Even as I mulled it over I could see where this was going to end.

And why not? Wasn't I trying, in setting up my Bourbaki, to become the exception—the man they couldn't retire? And hadn't all of this come about in the first place through Jocelyn? I didn't really have to decide—it had already been decided for me, it seemed, long before. All I had to do was acquiesce.

"I'll tell you what. You're graduating in June. Starting this summer, I'll be needing a part-time research assistant to help me with certain projects. It's unlikely to involve any lab work, but the person can pretty well arrange her own schedule. It won't be the same as working in my group—and I wouldn't be your thesis adviser. But if you're serious about getting a Ph.D. at Princeton and you can find a professor who suits you for your thesis research, there's no reason why you can't combine both."

I stood, reaching over the desk to shake her hand. Like most well-trained young Princetonians, she stood on cue; the handshake let me guide her out the door. I don't ordinarily encourage students to linger, but this time I was even more eager than usual to regain my privacy. As I strode back to the desk and pushed the intercom button, I realized that my Bourbaki train might actually be ready to pull out of the station. Not only have I found a research assistant, but she's probably the only one in the world who won't be surprised when she learns about the role of her grandmother in this affair.

"Jessica," I said into the intercom. "I'd like to dictate a letter to Professor Krzilska in Innsbruck."

A couple of days later, D_3 called. "Anything new on the Bourbaki front?"

"I've started to make some progress."

"Oh?"

I could sense her curiosity over the phone. "I've found a research assistant." It seemed Jocelyn hadn't told her.

"Is that all? Isn't that a bit like putting the cart before the horse? Sort of a baby carriage in front of a Clydesdale?"

I was tempted to retort that we do that all too often in the lab: placing minicarts in front of maxihorses. "Not really," I chuckled, then proceeded to tell her all about her granddaughter.

"I'll be damned! And she never breathed a word to me! I'm impressed."

I wasn't sure whether the last remark applied to Jocelyn's discretion or the fact that her granddaughter would be working with me. But, as usual, I didn't have time to find out: the next question was already on the way.

"Other than Joss, have you found any other people?"

"Not yet. I've written to Professor Krzilska, suggesting I might have something interesting to propose in connection with his retirement. I told him to expect a phone call from me in a couple of weeks. I didn't want to break it to him without some preparation."

"And what about the next two?"

"Diana, you act as if one could produce such people out of a hat." I was starting to get irritated. "I can't very well advertise."

"Of course you can't. I was just wondering how you'd go about it. If money is a problem at this stage, please let me know. Perhaps MacArthur can be of some assistance."

"Money?" I said slowly. "Actually, money could expedite matters at this point, but I think I know where to find it. For my present needs, I can probably tap the departmental seminar budget."

Diana's comment, back in her apartment, about the value of diversification had prompted me to consider throwing a wide net. The University of Tokyo, with its absurdly early retirement age, seemed a reasonable fishing ground. I didn't think I'd have much trouble convincing my department that Hiroshi Nishimura would be right for a special Bowman Lecture. The Bowman funds could entice speakers from just about anywhere in the academic universe.

The real problem was not money but how I could persuade Nishimura to accept. Flying to the States on short notice would be **49** more of a nuisance than an incentive for someone of his reputation, especially one who, like Hiroshi, spoke exceptionally good English and was therefore much in demand. He could easily turn the invitation down. How could I make it one he'd *want* to accept?

The annual meeting of the National Academy of Sciences was scheduled to start on April 24. The following day would be the business session, when the election of foreign associates would be announced. I had no idea whether Hiroshi knew that he was a candidate, and I certainly didn't want to appear to promise what might not come off. But why not insinuate something about his chances? I called one of my colleagues in the Physics Department who was also a member of the Academy. "Herman," I said, "I've been looking at the slate of foreign candidates. I see we have two Japanese, one of them a physicist. Can you tell me something about him?" It was not an unreasonable question: to ask about the qualifications of an Academy candidate in another field before marking one's ballot.

"Don't waste your vote. There are two physicists on the list, and the other one is from Venezuela. You know how the Council is always complaining that the sections only propose Europeans, Japanese, and the odd Israeli or Australian. The Venezuelan is a shoo-in." Before writing to Nishimura, I looked once more over the list of foreign associates. There were no other biochemists.

I ended my letter to Nishimura, *"Let me propose April 27 for a Bowman Lecture at Princeton. This way, you could also attend the annual meeting of the National Academy of Sciences in Washington, which is held earlier that week. All of the sessions are open, except for the business meeting where the new members and foreign associates are elected. Even that may be of interest to you. We can then ride together on the train back to Princeton. I'll bring the champagne, just in case."*

The last sentence was probably somewhat disingenuous, and I don't know whether it really made any difference. In any event, Nishimura accepted.

If I had thought D_3 would be satisfied with my progress, I was wrong. "What about the fourth member?" she wanted to know.

"Can't you find a woman?"

"It's difficult enough to find a suitable *man*," I groaned. "Where will I find a *woman?* Ready to retire and in our field, to boot."

"Just try," she said soothingly. "If you can produce an Austrian and a Japanese man, surely you could find an American woman. At least show that you tried. By the way, have you read my article yet? I sent you a photocopy."

Yes, I told her, I had read it. In fact, I'd found it rather charming: "*La Spectatrice:* A Secret Journal of Eighteenth-Century French Feminists." I'd even marked certain paragraphs for eventual after-dinner chitchat with D₃.

"And *A Room of One's Own?*" she added. "I sent it on impulse. I thought you might not have read Virginia Woolf before."

"Thanks for sending it."

"What did you think of the library scene?"

I don't like being quizzed; especially not when my facts are wobbly. I stalled: "Library scene?"

"Didn't you find it outrageous that not so long ago—in fact, within your lifetime—a woman couldn't enter a university library?"

"Oh, well," I said, trying to steer a neutral course, "you know the Brits."

"So you think that's all it was? The Brits at Oxbridge? Didn't you know that at Harvard, long after the Second World War, no woman could use the Lamont Library?"

"Is that true?"

"Do you want to see it documented?"

"No, no—of course not." And then I said something I regretted saying, but by then it was too late. "I'll see what I can do about finding a Nicole Bourbaki."

But I had told D₃ the truth: it's awfully difficult to find potential candidates, irrespective of gender, if one has to do it *in camera*. The most efficient way would be through the proverbial old boys' network, but that is hardly designed to uncover *female* candidates. For a moment, I toyed with the idea of asking Jessica to go through *American Men and Women of Science* and identify all the women in the biological sciences above the age of sixty-four. **51**

I even swiveled my chair around to look at the bookshelf behind my desk, but then I discarded the idea: eight volumes, each the size of a phone book. I couldn't possibly ask Jessica. My eyes were still scanning the bluish gray volumes of that compendium when I noticed the National Academy of Sciences Directory on the same shelf. That slim volume contains less than two thousand names: the elite of American scientists—at least that's what the members of the Academy claim, and who am I to argue otherwise? The mean age of the membership is probably over sixty—a gold mine of potential Bourbakis—and there can't be more than fifty women members altogether.

It took me all of ten minutes to collect the females of the relevant species: biochemistry, genetics, cellular and developmental biology. There weren't many women, but by the time I'd finished going through the directory, I was surprised that I'd assembled a list of nearly a dozen. I knew about half of them personally and most of the rest by reputation.

After that, it was a simple matter to look up their biographies in *American Men and Women of Science*. Not so long ago, the title of this directory didn't even include "and Women." Now, it wasn't long before I found the professional c.v. of a suitable Nicole. In retrospect, I'm still surprised at how quickly I felt she was the right candidate, even though I knew less about Charlea Cherith Conway, Professor of Mathematical Biophysics at the University of Chicago, than any other woman on my list. Her name was barely familiar to me, but that was not surprising: her field was so very different from mine. I didn't even know they had professorships at Chicago so precisely defined as mathematical biophysics. (Only later did I learn that the University of Chicago had obliterated that program by moving it into theoretical biology. Conway, however, had refused to alter her title, thus reinforcing her status as *avis rarissima*). Her c.v. was impressive: a substantial list of awards, lectureships, honorary memberships in learned societies—even two honorary doctorates, from Holyoke and Brown. But what made me zoom in on her biography were three seemingly minor entries: her unmarried—in fact, never-married—status, which might mean she was dependent on her own income; her membership on the editorial board of the *Journal of Theoretical Biology*; and her age: sixty-four last October. I picked up the phone and dialed her office number at the University of Chicago.

"Conway!"

Even if I know the person, this kind of response always puts me on the defensive. People who just give their last name, without any "Hello" or other mollifiers, usually do so in a testy tone. The implication is all too clear: *why are you bothering me?*

I got straight to the point. "This is Max Weiss from Biochemistry at Princeton. I'm calling to ask whether you're going to this year's annual meeting of the NAS."

"Weiss?" she asked. "Are you the one who published on the regulation of early T cell activation genes?"

Well, well, I thought, maybe Charlea Conway *is* the right choice. "Yes," I replied, trying to put some modesty into that three-letter word, "so you read that paper?"

"Uh-huh. You've got an interesting idea there, but I think you've got the actual regulator wrong."

I was about to ask her what the hell she meant by that, but she wasn't finished. "Yes, I'll be in Washington. Let's get together and talk about T cell activation. I'm working on some theoretical aspects of the process."

I could hardly believe my luck: I didn't even have to explain why I wanted to meet her. Now I could look her over and see whether she was a potential candidate. But how could we be wrong about our NFAT? There's no question that this protein is restricted to *activated* T cells. That's what NFAT stands for: nuclear factor of activated T cells. I was curious about what she'd have to say when I showed her our gel mobility shift assays. There's no question we're right.

8

The Royal Society of London, the Académie des Sciences in Paris, the Leopoldina in Halle, the Royal Swedish Academy of Sciences in Stockholm: none of these can beat our National Academy in terms of the breakfasts offered to the members and their spouses. In the center of the Great Hall of the Academy's building on Constitution Avenue in Washington, D.C., the huge round tables literally overflow with the freshest baby bagels I've ever tasted, accompanied by cream cheese, lox without a trace of oil, and exquisite tiny Danish pastries—none of that huge, doughy stuff served at conventions in hotel lobbies. The coffee is freshly brewed, the water for the tea is boiling hot, the orange juice squeezed that morning. Philip Handler, the first Jewish president of the Academy, instituted this tradition, and with minor changes it has flourished ever since.

This year, on the second morning of the annual meeting, I'd just finished my glass of orange juice and was backing away from the table with saucer and teacup in one hand and a full plate in the other, using my rump to push through the crowd, when my left elbow took a solid jolt: tea splattered my jacket.

"Dammit," I muttered, "see what you did?"

"So sorry," said a woman's voice lacking any sorrow. "Let me wipe you off." Before I could even respond, I was propelled to the periphery of the milling crowd, a napkin dabbing at my jacket.

There is one other distinctive aspect of the NAS meetings that I should mention: the identification badges. I have attended my share of meetings all over the world. I could write an essay on the variety of badges used on these occasions. I particularly dislike the self-adhesive ones, which leave one's lapels prematurely bald; and the badges without pins, only a fold, which is supposed to fit into your breast pocket—useless when you just wear a sweater, as I've been known to do. And then the print: either it's so small you have to lean way forward to read the name, or else there is so much ancillary information crowded onto the small space that there isn't much left for the bearer's name. The National Academy of Sciences—perhaps in deference to the failing eyesight of its aging members—uses good-sized cards, enclosed in plastic and fastened with a solid safety pin, which show solely your name, printed boldly and in huge black letters. Even at three paces you don't need twenty-twenty vision to be able to pretend to recognize whomever you've just bumped into.

When I heard "So you're Max Weiss!" I didn't have to bend down to read *Charlea C. Conway* on the badge of the short woman wiping the tea off my jacket. "I was wondering how we'd meet in this crowd," she went on, still scrubbing my jacket. "Somehow, I had a different perception of you. It must have been your voice on the phone."

"Oh?" I purred, thinking that the same was true of her. The peremptory tone she'd used on the phone had made me think of a tall, rather severe androgyne—not this stocky, carelessly dressed woman with the warm and amused look in her eyes. "And what did you have in mind?"

"Someone younger."

Well, I thought, I never said I wanted a diplomat. "How much younger?"

She shrugged her shoulders. "It doesn't matter. Say, what are you up to right now?"

"The business meeting is about to start. I thought I'd go. I'd like to know how the elections come out."

She eyed me curiously. "Unless some silly man decides to make a spectacle of himself and blackballs someone in public, it's all been settled by mail. You saw the preference order of the individual section ballots."

"Actually, I'm interested in the foreign associates. Remember? The Council picks them."

She gave a dismissive shrug. "You can find that out at the end of the session. Why don't we go out and talk? It's beautiful today. In Chicago, we won't see weather like this for another month."

It was a gorgeous, soft spring day, and the prospect of spending it inside a windowless hall was not an inviting one. Besides, my business with Charlea Conway was more important than the largely preordained business of the Academy. With her, I had work to do. "Okay," I said and headed for the C Street exit, which comes out across from the State Department.

She grabbed my arm and turned me around. "Let's go out to Constitution Avenue and sit by the Einstein statue, Max. I like looking at that giant head."

So I'm already "Max," I thought as I followed her through the gray-white sea of heads dotted with occasional shiny bald white caps. "Shall I call you Charlea?" I asked, wondering whether she went by that name, or perhaps "Chuck."

"Why, yes—just so you don't make it sound like 'Charlie.' I don't believe in titles—not after you've earned them."

"I see," I said, although I really didn't. What are titles for if not to be used?

As we approached the concrete ledge by Einstein's side, I gazed at the carpet of red, white, and pink tulips extending all the way to the dogwood trees in the background, their flat white leaves like Japanese prayer messages—blank and waiting to be filled. Conway sat herself by Einstein's right foot and reached over to stroke his bronze shin. That's when I noticed that her slip was showing. The stretch of white slip shone brightly in the sunshine, so brightly it seemed she'd pulled it down below the hem of her dark green skirt as a deliberate challenge: to show that dress or appearance simply didn't matter. She wore absolutely no makeup; her hair seemed to have been cut by a man's barber. What a contrast to D_3! But despite the contrast, they both seemed to know what they wanted, and neither wasted any time getting to the point. Charlea Cherith Conway, I found myself musing: C_3. I could just see myself introducing two chemical formulas to each other: "May I present the three deuteriums to the three carbons?"

"Let's talk about your T cell activation work. I've gotten interested in that subject."

"No," I said, "let's not. Let's discuss what I really phoned about from Princeton. Have you ever heard of Nicolas Bourbaki?"

C_3 leaned slightly backward, as if she wanted to get me into better focus. "Of course I've heard of Nicolas Bourbaki. What mathematician hasn't? But how come you have?"

I should have known better: C_3 wasn't just an ordinary biophysicist, she was a *mathematical* biophysicist. But I was still taken aback that the last two women to whom I'd posed the question had each answered in the affirmative.

"Personal reasons," I replied. And then I outlined the entire scheme to her.

"It could be amusing," she said pensively. "But why did you pick me? Did my being a woman have anything to do with it?" There was nothing amused or warm about her look.

"It didn't hurt."

"Did the fact that I'm a woman come first or last? I want a frank answer."

"First." I didn't see any point in denying it; I braced myself for the accusation, but none came.

Conway just sat there, slightly hunched, looking pensively at Einstein's huge head in its brown bronze patina, her right hand again slowly caressing the sculptured shin. Finally, she turned to me. "I'm still a few years from retirement. But my dean has been dropping hints lately. I suspect he'd make it pretty attractive if I agreed to leave early. And what you're proposing is enticing: a research gamble under another name. I'm already picking the faces I'd like to see if we can pull this one off. Our dean is one of them."

"Any other reasons?" Somehow, I felt cheated. It seemed too simple. She had to have some other motive.

"Do you need any more?" She gave me a quizzical glance.

"No, of course not," I said quickly. "But what about the name? Are you willing to trade anonymity for—"

She gave my lapel a slight yank. "Haven't we agreed you need no more grounds?"

"I'm serious, Charlea. How would you feel publishing under another name, a collective like Nicolas Bourbaki?"

"It wouldn't bother me too much."

I looked at my watch and realized that the business meeting might well be over by now. With Conway on board, it was time to concentrate on Nishimura. As we rose and walked past the sitting figure of Einstein, I noticed for the first time that the back of the retaining wall bore some inscriptions. I pointed to the one behind his left foot: *The right to search for truth implies also a duty; one must not conceal any part of what one has recognized to be true.* "Do you think Einstein would have categorized our project as concealment?" I asked.

C3 gave me a curious look. Wagging her finger, she intoned, "You're too preoccupied with the disguise. My guess is that Einstein would have concentrated on the *idea.*"

"And?"

"He would have liked it."

When we reached the Great Hall, we found the Academy members pushing through the open doors underneath the huge mosaic scenes from Aeschylus's *Prometheus Bound.* I headed for the first person I recognized to ask whether Nishimura had made it into the Academy.

"Here's to the NAS's newest foreign associate." I held up my glass. I was in a buoyant mood to begin with; when I had gotten a glass of champagne in me, my good humor was too much to contain. "I envy you your remarkable promiscuity," I grinned. Hiroshi looked shocked. "I mean your ability to work at the same time on such a diversity of projects," I added hastily.

Hiroshi looked relieved and then, sipping, eyes closed, at his glass, responded gnomically, "I'm just a tourist on my personal planet. I try to take in as many sights as I can."

"How would you like to fill out your itinerary with something new?"

He raised an eyebrow. The look he gave me was cryptic.

"Have you ever heard of Nicolas Bourbaki?" I began.

I was pleased at the speed with which Hiroshi took it in—even though he'd never heard of Nicolas Bourbaki—but his response surprised me. His attitude toward his impending retirement was hard for me to comprehend. Instead of moving to a private university in Japan—he'd already received several offers—he planned to drop research altogether.

"But you're just turning sixty," I protested.

He gave me a long, searching look. "You don't know much about our system, do you?"

"What makes you say that?" I asked. "I've lectured there several times, I know lots of Japanese scientists in my field; I even know about your absurdly early retirement age at the University of Tokyo."

Hiroshi reached over and touched me gently on the sleeve. "I mean from the inside: how we are trained, how our universities operate . . . what it is like to be treated as *erai sensei*."

"As what?"

"It's a Japanese term for 'great master.' "

"That sounds pretty good to me," I chuckled. "I wish my students would call me that."

"Don't say that!" His tone was surprisingly sharp. "It is meant, of course, as an expression of reverence, but with us, such respect carries with it the feeling that the person is beyond criticism. Most of our senior professors are treated that way; that's why they are so influential. But it's dangerous for a scientist to be beyond criticism." He took another sip of champagne and then put down the glass. "Furthermore, all that power is terribly time-consuming. Our national universities—we called them imperial universities before the war—are a combination of autocracy and democracy. In one sense we are too democratic: everything has to be settled in committees and in faculty meetings. We spend an unbelievable amount of time on administrative detail; we work ten or twelve hours a day, including Saturdays. And you know why?" Hiroshi didn't wait for an answer. "Because all of our national universities belong to the Ministry of Education—a terrible organization staffed by people who know nothing about research. They control everything from primary school through graduate education and haven't changed for decades. Do you know about our *koza?*"

I shook my head.

"It's an administrative and funding unit, created decades ago by that ministry, and the source of most of the authoritanism in our graduate schools."

"Authoritarianism," I corrected him.

That's when I finally got him to smile. "I have trouble with that word—in every sense. A *koza* is a unit consisting of a senior professor, an assistant professor, and a couple of assistants; it also resembles modern slavery. But even though you hear me condemn it, I never did anything about it. I just tolerated it—maybe because I survived to become a senior professor myself." He made a deprecating gesture with his hands. "*Your* young assistant professors, they are totally independent: they apply for financial grants on their own, pick whatever research topic interests them, and then get evaluated for their originality. With us, it is the reverse. The assistant professor in a *koza* is completely dependent on the senior professor; he spends many years supervising the students who do the senior professor's research; and eventually, when the professor retires, he gets his boss's job—not for his originality but for his service. At least that was the situation until about ten years ago. Now we are starting to change. Still, we do not switch universities—not even to take a postdoc elsewhere in Japan for a year or two. Our Ministry of Education does not understand the importance of postdoctorate studies or moving from one institution to another to avoid inbreeding. They finally started a modest program of postdocs in Japan, but do you know what they call them?" He challenged me with an accusing look. " 'Overdoctors,' because these positions are simply created to pay stipends to recent Ph.D.s who have not yet found a job. That is why so many of us go abroad—and especially to America—yet when we return, it is back into the *koza* system. And is it not embarrassing that you pay for our stipends in America, even though we are a rich country?"

I asked why he didn't consider moving from Tokyo to an American institution. Especially now that he was one of the very few Japanese foreign associates of our National Academy of Sciences. Many an American university judges its standing in the sciences by the number of NAS members on its faculty.

"You have never met my wife. She is very Japanese and speaks no English. At our age," he made a short bow, "it is very difficult to learn a new language. Also, she is a traditional Japanese painter. Quite well known. Here, that would mean nothing."

"But why retire? What about a research institute or industry?"

He shook his head. "Not after so many years in our best university."

And then he uttered one of those typical Japanese laughs of embarrassment that are immediately shielded by a hand over the mouth. "Did you know that I'm also a poet, Max? When I retire, I have planned to devote myself to my poetry."

"Poetry? At your age?"

"Ah," he sighed. "Age in poetry or art is very different from age in science. Are you familiar with the work of Hokusai?"

For a moment I had an idea of how people feel when I ask them about Bourbaki. I shook my head.

"He is one of the great masters of Japanese drawing, born in 1760. Let me tell you what he wrote. I know it by heart." Hiroshi leaned back and looked past me through the window. His voice had turned low, as if he were talking to himself. "*All I have produced before the age of seventy is not worth taking into account. At seventy-five I have learned a little about the real structure of nature—of animals, plants, and trees, birds, fishes, and insects. In consequence, when I am eighty, I shall have made still more progress. At ninety I shall penetrate the mystery of things; at a hundred I shall certainly have reached a marvelous stage, and when I am a hundred and ten, everything I do—be it but a line or a dot—will be alive. I beg those who live as long as I, to see if I do not keep my word.*" For a few seconds Hiroshi nodded quietly to himself. "You can say that about poetry, but not about science."

I knew when I was defeated. "In that case, good luck on your poetry for the next fifty years." I raised my champagne glass, ready to concede.

But Hiroshi did not lift his glass. He played with it, swirling it slowly so that the bubbles escaped to the surface. "Aren't you going to drink to your poetry?" I said, lifting my glass once more.

"I suppose you have not heard of *renga* or *haikai?*"

Again I had to shake my head.

"It is a very special form of Japanese poetry: linking poems composed by different poets. Not unlike what you want to do with your Bourbaki." A shy smile started to appear on his face. "Theoretical biology in the renga manner?" he mused. "Why not? It might merit a poem about the worthlessness of names." He raised his glass.

When he put it like that, suddenly I felt my fervor wane. "But isn't the worth of your name the whole game in science? Or almost the whole," I added lamely.

"Then why are you prepared to hide Weiss?"

"Revenge—pure and simple."

He laughed. "Ah, too simple. Too Western. Think of Kabuki, where all female roles are played by men. Think of the importance of masks for a Japanese: we wear them much of our life. The older we get, the more important they become. Imagine, just as I am about to start a new life as a poet, you offer me an entirely new mask." He laughed again. "How do you say it in English? 'Have a cake and eat it?' I already have a new cake and you now offer a second. I might eat them both!"

"How do you spell *renga?*" I asked. The idea of linkage intrigued me. Was that really a precedent for Bourbaki's mode of work?

He considered for a moment, then spelled out the English letters.

"Then let's toast the place where our new masks will work," I called out. "The Renga Institute of Theoretical Biology." I meant it as a joke, but the longer I thought about it, the better I liked it; I could feel my excitement return. "Could you recommend a book of Japanese poetry translations for me?" I asked Hiroshi.

He looked at me quizzically, as if wondering whether I really meant it. "I read a lot of poetry in English, but not many translations. I will see what I can find for you." He stroked his chin. "Here is one of the few Japanese poems I know in English, a *tanka* written almost eight hundred years ago by Minamoto Sanetomo. Maybe that will tempt you to read more:

> This world—
> call it an image
> caught in a mirror—
> real it is not,
> not unreal either."

9

I've been trying to pinpoint the moment when it dawned on me that D_3 had assumed one of Nedra's subtle but important roles in my life: captain of my cultural calendar. It was probably the long lunch at the Russian Tearoom shortly before the Academy meeting in Washington. We'd already eaten there twice—each time before a concert at Carnegie Hall.

We had been drinking tea and talking lightly about music—she had determined to educate me out of my prejudice (one I had imbibed, I realized, from Nedra) against Wagner—when suddenly the subject changed. Her tone grew serious.

"Max," she said. "How much do you know about women in science?"

"Not much. There aren't too many in my field. Except students, of course." I was determined to put the best possible face on things, but Diana wasn't impressed.

"I've been reading more about Bourbaki," she said. "Nicolas, that is, not my general. Do you know they never included any women? When they looked for new members, they invited potential candidates—*courbail* they called them—for a trial session to look them over. I gather that in the seventies, two of these guinea pigs were women, but nothing ever came of it. Why don't you try to be different?"

"I'll try," I said, hoping to put the subject to rest—at least for this lunch.

"Do, Max," she said. "If you knew some of the history of the question, you'd appreciate the need."

"Very few scientists pay much attention to scientific history."

"I was aware of that, but it's nothing to brag about."

"I'm not saying it to justify such ignorance. We're just so busy   **63** keeping up with the current literature that our historical perspective covers a very short range: in a rapidly advancing field, ten years is history."

Diana shook her head slowly. "Did you read my whole *Spectatrice* article, or did you just skim it?"

"I read it," I replied warily, wondering whether she would quiz me about some esoteric point. I had not found the subject matter—a minor feminist journal, published some two and a half centuries ago—very interesting. Still, as D₃ had uncovered the identity of the anonymous female editor, I had become intrigued, and I had intended to compliment her on her academic detective work.

In her paper D₃ had noted that during the early part of the eighteenth century, all publications in France had to pass the scrutiny of the royal censors, who frequently "denatured" tendentious writing. (I rather liked the use of that word, because in my own work I often denature proteins in order to take them apart.) In a neat switch on the old *cherchez la femme*, Diana's article had focused on one François-Denis Camusat, the royal censor who had allowed fifteen issues of *La Spectatrice* to appear in undenatured form. Diana's *recherches* in the *Bibliotheque de l'Arsenal* in Paris had uncovered a cache of Camusat's private papers. These included a torrid correspondence with one of the great *salonnières* of that period, with cryptic references to Camusat's "yielding" in return for *La Spectatrice*'s amorous favors.

"Do you recall my references to the Parisian salons of that period?" D₃ asked.

"You mean your discovery that the salonnière was the editor?" I replied quickly. For the life of me, I couldn't recall the name of *La Spectatrice*'s editor. I was lucky enough to have remembered the fancy name for "salon keeper."

"Not specifically," she said, with the sort of smile that I know students love to get. "I meant about the institution of the Paris salons in general. By the way, have you read anything by Londa Schiebinger?"

"Never heard of her."

"The Mind Has No Sex."

"I beg your pardon?"

Diana smiled, but I could see she wasn't in a joking mood. "That's the title of her book. It deals with women in the origins of modern science. I'll lend you my copy. It's the sort of thing every male scientific *pédant* should read."

Spare me, I wanted to say, but out loud I only uttered "Please!"

She patted my hand. "Relax, Max. I don't mean to sound snide. Not this time, anyway. But there is a connection between Schiebinger and the early Paris salons that interests me—and it *does* have something to do with science and—in a way—with your projected enterprise. Her thesis is that modern scientific institutions had their roots first in medieval monasteries and universities, and then in the Renaissance princely courts and royal academies. Now I ask you, Max, what did all these have in common?"

"Go on," I said, thinking with some envy of Nishimura's "great masters." I bet no Japanese woman would ask such questions.

"They were exclusively male institutions. Women had no chance in science at that time."

"So?"

"So along comes the institution of the salon—in its way as influential as the early European academies—and it breaks the restraints on women's intellectual life. Three of the most important *salonnières*—the Marquise de Lambert, Madame Tencin, and Madame Geoffrin—not only attracted scientists, these women had the power to make or break an academician's reputation. Contemporary observers—men, of course," she added—"weren't wild about this."

"Of course," I echoed dutifully. She stabbed me with a short glance to see if I was mocking her. I looked innocently back, all ears. And I *was* interested, though what this had to do with our research group I had yet to understand.

"Rousseau," she continued, "then a secretary to Madame Dupin, who herself ran a salon, complained that women were ruining French letters and arts: 'Every woman in Paris,' he wrote, 'gathers in her apartment a harem of men more womanish than

65

she.' We still hear this about women in power in industry or government: that they surround themselves with weaker men."

"Do you think that's true?"

She eyed me archly. "Do *you?*"

I shrugged, but before I could speak she said, "You know what the editor of *La Spectatrice* wrote in her very first sentence of the first issue? 'I sometimes admire the pride of men, who accuse us of inconsistency and levity. It seems to me that in ambition, in love, and in many other things, we want more than men, and when we want it, we persevere no less than they.'"

For a while, neither of us said anything. "The salons, of course, didn't survive the Revolution," Diana continued, moodily stirring her cold tea. "And I don't believe that women ever again had this kind of patronage in science. I rather fancy trying to revive it here, at the end of the twentieth century." She gave me a long look, so long that I finally looked away. "Except for feminist causes, I've never really gotten involved in social issues. I realize that your Bourbaki isn't a typical cause either, but it strikes a chord in me. And I think I like the idea of taking something utterly intellectual and giving it a naughty twist."

Was it the noise I made in my throat, which sounded a bit apprehensive, a bit embarrassed, that caused her to touch my hand? "Don't worry," she said. "What I want won't interfere with your research. It will just make it more elegant."

"And what is it you want?" I asked. Somehow, I felt that precision was important at this point, as if we were discussing the fine print in a legal contract.

"To reintegrate men and women in science; to reconcile science and the humanities, show them for what they really are: integral parts of something larger—something we hardly have a name for."

"Is that all?" I said, but she didn't smile.

"Until now—and it's getting somewhat late—scientists have not been part of my life. Meeting them as dean doesn't count: that was more of an adversarial process. I would like to see how you people operate. Mostly here, I mean," and she tapped me on the forehead with her index finger. The taps, all four of them, were firm. "And perhaps be your institutional glue," she added.

What we live on a scale of minutes or hours, we remember in picosecond bursts. Back home in Princeton that evening, I was indulging in one of my favorite pastimes: a long, hot bath before going to sleep. As I soaked and mused, I found myself wondering about my prospective colleagues: how would they respond to working in a modern salon? I didn't think I'd mind; so far, most of my contacts with D_3 seemed to have been one long tête-à-tête salon. I hadn't minded, not at all. But a few weeks ago, while sipping coffee after a good dinner, Diana had turned to me. "Tell me, Max," she'd said in a perfectly ordinary voice, "what kind of a sexual person are you?"

"You mean now or ever?" I stuttered, flushing. To hide my embarrassment—or perhaps to augment it—I turned toward the table on my left to see whether the couple eating there had witnessed this mammoth intrusion into my privacy. They didn't even meet my glance; they just seemed to be interested in each other.

"Well, both," she said brightly, as if she'd asked me some ordinary question such as my feelings about peanut butter. "But primarily the latter."

She can't be serious, I thought. I am one of those rare men—at least judging from the Kinsey Report—who's only had one sexual partner all his life. Nedra and I didn't talk much about sex, and during the past ten years or so, we didn't even have any. Nedra was pretty ill the last couple of years of her life. Since becoming a widower I'd barely thought about sex.

I guess my embarrassment must have shown, because suddenly I felt Diana's hand turning my face in her direction.

"Max," she exclaimed, "you're positively blushing." She held my face for another moment, and then the hand dropped and covered one of mine. "Don't read too much into it. I'd like to know what you, Max Weiss the scientist, are like as a human *being*. Besides—it's the *salonnière*'s duty to know something about the sexuality of her guests. Some of the great ones—Mademoiselle de Lespinasse, a particularly well-known case—took their lovers from their own salons." She raised her hand, seemingly to stop me from saying what had not even occurred to me. "Not all of them behaved that way. My *salonnière* actually attacked such promiscuity in *La Spectatrice*. Anyway, my question wasn't addressed to sexual *performance* but to attitude and feeling. A person can be very sexual and yet quite prim and proper. Take me, for example."

I felt my blush returning. In desperation, I focused on a faint stain on the tablecloth. If D_3 noticed, she didn't let on. "I've been a sexual person all my life, but I've been sexually intimate with only two men—my husbands. That doesn't keep one from fantasizing or even self-gratification . . ."

I think it was at that moment that I tuned out completely. I simply didn't want to know when it would be my turn to respond.

"Max," she laughed, "I never thought I'd see you so sheepish. Never mind," she added, giving my hand a squeeze before withdrawing hers. "I won't pursue it. Not today, at least. But I'll leave you with one thought. Sexual fantasizing—and whatever goes with it—is most common at the extremes of age: in youth, when a partner is not yet available; and in old age, when the partner is incapable or dead."

I pulled the plug and got out of the bathtub. But I didn't feel sleepy. Instead, I picked up the most recent issue of the *Journal of Biological Chemistry* to read the latest hot papers. Half an hour must have passed before it hit me that I hadn't absorbed a word of the text.

10

"So you have a full complement?" Diana asked the question coolly enough, but even over the phone I could sense her excitement.

"Indeed."

"You haven't even told me about your Austrian. How did he end up in your net?"

He jumped in, I wanted to say, but that wasn't really fair. The moment I mentioned the word *retirement* on the phone, a veritable avalanche of words came roaring down his alp of accumulated irritation. Some of it was almost funny: his dramatic imitation of an officious bureaucrat at the Institut der Biologischen Chemie. On the very day his retirement became official, Sepp claimed, he had found this bureaucrat marching up and down in his Lederhosen (or maybe I made that up), removing the legend *Professor Dr. S. Krzilska* from doors and wall directories wherever he could find it.

"And to think who established the reputation of this place," Sepp fumed. "They could not even wait a decent interval."

When I finished describing the Renga Institute, he demanded, "When do we begin?" I was a bit worried that my message about a collective nom de plume had not had time to sink in, but I decided not to belabor the point. That was one topic all of us would certainly have to discuss at length at our first meeting: a substitute for "Nicolas Bourbaki."

"And who is the fourth?" Diana asked.

I paused. I had been relishing this moment for days. "Professor Conway. A professor of mathematical biophysics at Chicago— and a member of the National Academy of Sciences to boot."

"Congratulations," she said. I could hear the disappointment in her voice. "It's too bad you couldn't find a woman."

"Professor *Charlea* Conway," I said, pronouncing the last two letters of her first name separately, the way C_3 had told me to do.

I would have loved to have seen Diana's face at that moment.

"Well, I'll be damned! What does she look like?"

"What a sexist question."

"You're right," she laughed. "But still: what *does* she look like? And when can I meet them? Do they know each other?"

"No, they don't—"

"That's marvelous!" she exclaimed. "So your first meeting will be crucial. Let's have it at my apartment. I'll hire a caterer and do it in style."

So we're starting right from scratch with a salon, I thought. Well, why not? "Nishimura will stay on the East Coast for another week before flying back to Tokyo," I told her, "and Conway could easily come here for a day or two. But how are we going to get Sepp here on such short notice? Impossible."

"I'll use some of my MacArthur kitty—"

"Don't be absurd," I interrupted her. "We can't allow you to use your money for such purposes."

"Whoever 'we' is should learn not to argue with a MacArthur-anointed genius. The beauty of these grants is that the genius does not have to account for their use."

"But . . . but," I stammered.

"No *buts*," she rejoined firmly. "Besides, all I'm offering is a supersaver Apex fare. My MacArthur can afford that."

It wasn't so much the long, narrow shape of Diana's dining room—long enough to accommodate the rectangular dining table with its surface of dark, smoky glass and the eight padded chairs, upholstered in brocade. Nor was it the mirror along one long wall, in which the diners across from it could watch themselves eating while simultaneously seeing their partners' faces and backs. Nor was it even that third, mysterious set of reflections shining between the place mats in the dark-mirrored surface of the table. What was distracting me, I realized, was the mirror on the ceiling. It was precisely the size of the table. Anyone looking up saw an entire dinner party eating upside down. Even though there were only five of us at this catered dinner thrown by our *salonnière*, a peculiarly crowded tableau met the eyes wherever they happened to fall.

Does her bedroom have one too? I wondered suddenly. From across the table, my own face gaped back at me—speculatively, then abashed.

"What do you think, Max?"

I blushed, momentarily thinking D_3 had read my mind. "About?"

"The name, Max. Hadn't you all agreed to settle on that tonight?"

For weeks now, I'd been thinking seriously about that question, realizing that we couldn't start with a nameless cabal. I'd toyed with various possibilities, including some acronyms, but then I had arrived at *Skordylis*. I would never have thought of that urname of the Bourbaki clan if it hadn't been for D_3's New Year's present.

"Skordylis."

"Greek?" Charlea Conway had beaten everyone to the punch. "I don't get it. Why?"

After I told them the origin of the Bourbaki name, I ended with a mock bow toward D_3—a gesture of homage that was reproduced across and above me in the mirrors.

"I like it," C_3 said. "But you talk as though Skordylis is a man. What's wrong with a woman?" I glanced around the group and then up to the ceiling, where I watched C_3 spooning her soup upside down.

For the next five minutes we behaved like expectant parents arguing about a first name. In the end, Conway won by proposing "Diana." It wasn't really Greek, she conceded, but why not pick the goddess of hunting and childbirth? Didn't we intend to hunt for problems and then give birth to solutions? I hoped that D_3, who hadn't said a word, would interpret the choice as I did: discreet homage to our Bourbaki's muse.

That went rather well, I thought: barely past the soup and we've already got a name. Before the conversational ball had come to a complete stop, C_3 had picked up it up again.

"Tell me, Dr. Ditmus—"

"Why don't you call me Diana?"

"Diana, then," Charlea continued, "what field are you in?"

"French history. The *ancien régime*."

I was waiting for more, but when D_3 stopped, I decided to try to help out. "And a fascinating topic: *La Spectatrice*, a feminine journal published by an anonymous woman editor."

"Feminist, Max—not feminine," D_3 rebuked me mildly. "There's a difference."

"Of course," I said. "*Excusez-moi pour le faux pas.*" I thought the attempt at French would produce a smile. It produced nothing. "You all ought to read Dr. Ditmus's article about how she uncovered the identity of the editor," I hastened on, trying to fill a silence that seemed to deepen by the second. "It's quite a story."

"Why feminism? Do you call yourself a feminist?" C_3's jaw had taken on a truculent set.

"The way I define myself to women like you," Diana said casually, "is to say, 'I'm not a feminist, but . . .' That's the way to enlist women who forget that if they don't stand up for what they want, few men will do it for them."

"And what makes you think I didn't, or don't, do that?" For once I couldn't titrate Charlea Conway's tone: was she irritated or was she just egging on Diana?

"Doing it alone is not enough."

Brava! I wanted to exclaim. Diana may not have been with me in Washington, but she'd obviously gotten C_3's number.

"Unless you organize a critical mass, a constituency that can exert political force, all you have are . . . private deals." I could see C_3 straighten, ever so slightly, in her seat. "If you're going to change anything," Diana continued, "you have to change everything. From the nursery to the workplace, from clubs to faculty senates." She leaned back in her seat, her eyes dropping to the table surface. I wasn't sure whether she simply wanted to break eye contact with C_3 or was using the table's mirrored surface for a different perspective on her audience. When she spoke again, her tone was lower, less bristling. "It took me years to learn to articulate these problems, Charlea—first in my own mind, and then out loud. My husband's financial security had shielded me from so many problems faced by the vast majority of women. Take motherhood: my daughter was born just before the outbreak of the war when there was household help to be had—and not just for the rich. My seminal year—"

She flinched and rearranged the silverware around her plate. "Perhaps not the best word—was 1950, the year after Simone de Beauvoir's *The Second Sex* came out in France. I read it that summer in the Dordogne. It had an enormous impact on me, including the eventual choice of my dissertation topic. To oversimplify and even romanticize my motivation: I was visualizing the editor of *La Spectatrice* as an earlier incarnation of de Beauvoir. I have no doubt that delving into eighteenth-century questions of feminist and feminine issues," she threw me a knowing glance, punctuated by a smile, "raised my awareness of twentieth-century women's problems.

"As Max knows, I got married again, when my daughter was eleven, and moved to New York—right to this apartment. My husband was a corporate lawyer with an office downtown, my daughter went to private school, and I decided to go back to school myself and get a Ph.D. At Columbia, which was a very easy commute."

C_3's nod, though slight, seemed to imply sympathy. "So what made you decide to get a Ph.D.? I mean at an age—"

"Simple," D_3 broke in, with a speed that I could only attribute to a desire not to have the question completed. "It was very much related to my lack of professional credentials. I wanted to demonstrate to myself that I could use my mind. I value knowledge for its own sake. Like many women, I take pride in that knowledge. Most men, it seems to me, use knowledge differently: they feel they *must* use it." For a second, her eyes met mine in the mirror. I was startled: was that an accusation addressed to me, or just a general observation? This was not the time to ask, but I decided to file it for future reference.

"What then?" Clearly, C_3 was out to get the entire biography.

"I was lucky," observed D_3. "By the time I got my Ph.D., demonstrating to myself—or my husband—that I could use my mind   **73** was not enough: I wanted to launch my own professional career."

"Like men?" I couldn't interpret C_3's tone well enough to tell whether she'd meant it sarcastically.

For a moment Diana looked startled, but then she laughed. "I guess you're right. As I said, I had luck. I wasn't really mobile: in those days, husbands with established positions were not expected to move if their wives got a promising job elsewhere. I found something temporary at Hunter College and a couple of years later a tenure-track position at NYU."

"Where eventually, she ended up as dean of H and S," I announced proudly.

Hiroshi had sat silently, taking it all in. "H and S?" he now asked.

"Humanities and sciences. Even the science bonzes had to bow to her," I couldn't help adding.

"Ah so," he exhaled, bowing from the waist. "It could not have happened in Tokyo."

"But enough of me." Diana put her index finger across her lips. "I suppose I'm telling you my own secrets because all of you are here to start on a secret life." She took a long look around the room, stopping for a moment on each of our faces. It made me uncomfortable, I know: as if I was being put on oath. When her look came around to Charlea, it was C_3's gaze that broke away first. "What kind of a feminist are you?" asked D_3.

A brief shake of the head, coupled with a frown, preceded C_3's response. "I'm not a feminist. Not in your sense of the word. I haven't got any quarrels with it, except for affirmative action—I simply don't believe in that, especially not these days. If a woman is competent enough, she can make it in just about any field."

"Aren't you ignoring something?" Diana's face had started to redden. "Suppose you want to combine a professional career with motherhood and aren't financially independent?"

"That's a tough call," admitted C_3. "But it'll take more than affirmative action to solve *that*."

"How did *you* manage to solve it?" Diana asked.

For a moment, C_3 looked puzzled. "I have no children. And no

74 husband, either. I never wanted them. But if I'd had to choose

between science and family, I know which would have won out."

"But isn't that quite a sacrifice?" persisted our hostess. "One only women have to make?"

Charlea shrugged. "It wasn't a sacrifice for me. Scientific research is addictive in the most positive sense of the word. I've never cared much for men—not now or earlier. Don't misunderstand me," she looked briefly at me and then at Sepp and Hiroshi, both of whom stared back stonily. "Some of my best friends are men." For the first time that evening she gave a hearty laugh. "Not that I have much choice in my field."

The smile faded and she turned back to D_3. "I'm not knocking companionship: I happen to be living with a woman now—which, incidentally, is much easier done these days than fifteen years ago." Her gaze dropped down to her folded hands and remained there for what I imagine were only seconds but seemed like minutes at the time. For a moment I thought she was praying, but then I realized she was purposely letting her words sink in. When she looked up, it was in the direction of D_3. "You mentioned embarking on a secret life. Let someone who knows tell you something: most of the time, secret lives are for the birds."

11

Charlea turned to me. "But as long as we're going to have a secret life, Max, maybe you'll tell us: just what have you got in mind?"

"Well," I hemmed. "What I really have in mind is a form of revenge on the academic establishment."

"Absolutely!" Sepp nodded vigorously. "That is exactly what attracted me in Max's proposal. Just imagine . . ."

As unstoppable as the Ancient Mariner, Sepp recounted the tale of the bureaucrat's assault on his nameplate. Charlea waited impatiently for him to wind down, then said dismissively, "Consider yourself lucky. It could have been worse. Erwin Chargaff— **75** the nucleic acid man at Columbia," she added in an aside to Diana, "found his office lock changed as soon as he retired from the chairmanship of their biochem department. You know, if he'd been born a bit later, he might have been a good candidate for Max's plan."

Charlea reached out to pat me on the hand. "But revenge isn't everything. I'll admit, though, that the idea of trying something new does tempt me mightily." She turned to see whether Diana was listening. "I've thought a lot about this since Max first approached me in Washington. In the end, it's the idea of doing it under an assumed name that appeals to me most. It's not so much revenge as thumbing your nose—and not just at the establishment. What about us?" Her fork swung around in a half circle. "We've spent lifetimes building reputations. I'd like to know if we've still got what it takes to carry it off as unknowns." She looked across the table at Hiroshi. "What about you? I gather at Tokyo, you've got to retire at sixty. How revengeful do you feel?"

The discomfort in Hiroshi's face was unmistakable. He cleared his throat. "Japan is different."

"You mean the Japanese have better manners," she interrupted with a laugh.

Hiroshi wagged his head. "Possibly." I admired the diplomacy of his response. "The retirement is no surprise; you are prepared for it; and . . . I was treated very respectfully," he said after some hesitation. He blushed. "Last month I received the Imperial Prize."

"Congratulations." Charlea pronounced the word slowly, emphasizing each syllable. I was about to interrupt—to ask why he hadn't told us earlier—but C_3 gave me no chance. "So why are you here, Hiroshi?"

He looked startled; clearly he had not expected to become the center of attention. "Max knows."

I could see he wanted my help, but what could I say? That I had misjudged him when I first broached the subject of Bourbaki? That he had surprised me with the frankness of his criticism of the Japanese educational system, with his talk of poetry? In fact, now that I thought of it, with his acceptance of my invitation?

76

I decided to give it a try. "I think Hiroshi was tempted by the idea of getting away from the Japanese system."

He nodded. "This way, I can do that and still live in Japan."

"And the anonymity?" Charlea pressed.

Why is she pursuing this? I wondered.

He stroked his chin. "It does not bother me. More than two years ago, I had decided to use my university retirement to embark on a very different intellectual life, outside science. Whatever I might publish in that new life—even if I did it under my own name—would in a sense be anonymous: the name would mean nothing to my new audience. And my former scientific colleagues? They would be unlikely to read what I would then be writing." He opened both hands in a gesture of revelation. "Because I had already accepted that, Max's suggestion was not such a big step. Actually, it intrigues me. In the same way that you described it, Charlea."

"And the Kabuki aspect?" I asked. "Back in Washington, you said that wearing a mask was part of being Japanese."

For a second, Hiroshi looked surprised. "So you remember that? Yes, it's true about the masks, though in Kabuki, makeup and acting take the place of masks." He nodded at Charlea, then expanded the gesture to include us all. "In Kabuki, the made-up face and the gender of the real one may not be the same."

Diana, who'd been listening quietly, broke in. "So you look at it as a play?"

He frowned. "Kabuki is not really a play—it is a stylized way of describing life. Diana Skordylis will be a stylized way of doing science—"

"Rather different from the usual style," Charlea interrupted.

"Agreed." Hiroshi nodded vigorously. "That is what interests me. And that I can do it as a woman character."

Sepp looked completely perplexed. He was shaking his head. "Sex has nothing to do with science—"

"I'm sure it does," observed Diana, smiling to herself. "But I think you mean 'gender.'"

C3 growled agreement. "*Both* sex and gender have plenty to do with science. Just look at you, Hiroshi: you, a man, want to 'play' the woman scientist Diana Skordylis. And you," she looked across the table at Sepp, "you want to make her sexless or genderless. Yet aren't we all androgynous?"

An awkward moment of silence extended, broken finally by Diana. "How do you people go about choosing a topic for your research?" She seemed to be paying more attention to the position of her wineglass than to the question.

"We haven't discussed that yet," I said gratefully. "That's probably the key item we ought to focus on."

But D_3 hadn't been attempting to push the meeting along. "I didn't mean as Diana Skordylis," she continued in the same slow, distracted way. "I meant any of you as scientists. How do you decide what to work on?"

Hiroshi exhaled so audibly that I knew exactly what he was feeling: how does one explain a process that one barely understands oneself, and that doesn't really happen in words? "It depends," he started, and then fell silent. The three of us were nodding to ourselves—but I noticed none of us rushed to fill in the gap.

"On what?" Diana put one of her elbows on the table, cheek in hand. She was prepared to wait.

"Well," he began again, glancing at me. All I offered was my sudden attention to a particular sliver of mushroom, an inspection so intent that I could have been involved in a major unsolved problem in fungal taxonomy. "It depends on who you are," he said lamely.

"Yes?" She prodded.

"Your field," he said in a rush. "The size of your group, the stage of your career, financial resources. Many factors. It is not like turning on a faucet; new ideas do not just pour out. They come in . . ."

He seemed to be searching for the right word. "Spurts?" I offered, returning quickly to my mushroom. I wanted to add that I would put a person's age high on the list. I wondered if he would include that.

"But what about you, Hiroshi?" I was struck by the gentle tone of D_3's voice. "How does it work with you?"

"Ah." His face had adopted the rigid grimace I had seen him use before when confronting some difficult problem in translating from the Japanese. "When you have spent years in a certain field," he started again, "Max's, mine, the others—it is like working on the construction of a complex building. You keep adding wings, extensions, towers, bridges. You do so as the need arises, but the manner in which you make those additions is partly controlled by what you have already built. If the main structure is made from brick, you are unlikely to use bamboo for the addition. You may come up with interesting variations, new construction techniques, perhaps even new engineering principles, but you are still influenced by the original building."

"That doesn't seem to leave much room for innovation, or even originality."

He nodded—a short, curt, oddly formal gesture. "Certainly, that is a risk. There is a great temptation to stay with a topic with which you are very familiar. You can fall in love with one project and stay with it all your life. That's where a bright young scientist has a certain advantage over an older one: he can come up with wildly original plans using every type of material available: brick, tile, wood, plastic."

"But will he?" I asked. I felt Hiroshi was overstating the case for youth. *Wildly original?* "There are plenty of young scientists who are not risk takers. Besides, older scientists, especially experienced ones, get a feeling for problems that are ripe for solution; they understand which ones should be dropped completely and which should be left for later."

"As I said earlier, it all depends." Hiroshi gave me a faint smile and then turned to Diana. "Remember, Diana Skordylis is no— what is the expression?—spring fowl."

I was not going to let him have the last word—not on this issue. "It's 'chicken,'" I said. "And just a couple of months ago, weren't you quoting a Japanese artist about the powers of old age?"

He gave me a long, ironic look before replying. "I was speaking of wisdom, understanding, beauty—not innovation. About poetry, not science."

"Did you say poetry?" exclaimed Diana. "Are you also a poet?" **79**

Hiroshi raised his hand, fingers outspread, as if he'd just snapped open a fan to hide his face. "Trying to become one," he said, giggling slightly.

Diana reached over and pulled down his hand. "Tell me about it."

He shook his head, giggling harder. "Not now."

"Is that the new life you are embarking upon—where you can publish as an unknown?" Charlea's interest had been rekindled.

He nodded.

"Poetry?" She guffawed. "You can't be serious."

Hiroshi looked at her, his thin eyebrows arched. "Why not? What is wrong with poetry?"

"I beg your pardon," Charlea said quickly. "I know nothing about Japanese poetry—or even our own. It's just that you surprise me: it's quite a jump from biochemistry to poetry."

"How did you come to write poetry, Hiroshi?" Diana asked.

"I have always been interested in Japanese poetry—since my middle school days," he began, face turned toward his hands, which were folded before him on the table. "Several years ago, I started to translate some American poets into Japanese, to get a feel for your prosody."

"What does 'prosody' mean?" whispered Sepp.

"It has to do with poetry," I whispered back.

"But what?"

I ignored him. "Did you publish them?" I asked the scientist's inevitable question.

Hiroshi looked shocked. "Oh no. I did this for myself. We learn very little American poetry in school, so I did nothing very systematic or logical. I was only learning phrasing and rhythms. I picked a big anthology and started browsing. And who do you guess I chose first? All by myself." He looked around, waiting for us to guess.

"Frost?" I blurted. Probably because his reading at the Kennedy inauguration had been my last exposure to poetry.

"Robert Frost?" Hiroshi sounded surprised. "What makes you say him?"

I shrugged. By throwing out a name, I had hoped to claim

some knowledge and at the same time be excused from further participation. Poorly prepared students often try this tactic, but experienced teachers—like myself—often catch them. So why did I think that I could get away with such a silly stunt?

I fell back on the next line of defense: answer a question with a question. "So whom did you pick, Hiroshi?"

"William Carlos Williams."

"Who is he?" Sepp whispered in my ear.

Diana saved me from any further need for prevarication. "Why Williams?"

"To a Japanese, his poetry sounds familiar: his minimalism, his vivid, concrete images, his aesthetic ideal: 'no ideas but in things.'" For a moment, he sat there quietly, elbows on the table, his arms forming a triangle that supported his chin. "Also because he was the closest thing to a scientist in the *Norton Anthology*. For me, the important discovery about Williams was that his field—medicine—played hardly any role in his poetry. At the time, I did not want my science to interfere with my poetry. Now," he ran his hand through his hair—a gesture I had never noticed before in him—"I am not so sure anymore.

"I thought I would find it easy to translate Williams, and mostly it was, because he uses simple language. I still remember some lines from the first poem I translated:

> All this—was for you old woman.
> I wanted to write a poem
> that you would understand.
> For what good is it to me
> if you can't understand it?
> But you got to try hard."

Once more he stopped, nodding slightly to himself. "Only when you recite poetry out loud can you get a feel for the rhythm, the accents, the technique of the poet. When you do this often enough—and especially if you translate that poem into another language—you get to know it by heart."

He saw me shake my head in wonder. "I am sure you could do it, Max. It just takes practice."

"Will you recite one for us?" asked Diana.

"No!" Hiroshi's answer came almost explosively. "No," he continued in a calmer voice, "I cannot. I recite only to myself. I am too embarrassed to do so in public."

I was tempted to remind him of the time he had grabbed the microphone at a geisha house in Kyoto and started crooning, in a creditable imitation of Tony Bennett, "I Left My Heart in San Francisco." By the time the little cable cars got halfway to the stars, he had started to bellow so loudly that one of the geishas discreetly turned off the amplifier.

"But Hiroshi," I said instead. "You do this all the time when you give lectures. And in English, no less."

He dismissed me with a slight wave of his hand. "That is science, not poetry. In science, the language barrier exists only for the listener, not the speaker. Not so in poetry: the way you read poems makes all the difference in the world. If someone reads to you a scientific paper in Nipponese English, heavily accented, just barely understandable, as long as the science is good, you will still be impressed. Just imagine what would happen if a poem were presented that way."

I was not going to let him off that easily. "But your English is excellent. You have only a little accent."

"Max, you do not understand. My English is not good enough for reciting poetry . . . at least to this audience." He nodded to Diana.

"Do you feel that way about reading poetry in Japanese?" I asked.

"No, that I can do in public. Especially if it is my own."

"Why don't you let us hear one in Japanese, then?"

He shook his head. "Why? You would not understand a single word; none of the subtlety or structure; nothing of the beauty of the poem. You probably would not even get the rhythm. It would be like a circus performance."

Diana had not said a single word, but I noticed that she had not taken her eyes off Hiroshi. "Let's give Hiroshi a chance to finish his dessert," she said. "And then," she directed her gaze to him, "you can at least *tell* us some more about your poetry. What kind is it you write? What sort of prosodic practices have you adopted?"

I seemed to detect a touch of apprehension in Hiroshi's eyes. "*Mine?*" He shook his head. "But I could try something appropriate for our . . . salon? Could I have a piece of paper?"

While Diana went out to get it, I wondered about his reference to our salon. Had Diana talked to him about French salons? For a moment, I felt a tinge of jealousy.

He fingered the sheet absentmindedly before jotting down a line. "This is a *hokku*—the opening line to a *renga*." He glanced at me; the good student, I smiled back, nodding. "*Renga* are linked verse, composed in one sitting, each stanza by a different poet, quite often by as many as five." Hiroshi swung his index finger around our circle, as if he were counting.

"The important part about the *hokku* is that it refers to the actual situation and time of the composition." He looked up at us from the page. " 'A man on a chair cannot climb a mountain.' Who will be next?" Hiroshi held out the page. "We shall not worry about rules concerning syllables and lines. But we will observe one tradition: each poet has two minutes to respond."

I always panic when I find myself at an event where the audience is asked to participate. "How many stanzas?" I croaked.

"Only five—one for each of us. Who is the first volunteer?"

"I."

I looked at Sepp in astonishment; I would have thought he'd be the last to volunteer.

"There are trees on the mountain and branches on the tree." He leaned back, looking pleased with himself. I suspected him of cribbing from some Austrian bard.

"Not bad," murmured Hiroshi, writing down Sepp's stanza.

The next line came from Charlea. "A woman slaving in the kitchen doesn't think of mountains."

Hiroshi looked up, puzzled. I could understand his confusion: was it a comment or a contribution?

"Write it down, Hiroshi," Charlea said, "that's my stanza."

I started to sweat. The last thing I wanted was to be last. "Thinking of summits keeps me climbing," I exclaimed. As Hiroshi transcribed, I wondered where that had come from.

"I ride up the mountain on my choice stallion," Diana said coolly.

"This is getting to be quite a *renga*." Hiroshi looked at his watch. "Amazing. At this rate, we could produce a *hyakuin* or a *senku*."

"Which are?" Diana asked.

"A one-hundred- and a one-thousand-stanza *renga*."

"Too ambitious," I declared. But, stimulated by our success— I was getting into the swing of our catch-as-catch-can variety of *renga*—I suddenly came up with an idea on a completely unrelated topic that had been troubling me for a while. "When I saw Hiroshi in Washington," I began, "he told me about *renga*. We are going to need some institutional name once we start publishing. Since the principle of the *renga* bears such a similarity to our own concept, why not appropriate the term? How about 'Renga Institute of Theoretical Biology'?" I looked around the group, perhaps a bit too disingenuously.

"I like it," Charlea said, with barely a moment's hesitation. "But not 'theoretical.' It's too pretentious. And we all know that Diana Skordylis isn't all that theoretical. At least not yet."

"I agree with Charlea," said Sepp. "It is too specific."

"Hiroshi?" I asked.

He nodded. "Remove 'theoretical.'"

"All right," I proclaimed. "Then we have a name for our institution: the Renga Institute of Biology."

"But why 'biology'?" Charlea mused. "I'm a biophysicist, you're a biochemist . . . who knows where Diana Skordylis will publish most of her papers. 'Renga Institute' sounds concise; it's easy to pronounce, yet limitless in scope. I bet people will try to guess whether RENGA is an acronym. Let them."

"Did you ever think that your poetry would become so useful?" I asked Hiroshi as we headed for the elevator.

He stopped and gave me a long look. "Yes," he nodded, "I was always sure of that."

12

Throughout the dinner at Diana's apartment I'd found Sepp uncommunicative—an uncomfortable observer. Strange, I thought: the Japanese feeling more at ease than the European. But my thoughts on that subject were scattered away when D₃ took me aside at the end of the evening.

"I won't interfere in your deliberations," she said. "But I'd like to be present when you decide on the rules of your Bourbaki. I promise not to dominate the conversation."

I was about to offer a disclaimer about the possibility of her dominating the conversation, but she didn't let me. "Have the meeting at the Century Club," she added. "It's convenient—in midtown Manhattan—"

"What's wrong with the Princeton Club?"

"Nothing. It's just . . ." she hesitated. "I would like to host your meeting tomorrow."

"Are you a member of the Century Club?" I don't belong to any clubs other than my Princeton affiliations, but I had some vague recollection that the Century Club was very much a male bastion. "Are women . . . ?" I didn't know how to finish the sentence without treading on shaky ground.

"Welcome? Not very," she shrugged. "Tolerated? Yes. Admitted? Finally—after a full-blown legal battle. That's why I would like you to hold that meeting there tomorrow. And for Charlea's sake," she added as a seeming afterthought.

"How so?"

"I just wanted to make a point with her. A minor one."

"You certainly seemed in good form last evening," I said to Hiroshi when I found him waiting in the lounge the next morning. "But I noticed you were very quiet during most of that conversation between Diana and Charlea."

"I was wondering what my wife would have thought if she had been there. I do not believe she would have understood. Even if she knew English," he added in a pensive tone.

"What about you, Hiroshi?"

"I did not understand. Perhaps because I do not approve."

I suddenly realized that however much I knew of Hiroshi's work, there was much about him personally that I did not know.

"Of all?" I asked.

He rocked his head side to side. "To you I am probably old-fashioned. No, I did not disapprove of everything. But Max," he leaned forward without looking me in the eye. "Professor Conway, when she spoke about a companion, does this mean . . ." He didn't finish, the resulting silence embarrassing us both.

"Hiroshi," I said, "we're living during the last gasps of the twentieth century."

He nodded. "Yes. But Japan is not America. And I have two daughters."

"How old?"

"Twenty-four and thirty."

"Married?"

"No," he said. "No," he repeated, looking past me toward the entrance.

"How would they have felt if they'd been present?" I was surprised to find myself pursuing this line of conversation, considering the undercurrent of discomfort.

"I don't know. We do not discuss such questions. Why do you ask?" For the first time he looked me fully in the eyes.

"Curious, I guess. And your mentioning the differences between Japan and us. I have heard it said that one can learn about a society by studying its children. It's even a way to learn something about the parents."

"How many children do you have?"

"None."

"So one can only learn about you from you?"

We were probably both relieved when we saw Sepp enter the room, right hand outstretched. "Good morning, Max," he shook my hand so vigorously it hurt. "And good morning, *Herr* Professor Nishimura." He beamed at us, his white teeth appearing even brighter against the rosy cheeks of his Gothic, triangular face. "What a morning," he exclaimed. "I have discovered a gymnasium in my hotel. Bicycle, weights, cross-country skiing machine—for a moment I felt I was back in Innsbruck. I have been up since six." He grinned a bit sheepishly. "I was beginning to wonder: first the jet lag. And then that dinner discussion," he rolled his eyes heavenward. "But now," he patted his flat, firm stomach, "I feel good. Let me get some coffee."

"You were very quiet during the dinner," I observed when Sepp rejoined us. I was wondering if he would elaborate on his earlier remark.

"*Ach*," he shrugged. "You were the only person I knew, Max. And I was curious about *Frau* Doctor Ditmus. From what you wrote, I thought she was just a society lady. You never told me about her *Doktorat*. What a combination: elegance and intellect! *Fabelhaft!* Tell me, how old is she?"

"Late sixties, I would say."

"Tsk, tsk," he sounded surprised, "So old? Ah well, wealthy women do not wilt as fast as we." The number and proximity of *w*'s gave him trouble: he compromised on a new consonant, midway between *v* and *w*. "At least she seems wealthy."

I was beginning to think his earlier eye rolling had been simple admiration of Diana and her doings when he continued. "But Professor Conway!" Again his eyes moved heavenward. "I did not expect a lesbian in our group."

"Now wait a moment, Sepp," I started. "How do you know . . ." she is a lesbian, I wanted to say, but then stopped. "What difference does it make?" I added more feebly. "I hardly think sexual preferences will matter." Or will they? I wondered, recalling D_3's question about my sexuality. "I think it's high time for the four of us to start discussing our project."

"But *Frau* Doctor Ditmus said . . ."

"Sepp," I interrupted, "forget about the *Frau* and *Herr*."

"I apologize," he said formally, bowing slightly from the waist, "I have not been in America for quite a time. This," again he moved his hand around the room, "will also be good for my

English. And I agree: it is high time—is it high time you say?—
we started."

I had just risen to offer Charlea Conway my chair and was wondering where D₃ was when the concierge—or whatever they call
the Century Club's gatekeeper—approached us.

"Dr. Doyle-Ditmus is delayed. I am to lead you to your party's
private room. And I'll send a waiter for drinks."

Once we had settled in, Sepp's earlier questions prompted me
to break the conversational pause by describing D₃'s credentials.
"Do you know that last fall she got a MacArthur?" I announced.

"Well, I'll be damned." Charlea looked impressed. "And she
never mentioned it."

"Would you have, if *you'd* gotten a MacArthur?"

C₃ waved my question aside. "Let me tell you *my* MacArthur
story. A couple of years ago, I got a Federal Express letter from
the MacArthur Foundation with *private* and *confidential* marked
all over it. I was so excited I could hardly open the envelope. Do
you know what it was? A request for an evaluation of a candidate.
I was so pissed off I gave him the 'sound man, but . . .' treatment."

Only after we both stopped laughing did we notice Sepp's and
Hiroshi's blank expressions. "*Unglaublich,*" pronounced Sepp
with a dazed shake of his head when the $350,000 grant was
explained to him. "You Americans with your superprizes."

"We poor Americans need them, because we have no emperor." Charlea was in a bantering mood.

Hiroshi drew back, startled, as C₃'s index finger pointed at his
nose. "Tell us about your Emperor's Prize."

"For that I need a drink." Only after he'd downed nearly half
the contents of his tumbler would he allow the subject to be mentioned. And even then it took the combined appeals of the three
of us to induce him to speak.

"*Aota-gai,*" he said finally and drained the other half of his
glass. "It could be a useful word in English—the way you have
accepted *hara-kiri* into your vocabulary."

We were standing around him in a wide circle, drinks in hand,
88 incomprehension plain on our faces.

"*Aota-gai* is the practice of harvesting rice while it is still green," he explained. "You do it so you are first in the market. Now we use the word in the general sense of 'beating the competition.'" He lowered his voice to share a secret. "I confess: it was *aota-gai* that got me the Imperial Prize." He nudged me with his elbow. "But you are quite a rice merchant yourself, aren't you, Max?"

"Aren't we all? But *you* got a prize for it. And why didn't you tell us earlier?"

"It just happened."

"But you must have known about it long before. Didn't you?"

He inclined his head. "It is not good manners to talk about it before the actual ceremony."

"What was it like? Surely now you can tell us." I'd heard vaguely that this was the greatest distinction a Japanese scientist could receive, but not much more than that. What scientist is not curious to hear about new kudos? And especially to learn how much money was involved. "Did you have to prostrate yourself when you approached the emperor?"

"Max!" Charlea giggled. "Prostrate!"

"All right," I conceded. "Just tell us what happened after you bowed deeply."

"Where do you want me to start?"

"Who gives the award?" Sepp asked.

"The Japan Academy."

"Are there any women in your Academy?" Charlea, I swore under my breath, let the man talk before you interrupt.

Hiroshi appeared startled. "No," he said, after a moment's reflection. "No women."

"Why not?"

"They just . . . have none," he stammered.

"Suppose you were a woman, Hiroshi, with your c.v. Would you have been elected to the Japan Academy?"

"No," he said, relief appearing on his face. "Absolutely not!"

"Why that's terrible," Charlea cried. "But how can you be so sure?"

"Because *I* am not a member. And if I, Hiroshi Nishimura, . **39** cannot be elected, then surely Charlea Nishimura has no chance."

He obviously thought this was funny, and I have to admit that the thought of a Charlea Nishimura made me smile. But how come Hiroshi—a foreign member of *our* Academy—can't get elected to *his?* For once, I didn't have to ask the question.

"But why?" asked Sepp and C3 in unison.

Hiroshi emptied his glass and looked around for the bottle.

"Very simple," he said, pouring himself a full glass. Hiroshi's ability to metabolize astounding quantities of ethanol was well known, but I was starting to worry. "I am too young. Of the 131 members, the average age is 79.5. The sole biochemist, Hayaishi, is in his 70s. The only two organic chemists, Nozoe and Akabori, are around 90 years old."

"You certainly know the statistics," observed Sepp dryly.

Hiroshi shrugged. "How else would you calculate the odds? In our Academy, a member has to die before a new one can be elected. Besides, the 131 members do not come just from the natural sciences. We also have three sections of 'human science.'"

"Which is?" It was Diana's voice. We had been so mesmerized by Hiroshi's tale that we hadn't noticed her quiet entrance.

"The Academy considers human science as literature, philosophy, history; also law, politics, and economics; even business."

"So you have a double chance," said D3. "If you don't make it as a biochemist, maybe you'll enter as a poet."

"Completely impossible," he said emphatically. "You do not understand how the Japan Academy functions: its sections correspond to the various faculties in Japanese universities. A member's category is based solely on the subject in which he received his degree—decades ago—no matter what the subject in which he made his professional reputation. This may explain why there are no women," he bowed apologetically to Charlea.

"Could there be a woman academician in literature?" Diana asked.

"I have no idea," Hiroshi said flatly. "Maybe our literary women are not distinguished enough."

"Hiroshi," she struck his arm in mock anger. "What about *The Tale of Genji?* That was written by a woman. Is that not distinguished enough for you?"

"Murasaki Shikibu lived during the mid-Heian period. The Japan Academy did not exist then."

"What about women and the Imperial Prize?" Charlea was still not ready to yield. "Since you don't have to be an Academy member to win one, couldn't—?"

"Charlea," I whispered to her, "why don't you give up? You must know the answer by now."

But I was wrong. Hiroshi, anticipating her question, nodded vigorously. "Yes, there was one: Aki Ueno, in 1960. She did the restorations of the murals in the pagoda at Daigo Temple."

That seemed to satisfy C_3, and for a while Hiroshi was able to proceed at his own pace. It was poignant to hear him tell the story of his recent award. His pride, his eagerness to tell it—his earlier reticence had vanished entirely—were all too apparent. And why should he not be proud? We academic scientists are all infected by kudomania, a word I coined that very moment and decided to store for future reference.

Hiroshi, we learned, had done exceptionally well on the kudo front during the year of his official retirement. He had actually bagged *two* honors: the Imperial Prize *and* the Japan Academy Prize. He explained that the latter is given annually to fewer than a dozen scholars working in the fields covered by the Academy. Out of this exalted company, one or two are additionally anointed with the Imperial Prize—Japan's highest award.

"I learned in January—unofficially—that I was likely to be one of the Japan Academy Prize winners. On February 13 I was notified officially that I had won both an Academy Prize *and* the Imperial Prize." Hiroshi's tone veered from enthusiastic to sarcastic. "At the press conference that day, the reporters asked me to explain my work in two minutes in simple words. Then they asked what I thought was the difference between Japanese and American research."

That intrigued me, remembering how bitterly he had complained to me just a couple of months ago. "What did you say?" I asked.

He shrugged. "I was diplomatic. I said that, on average, our education is more rigorous than yours, but that you had some advantages when it comes to support of basic research, postdocs, that sort of thing."

"The operative word is *had*. We *had* some advantage," Charlea sounded bitter. "But just look what's going on now with our research funding. My damned NIH grant, and everybody else's in the country, was cut by 11 percent."

Hiroshi clucked his tongue in sympathy.

"Never mind that," Sepp said. "Tell us about the award."

"The ceremony? That was held last week, at the Japan Academy building in Ueno Park, in the presence of the emperor and empress, the minister of education, all the Academy members. And guests, of course."

I had been imagining the swishing of kimonos and ornate ceremonial robes among the soft shuffles on tatami mats, but Hiroshi demolished the illusion with one sentence.

"It was all quite Western: the Academy building is International School, the furniture is European, all the men wore striped pants and tails, and the music came from a loudspeaker: Mendelssohn."

Before I could feel too sheepish at my cultural stereotyping, Hiroshi added, "The ceremony itself *was* quite formal, and we had to rehearse everything the preceding day, right to the minute. We assembled at 10:20 in the room holding the exhibits illustrating our work, to be ready for the arrival of Emperor Akihito and Empress Michiko at 10:33. At 10:39, starting with me, each recipient had three minutes to explain his exhibit and two minutes to reply to questions by Their Majesties. It all ended at 11:29." Hiroshi grinned at our skeptical looks.

"The official award ceremony in the auditorium of the Academy started at 11:33. The emperor and empress—the first time in the Academy's history that an empress had appeared—sat on the stage. The award winners were in the first row, our personal guests in the row behind us, and then the rest."

"All your guests in one row?" asked Diana. "How did you fit them all in?"

"No problem," he assured her. "Only three. We were not permitted to bring more."

"Only three? What about children, sisters, brothers, parents?"

"Ah." It was the first time this evening that I had heard Hiroshi inhale audibly. "Parents." He let the breath out and took another drink. "Except for the mathematicians, probably very few still had parents living. My wife was there."

"And your daughters," I guessed.

"No, not my daughters. My wife, my older brother, and my uncle—my father's youngest brother." He waved his hand as if he wanted to erase that image. "On one side of the stage was a podium, where the president of the Academy—he's ninety-one years old—stood, partly facing the emperor, and partly us. A clerk read out the names, just using 'Mister'—no other titles."

"Good for them," whispered Charlea.

Hiroshi blinked at her, then looked at the ceiling, as if reliving the event. "Since I had also won the Imperial Prize, I was the first to be called. I approached the center of the stage, bowed to the emperor, went up the steps, bowed again, and then turned to the president. He gave me two diplomas for the two awards and a wooden box containing the Academy Prize money. In cash—not a check."

I had been wondering all along whether money was involved. Now that I knew, I wondered how much?

So, apparently, had Sepp. "That must have been a giant box," he said. "With 130 yen to the dollar."

He shook his head. "A small box, quite small. And not even lacquered."

My mental calculator was going full steam: the Nobel Prize is worth about $1 million, the Wolf Prize in Israel $100,000; even if the Japanese are no more generous than the Israelis, that would still make it 13 million yen. How could so much paper money possibly fit into a small box?

"How much money actually goes with the prize?" Charlea's voice was cool and precise.

Hiroshi curled his lip. "Five hundred thousand."

"Yen?" Surely it could not be that, I thought. That would make it barely one-hundredth of D₃'s MacArthur.

But Hiroshi nodded. "Yen."

"And the Imperial Prize?" For once, Charlea was asking all the right questions.

"A beautiful silver vase. Quite tall." Hiroshi leaned over and held out his hand with the whiskey glass to indicate its height from the floor. "I would guess at least seventy centimeters high. And embossed with a golden chrysanthemum—the sign of the emperor's family."

"I think that's rather charming," exclaimed Diana.

Only a MacArthur recipient would say that, I thought, remembering the biggest award I had ever received, the National Medal of Science. No money, not even a silver vase. Just a diploma and a medal—bronze—were all I clutched as I departed from my only visit to the White House: those, and the tactile memory of Richard Nixon's handshake lingering on my palm. "What happened then?" I asked.

"I went back to the emperor, who this time stood up. I bowed, returned to my seat, and the whole procedure was repeated with the others. At 11:48, the deputy prime minister and the minister of education each spoke about fifty words, and at 11:52 it was all over."

"And that was it?"

"Then we had beer and sandwiches."

Sandwiches! I thought of sushi, of the freshest sashimi delicately arrayed on pale wood, and couldn't help thinking this the biggest letdown of all. But Hiroshi was not finished.

"I only had time to down a beer, because then we had to change into informal clothes for our visit to the palace. We were due there at 2:15—the award winners and the fifteen newly elected members of the Academy, most of them in their seventies. Max," he grinned at me, "how do you think we were transported to the palace?"

"Horse and carriage?" I asked hopefully.

Hiroshi roared with laughter. "Through Tokyo traffic? One more guess."

"A stretch limo, then."

"Not a bad guess. You Americans take these to go to the airport." He paused, savoring something tart. "They stuffed all the men into a couple of minivans."

"And the women?" Charlea had lost whatever amusement had still remained on her face.

"What women?"

"Your wife, the other women guests . . ."

"Women were not invited to the palace."

"Jesus Christ!" Charlea's tone sounded so ominous I couldn't look at her. But Hiroshi chose not to hear. He continued, undisturbed.

"The lunch was the most memorable event. The emperor had insisted that everything should be as informal as possible. We were distributed over six tables, with members of the imperial family at each. I was at the table with the emperor and empress, another had the crown prince, a third Prince Hitachi and his wife, and so on. After each French course," I could see his eyes twinkle with amusement at having guessed correctly our disappointment at the imperial culinary choice—"as the waiters cleared the dishes, the imperial family switched tables. The emperor is an ichthyologist, so we talked about color vision in fish. Charlea, you would have been interested in Prince Hitachi. He is a molecular biologist at the Japan Cancer Research Institute. He probably would have talked to you about lymphokines."

"I wouldn't have been invited," she growled.

"If you were Japanese, you probably would have won an Academy Prize," he said diplomatically.

"Not the Imperial Prize?" She shot back.

"Hiroshi," Diana intervened. "What an award for a theoretician!"

Hiroshi held up a hand. "I don't claim to be a theoretician."

"That's not a claim. For a biochemist, it's an admission."

Hiroshi gave Charlea a bewildered look.

"Maybe it is this wonderful Scotch," he raised his empty glass, "but I don't understand. I *admit* I am a biochemist. I *claim* that, on occasion, I have done theory. You are the only real theoretician here, Charlea. The rest of us are only . . . how do you call a man in a woman's dress?"

"A transvestite," Charlea said suspiciously.

"Exactly." The Japanese in him could not repress the small bow of acknowledgment. "We are theoretical transvestites." He said the words carefully, with an expression of delight. "But Diana," he added, playing the pedagogue once more, "a theory can only give you an answer if experimentalists establish boundary conditions. Without boundaries, there can be no theory, and Charlea would then be unemployed. We three theoretical transvestites," he waved an arm that included me, Sepp, and himself, "will provide the boundaries. A very important function!" He gave another small bow, this time to Charlea.

"Why did you say *three* transvestites?" Diana looked from Hiroshi to me and Sepp. I couldn't tell if her eyebrows were raised at Hiroshi's metaphor or at something else.

"Because Max and Sepp are like me. If you look at our publications, you will find that we are primarily experimentalists. We dabble in theory."

"Max!" Diana exclaimed. "I didn't know you men were all *dabblers!* How will you prevent Diana Skordylis from becoming one too?"

Before I could defend my credentials as a theoretician, Charlea intervened.

"Don't worry, Diana. I'll keep DS an honest woman. Besides, Hiroshi was too tough on himself . . . or too modest. When it comes to theory, he's neither a dabbler nor a slouch. It's just that he's not *pure*."

"Meaning?"

"As a 'wet' scientist—an experimentalist—he operates within the marshy margins of theory: he himself establishes the boundaries for his theoretical work. The *pure* theoreticians wouldn't dream of getting their hands dirty."

"And what about your hands?"

Charlea raised her left hand and gave it a mock inspection. "Not lily white; just barely dirty, but the dirt can't be washed off."

I began to wonder. Where do Sepp and I stand on the Conway dabbler-slouch scale? And why am I curious? In spite of her sarcasm, I was impressed with C_3: there was something tough, almost athletic, about her mental energy—a surprising contrast with her rather chubby frame. I found myself thinking she might be right about keeping Diana Skordylis honest.

As we sat down to lunch Diana produced a yellow legal pad. "I'd promised Max I wouldn't interfere with your deliberations today," she began. "But while we have lunch, I thought I might fill you in on some of the historical background to your project. There are some important differences between what you're attempting here and what your predecessors have done. Bourbaki's original intent was to compose a rigorous textbook of mathematics, a modern *Cours d'analyse*. They certainly had no intention, at first, of elaborating new theorems, much less publishing them. You, on the other hand, intend just that. Especially," she flashed me the briefest of smiles, "to publish. Now, whereas the Bourbaki group needed very little outside support—"

"How do *you* know all this?" C_3's challenge had the sound of an examiner finding questionable results in a doctoral dissertation.

"I'm a historian," Diana explained complacently. "When I first heard from Max about Nicolas Bourbaki, I decided to do a bit of research. It's what I do, after all, Charlea." She reached out a conciliatory hand and laid it on the table top halfway between them. "Do you want to hear about some of the similarities between the two operations that I discovered recently?"

Charlea hadn't taken her eyes off Diana. "Go on."

With a gracious nod, Diana picked up the pad and started

to read—the image of a good graduate student performing for a tough examiner. Only the similarity in their ages contradicted the illusion. "The Bourbakis, or NB as they refer to themselves in the singular, hold three annual meetings—*congrès* they call them—for seven to ten days. The only difference here is that you'll meet for longer periods, or am I mistaken?

"I'm quoting now: 'At these congrès, NB chooses remote and discreet sites, offering great charm and sensuous pleasures: landscape, cuisine, wine . . .'" She looked up, grinning. "'NB's operation calls for thinking of the most aggressive kind. Nothing, nobody, is sacred. There is no authority except an intellectual one: the *provisional*,'" she raised her finger for emphasis, "'consensus emerging from a free combat of ideas. But how can one design conditions whereby such intellectual debate does not destroy the friendship of such an intimate ensemble?'"

What is Diana reading? I kept thinking, barely able to keep from interrupting.

"'NB's anonymity is one of the prerequisites making this enterprise possible,'" D_3 read. "'Another is the absence of any internal authority structure.' Max had already mentioned to me that this would also apply to you people," she observed in an aside. "'There is no functioning chairman. The only figure with any authority is the adjutant, whose task it is to ensure that people wake up on time,'" again she grinned while her index finger wagged to and fro, "'and assemble promptly for working sessions. The adjutant also takes notes of all decisions made; otherwise, except for collectively planned agenda, each session is a free-for-all.'

"Now what do you think of that?" she asked, putting the notepad down. "I guess you'd better pick an adjutant."

"Where did you get that?" asked Charlea. The tone was suspicious, belligerently so. "What were you reading?"

"My notes."

I could tell that D_3 was enjoying herself—but be careful, I wanted to warn: the female of the species *Homo scientificus* may not be as easily handled as the male.

"Notes? Of what?"

"Of an interview I had this morning. With Professor Hyman Bass. That's why I was late."

"Oh."

I couldn't tell if C₃'s single syllable was confirmation or a question. Did she know who Bass was? I had never heard of him.

"You know, Charlea: the math professor from Columbia."

That was well done: pretending to acknowledge Conway's familiarity with Bass and feeding her the right answer at the same time. A smart aleck would have said, "You know Bass, don't you Charlea?" and then waited for the answer.

"Come to think of it, Max," she turned to me. "You must have met him. He's a member of the National Academy of Sciences."

"There are nearly two thousand NAS members," I countered. "You can't know them all. Besides, I have nothing to do with the math section. Do you know him, Charlea?" As long as we were putting each other on the spot, I thought it was my turn to find out how much C₃ knew about Bourbaki—or if she had been bluffing.

"The people in the NAS math section are all *pure* mathematicians; I don't even know all the sixty-odd members of my own section."

She's never heard of Bass, I concluded with some satisfaction; she just won't say so.

"I had to interview him, of course, as soon as I realized I had discovered an *American* Bourbaki."

"What do you mean, 'American Bourbaki'? How on earth did you discover *that?*" Charlea demanded.

"Simple. I looked him up in *Who's Who.*"

"And it said *there* that he was a member of the Bourbakis? I don't believe it," I said flatly.

"Here," Diana said, reaching into her briefcase and producing a photocopy. "Read it yourself."

"BASS, HYMAN, *mathematician, educator; b. Houston, Oct. 5, 1932,*" it read, followed by the usual personal information about first wife, second wife, names of children, education. "My God," I exclaimed, "Charlea, listen to this: he got his B.A. at Princeton and—get this—his Ph.D. from Chicago. Do you think we might have had him in our classes?" As I skimmed the rest, periodically I read out loud the astonishing list of honors and travels—it seemed he had been at every institute and think tank on the planet. "I thought *we* traveled, but look at these mathematicians! When is he ever at Columbia?" Then I saw it: "*Collaborateurs N. Bourbaki.*" "I'll be damned! Here it is!" I reached across Hiroshi to pass the paper to Sepp and Charlea. "Down at the bottom. Can you believe it? And in French to boot."

For a minute, everybody was silent while D_3 preened herself—deservedly, I thought. Charlea handed back the photocopy with a chuckle. "You've got to hand it to the mathematicians: they've got class. How many *Who's Who* readers do you think have the faintest idea what 'N. Bourbaki' means? Even most mathematicians don't know who belongs to this ultimate 'in'-club. I'd been under the impression every Bourbaki was French. Diana, congratulations for coming up with all this inside dope. Especially about Bourbaki's 'sensuous pleasures.' Did this really come from Bass?"

Diana nodded vigorously. "I got it just this morning. Right in his office. But there's another thing about Bourbaki you ought to know."

"What's that?"

"They have one rule, although it's been broken a few times: retirement at age fifty." She glanced down at her notes again. "How did Bass put it? Oh yes, here: 'an age sufficiently shy of diminished faculties to avoid any awkwardness.'" She looked up from her page. "Rather delicately put, isn't it?"

Charlea muttered something I didn't catch; Sepp looked grim; I found myself recalling that inexcusable memo announcing my "promotion." Only Hiroshi maintained an unreadable silence.

"The best prescription for diminished faculties," Charlea growled, "is to keep an open mind. Let's make that our rule, and not some arbitrary age limit."

"I think we've heard enough about Nicolas Bourbaki," I said.

I was about to continue when Hiroshi stopped me. "Just one more question, Diana. I already heard from Max where the name

'Bourbaki' comes from," he smiled self-consciously at his problem with the name, "but why did they pick 'Nicolas'?"

"I don't know." It was the first time today that I had heard such an admission from Diana.

"But I do," interjected Charlea. "It's supposed to be based on Saint Nicholas, bringing gifts to the mathematicians."

Diana headed for the sofa as the four of us settled around the table in our private room.

"Why don't you join us?" asked Charlea.

"I promised earlier not to interfere. It's time for you scientists to decide on your modus operandi. I'll just listen from here."

"No, join us."

"You mean you need another woman?"

"I do *not* mean that," replied C3, "but I'm starting to see how it might be useful to have a historical perspective."

"I already told Diana that," I added. "Besides, as an ex-dean, she might give us some financial pointers."

"I suggest we first talk a bit about the Skordylis persona," Charlea said. "Diana Skordylis can't just appear out of nowhere —publishing a paper and then disappearing. It wouldn't really accomplish what we're attempting to do: too ephemeral."

Sepp looked dubious. "Why? What if we publish a really *brilliant* paper?"

"Be realistic. We need to get people accustomed to seeing the name in the literature. I think she should publish a number of papers over the next couple of years—on somewhat related topics, of course—whether or not they are *brilliant*."

Sepp bridled at that last touch of sarcasm, but Hiroshi intervened. "What about coauthors?"

"That *is* a tricky question." Charlea looked at the rest of us, eyebrow cocked. "Any suggestions?"

"Excuse me," Diana interrupted, shaking her pencil. "You said 'publish a number of papers during the next couple of years.' How many is 'a number'?"

Charlea looked irritated. "What's the difference? Say half a dozen." She started to turn away from Diana, but it didn't work.

"Okay, half a dozen," D_3 pursued. "And how long does it take in your field for a paper to appear in print after you've submitted it?"

"A couple of months, minimum," Charlea's voice was curt. "Sometimes a year or longer. It all depends on where you publish, whether it's a 'preliminary communication' or a full paper with all details, whether you have problems with the referees, and, of course, how well known the author is in the first place. Which is exactly why DS had better publish several papers fairly quickly. We—meaning she—haven't got much time. I suspect," she threw a meaningful glance in Diana's direction, "that five years may well be close to the maximum for achieving everything: Sepp's brilliant idea, Max's revenge . . ."

"But don't you have to do some work—I mean *scientific* work—first? I still don't see how DS is going to produce six papers in two years."

Charlea gazed at her thoughtfully. "I'm starting to think we should follow Bourbaki's example and elect you adjutant." I could see from Diana's expression that she had taken Charlea's remark as a compliment. Then she turned to the rest of us. "I'd like to propose that we launch Diana Skordylis in life by having each of us contribute to her dowry."

"Dowry?" Diana asked. The reference to Skordylis's marital status seemed to have piqued her curiosity.

"If we are going to solve the practical problem that our adjutant has just raised," she threw a surprisingly affectionate glance at D_3, "how about each of us contributing some projects of our own—ones that are complete or nearly so but not yet published? It wouldn't take us long to collect half a dozen manuscripts that way, would it?" She raised a hand to still the murmur rising around the table. "Of course, they will have to be problems you have worked on alone—rather unlikely, I suspect, among the three of you—or at least ones where you don't feel an authorship commitment to somebody else."

"How could that be?" Sepp asked suspiciously.

"We've all worked long enough: cumulatively, well over one century." I pretended to shudder, but she ignored me. "During that time surely each of us has published some experimental or theoretical work that merits amendment—or, God forbid, even more serious correction. Max," she turned to me, "take your NFAT work."

"What's that?" Diana asked.

"Nuclear factor of activated T cells," I said uncomfortably. "Charlea, you can't be serious."

"About giving it to DS, or about correcting it?"

"It doesn't *need* correcting."

"Oh, get off the high horse. *If*—and I'm saying it now just for the sake of argument—*if* your NFAT work merits another look, what would be wrong with the two of us doing it jointly? And *if*— just suppose again—we indeed found something in your original paper that required some modest, but not insignificant, correction, what would be wrong if we published it under the name of Diana Skordylis? It would certainly be better than if somebody *else* discovered such an error and published it."

Until a few moments ago, I wasn't sure whether she was pulling my leg. She certainly had that look about her; but now I could see she was in earnest. "Don't think I'm picking on you, Max," she added. "I just happen to have read your NFAT paper. I'm saying we should *all* look over our collective corpus," a momentary flicker of amusement crossed Charlea's face, "to see whether we can come up with contributions to DS's dowry. Let's look into the halfway house section of our files to see what's hidden there. We need to start learning how to be generous with our intellectual property. If we can't do that, Diana Skordylis hasn't got a chance."

"Agreed," said Hiroshi.

"Agreed," echoed Sepp.

"I'll go along," I said, looking at Charlea, "provided that in the minutes *corpus* is replaced with *opus. Corpus* sounds too much like *corpse*."

"You win that one," Charlea said solemnly, writing a single

word on her pad. She gave the impression that she wasn't taking notes so much as keeping score.

But searching our respective oeuvres for minor errors or even major gaffes could only launch Diana Skordylis on her career. It would require something very different to make her a scientific sensation: some highly original work, unconnected with our recent or current research. After all, what scientist would offer the prize diamond he'd already found and cut to someone else for polishing, just so it could be sold under another name?

"We could proceed along the obvious line," observed Charlea. "Starting here and now, any *new* research occurring to any of us should be thrown into the Skordylis basket. For a start, let's give each other a reasonable deadline: say three months?"

"Then what?"

Charlea looked at Sepp. "When we meet again, we'll take these proposals apart: no holds barred, the way Diana described the Nicolas Bourbaki sessions. Any project that survives will become the intellectual property of Skordylis."

"And then?"

"Then we'll work out who does what, where, when, and how."

"Fair enough," I said.

Sepp leaned forward, vigorously shaking his head. "That is easy to say for the two of you. You, Charlea, are not even retired. And you, Max, can still work at Princeton. In Innsbruck, at the university, I have nothing—not even an office."

Like a polite student waiting to be recognized, Hiroshi raised his hand. "Sepp has pointed out something important," he said. "We are not like your mathematicians, Max. Our efforts are not directed at a single project, like a textbook." He folded his arms before him, his expression hardening. "This is about our lives. How are we to work together—the four of us as one person— when our circumstances, our abilities—our lives—are so different?"

Next to me, Sepp was clicking his thumbnail against his teeth —a low, annoying sound. Now he stopped. "I am starting to realize this project will require real discipline."

"And altruism," Charlea interjected.

"Excuse me?" Sepp frowned.

"Lack of selfishness."

Sepp shrugged noncommittally. "Let me make a suggestion which would be good for our . . . altruism," he nodded at C_3, "and *also* good discipline. We now have a mechanism for rejecting proposals. But what if we are left with too many good ones? We'll need some priority system."

Good God, I thought, are we going to reinvent the NIH? "You've probably never applied for financial support to our National Institutes of Health," I started.

"I have," he interrupted. "They turned me down."

Sepp's reply threw me off. I wasn't sure how to handle it. "The point I wanted to make is that when you start talking about priority scores, you're starting to outline the procedure that NIH study sections go through when they review grant applications. I thought we were trying to get away from all that red tape and bureaucracy."

"There is nothing wrong with discipline—"

"Hang the discipline," I grumbled.

"Cool off, Max," Charlea said. "All he means is the discipline of evaluation. There's no other way to maintain standards. Besides, there is one big difference between this and any other evaluation panel: we sit around and criticize our own ideas. Right, Sepp?"

Sepp's grunt apparently meant yes. He sounded miffed. "When Max interrupted me, I was about to make a suggestion to help Charlea's altruism rather than to add to Max's red tape."

"I'm sorry," I said. I wondered if I sounded as ungracious as Sepp.

"Suppose we had to decide between two very good proposals: one by Max, the other by me," Sepp said.

"Suppose," I offered cautiously.

"I would have to defend Max's to the group, and he would have to do the same for mine. Only then would we settle on a priority. Do you follow me?"

He looked at Hiroshi, who nodded. Charlea, perceiving that

nothing further would issue from his corner, passed the ball to me. "It's worth a try. What do you think, Max?"

"I'd like to think about it a bit." I was somewhat taken aback by the operational minutiae starting to come out of the woodwork; when I had worked all this out in the Virgin Islands and back at Princeton, none of these things had ever entered my mind.

"Am I permitted to make a suggestion?" Diana sounded surprisingly hesitant. "When you have reached the stage Sepp just described, how about making the presentation to me? In language I can understand? Perhaps you could even address some of the societal issues that might arise. Unless, of course," she finished, looking directly at me, "your work is totally impractical."

To me, the word *impractical* always carries a pejorative ring. I don't know what my face looked like at that moment, but she must have misread my initial response, which was, at best, lukewarm.

"Max, I'm offering to act as an honest broker. And besides, if you people can't make Skordylis's work understandable to me," her gaze dropped to the table, "then isn't there something wrong with *you?*"

If that was a gauntlet being thrown, then I wondered who'd be the first to pick it up. I knew I wouldn't.

Charlea placed her hand on Diana's, the one holding a pencil. It looked almost as if she wanted to prevent her from using it. "A patron should understand how the money is being spent. Is that what you mean?"

Diana drew her hand away. "I had *not* meant it that way, because I am not your patron—much as I might enjoy serving that function. But now that you ask, why not?" She gave a quick, hard tap with her pencil. "I've heard all you talking about grants; applying for them, not getting them." She glanced guiltily at Sepp, who did not look back. "But I've never heard any of you mention who pays for them. You've always had a patron—it's society."

"So?" Charlea demanded.

"So patronage isn't a one-way street," she said heatedly. "It never has been. If you want patronage, participate in the exchange. Take the effort, at least, to explain your ideas in layman's language."

"Why not? Let's."

Diana stared at Charlea. "You mean you agree?"

"Sure," grinned Charlea. "What made you think I didn't?"

"Well," D_3 stammered, "I just thought . . ." I could see that Diana had been warming to a fight; now that it had been taken away from her, she couldn't do much more than trail off, like a teakettle taken from the flame.

"It's an issue in my country," remarked Hiroshi, but then he stopped and gazed at his hands. Did that mean he didn't want to deal with it? "But I do not understand how this will help our problem. We four need some way to decide among ourselves . . ."

"That's the problem," Diana countered. "Scientists always say that. But you may not be able to decide right away among yourselves. By reviewing the material before a relatively disinterested party, you will at least simplify matters."

" 'We should make things as simple as possible, but not simpler.' Do you know who said that?"

The tone was pure *Herr* Professor Krzilska addressing the student *Frau* Doyle-Ditmus, who just shook her head.

"Einstein! And I agree with him absolutely. Now, who should conduct the simplification on behalf of Diana Skordylis?"

If Sepp meant the question for Diana, it did not register: she had started to doodle on her pad.

Charlea came to her aid. "Obviously, you and Max should do so—assuming we are dealing with projects proposed by the two of you."

"And Dr. Doyle-Ditmus will then make the final decision?" Sepp's eyes narrowed. Diana's doodling had stopped.

"Why not?" C_3 shot back. "If we're down to two projects—both of them equally worthwhile—why not have an outsider pick?"

"On what basis? Whoever succeeds in making his project zound zimpler?" Sepp's irritation started to acquire a German accent.

It was time to put a stop to this. Charlea may have been teasing, but Sepp seemed to be taking it seriously. And I had no idea what Hiroshi was thinking. "This is getting counterproductive," I said.

"This?" Charlea's eyebrows started to rise. "What? Sepp's contribution to our altruistic training? Diana's proposal to have us present an intelligible version of our ideas? Or having her be the final judge?"

I took a deep breath and started to count. This was not the time to lose my temper. "Am I permitted to have my say now?" I asked, trying to sound merely arch. "We can certainly give Sepp's idea a try, but let's not set it into stone. And to you, Diana," I stared in her direction until she finally looked up, "I want to say that there is nothing wrong in presenting our scientific ideas in salon language." I glanced at Sepp. "Einstein would applaud that from his grave. But when it comes to Diana actually *deciding*," my eyes moved heavenward, "well . . ." I can't be any more diplomatic than that, I told myself, and stopped.

"Max," Diana said, "and Sepp. You must be wacky. I wouldn't dream of doing that. I do not have the background to make such a decision, nor do I want the responsibility. I've reached the stage in life where I'm getting tired of making decisions for others. I am supporting your plans because the idea behind your enterprise intrigues me. I enjoy being an observer, perhaps even your collective confidante or friend—but nothing more. You people better caucus some more about collective decision making. *C'est tout, mes amis*," she announced and rose from her chair.

"Well, there is our answer," I murmured.

"Eine fabelhafte Dame," concurred Sepp.

14

"I'll walk you to your hotel," I told Sepp. "I need some fresh air." What I really wanted was a bit of time alone with him. If there was any residual tension from this afternoon, I wished to allay it.

"Where are you staying?" he asked as we headed north on Fifth Avenue. It was an innocent enough question, yet I found myself tongue-tied. I didn't want to admit that I was sleeping in D₃'s guest room.

"At a friend's," I said quickly. I was about to change the subject when Sepp took me by surprise.

"How did you meet the *Frau Doktor?*"

"Which one?" I asked disingenuously, stalling for time.

Sepp was a good three inches taller than I, and as he looked down on me with a slightly provocative grin, he suddenly seemed intrusively threatening. "Certainly not Charlea," he said. "Are you two just friends?"

What was *just* supposed to signify? I wondered. Do we look like a couple? "Just friends," I nodded. "We met on vacation."

"And now? Do you meet often?"

I was about to say that it was none of his business when he stopped abruptly before a Mark Cross display window. "A Filofax?" he read, pointing to a leatherbound volume. "I will buy this for my son. I want to bring him something from America, and this he can use in his work."

"Your son?" I asked, grateful for the change in subject—and curious to be learning something about Sepp's personal life. "How old is he?"

"Forty-two. He was always interested in America. When he was a young boy, we used to read together about Indians, totem poles, buffaloes—the sort of things we Europeans romanticize about your West."

"What does he do now?"

"He's a psychoanalyst, a Jungian."

"Really?" I said, making the noise one makes when presented with a fact that doesn't seem to lead anywhere. And then, for no reason I could understand, I asked, "Have you ever been in psychoanalysis?"

But Sepp didn't seem to think the question was prying. He just shook his head. "Takes too much time."

Now what does that mean? I wondered. That he would have gone into psychoanalysis if he'd had the time?

"And you, Max?"

"Eh?"

"Have you ever been in analysis?"

"No," I said emphatically. "I've never felt the need for a shrink."

"Ah," Sepp said, eyeing me speculatively. "*Klapsdoktor*. My son hates that word. He says people who use it are insecure."

Suddenly uncomfortable under Sepp's gaze, I asked, "And you? Have you ever felt the need?"

"Yes," he said, and his eyes turned inward. "Especially recently."

I waited for more, but he just ran one of his fingers absent-mindedly through his still-sandy hair.

"Because of your retirement?" I nudged him.

"Before."

"Oh?"

"When my marriage collapsed." He stopped caressing his hair and gave me a searching look. "After nearly forty years . . . it's a long time."

I tried unsuccessfully to call up a visual image of Sepp's wife. I'd met her once when he visited Princeton, but no image returned. "It's certainly a long time," I said awkwardly.

As we left the Mark Cross store to continue uptown, a delayed train of arithmetical calculation pulled into my mental station. "Nearly forty years," Sepp had said. But hadn't he also said that his son was forty-two? "Sepp, have you ever been married before?"

"One wife, two sons. *Das ist Alles*."

What business of mine was it whether his elder son was illegitimate? Yet I behaved like a dog who would not stop sniffing. "How old is your other son?"

"Thirty-eight. Ludwig's love is the classics—he even took Greek in the Gymnasium. Now he is an antiquarian in Vienna. So you see: a Jungian elder, and an antiquarian younger." Sepp chuckled. "But enough of my family. You have no children, do you?"

"Just one wife. And she is dead."

There was something lacking during dinner. Was it that we dealt only with science or because there were only four of us? And the others—were they also missing D_3? We seemed to be speaking mostly past each other as we covered the sole remaining operational item, the need for experimental support. Except for Charlea, we had always depended on laboratory verification of our theoretical speculations. Now, as we confronted the effects our new situation might have on our work, we realized that we were too old—"too set in your ways," Charlea had put it in one of her more diplomatic moments—to metamorphose into pure theoreticians.

"But how will you reconcile the need for laboratory work with the necessity for secrecy?" Charlea was good at producing succinct summaries. "I gather none of you has actually worked in the laboratory for years."

"Decades," I admitted.

"So how will you do it? Surely you can't expect lab assistants to keep a secret."

But I knew the answer to this question—in fact, it was a question I had held the answer to for weeks, before the problem had even arisen. One of the problems of working with collaborators is that sometimes you have to let them wrestle with a problem first.

Charlea's fingers played with her lower lip, as if she were trying to draw out a solution. "There are plenty of experimentalists in my neighborhood: Chicago, Northwestern, U. of I. . . . I could tell one that a theoretician had written me about an idea that warranted experimental verification. I could get them interested that way."

"But suppose they had questions," interjected Sepp. "They try to contact this theoretician, no?"

She shrugged dismissively. "Let them. They can write to the Renga Institute. We won't have an address—just a post office box in a big city, say New York or Chicago."

Sepp seemed unconvinced. "Suppose they called instead? You could stall them once or twice, but what if they insisted on speaking in person?" He picked up his spoon and started to tap impatiently on the table surface. "And even if everything goes according to plan—a hot theoretical problem, a successful confirmation—I do not see how we shall be able to hide when your experimentalists proceed to write up their work for publication. Will they not want to consult then with Skordylis?"

Hiroshi leaned forward, elbows on the table. "We could use a Japanese scientist. I know just the man. He is in Niigata, a small university on the west coast of Japan. He has excellent technique, but his English is terrible. And he is quite shy: if you introduced him to Diana Skordylis, he would just stare at the floor. He would not dream of bothering an *erai sensei* for more information." Hiroshi mimed the stern face of an *erai sensei* refusing to be bothered.

"I don't know," mused Charlea. "It's hard enough dealing with experimentalists who speak English."

A stubborn silence followed. None of the experimentalists at the table seemed to be willing to rise to Charlea's bait.

"Wouldn't it be best to find one we didn't have to hide from?" I said. "One who could join us on occasion when we all get together?"

"Now *that* would be damn useful," Charlea broke in. "But we don't want too many people in on this, do we?"

"That's why I suggest we keep it in the family," I replied, smiling benignly at Charlea, "and use Jocelyn Powers: our Diana's only grandchild."

There were, of course, objections. How would such experiments mesh with her own work back at Princeton? One couldn't expect her thesis adviser to allow her to pick up new projects on a whim. Nor could we expect Jocelyn to work in secrecy. No, I explained, we could not. If Jocelyn was going to be our experimentalist, I would have to help provide her with that cover. I would have to take her on as a graduate student.

"And how are you, an emeritus professor, going to accomplish that?" snorted C_3. "At Chicago, if an emeritus asks to act as Ph.D. thesis supervisor, the answer will be a resounding no."

"Absolutely," Sepp chimed in. "If I were to ask such a thing, I know what I would hear: *nein, nein, und wieder nein.*"

I couldn't help but smile at their enthusiastic pessimism. But I thought I knew my possibilities at Princeton better than they did. I'd be able to swing it. All it would take was a small lie— or, if necessary, cashing in the IOUs I still held in the department. The lie was simple: I'd claim that I'd committed myself to serve as Jocelyn's adviser prior to my formal retirement. If that didn't work, I was sure that one of my departmental colleagues would agree to serve as pro forma adviser while leaving the de facto functions to me.

The group seemed satisfied, but then C_3 raised another question. "There's a further issue we haven't considered, beyond the need for publication. If DS is successful—if we four make some brilliant discovery—isn't the ultimate objective—at least for Max and Sepp—the immolation of Diana Skordylis?"

"Immolation?" asked Hiroshi. "What do you mean?"

"She means burn her up," Sepp explained.

"Yes, yes, I know," Hiroshi said. "But why?"

"To make Max's ultimate point about the intellectual capacity and originality of some . . ." she hesitated momentarily, "pregeri- atric scientists—"

"Ha," I exclaimed, "that's a new one."

"I didn't want to say 'older.' But anyway: to really make your point, Max, eventually some announcement will have to be made that we four are Diana Skordylis, and that will be the end of DS. But what would happen to Jocelyn in the meantime? We can't risk having her name on a paper with Skordylis as long as DS's identity has not yet been revealed. What if people asked Jocelyn about her collaborator from the Renga Institute?"

"I think we can get around that," I said. "Jocelyn will publish her thesis research completely alone—without any coauthors. No 113

Max Weiss, no Diana Skordylis—just Jocelyn Powers. It will certainly be of some advantage to her. She will be one of the few graduate students in biochemistry publishing alone."

"Sounds reasonable," Charlea said. "*Assuming* Jocelyn can do the lab work alone, and that she knows when to keep her mouth shut. But it will only do for something pure—for experiments based on a new idea. What about the projects we've all been thinking about during the last couple of days, the initial 'cleaning up' we're going to publish under DS's name? If they need experimental support, Powers could hardly participate. She'd be automatically inheriting some coauthor—at the very least D. Skordylis. What then?"

"In that case, I guess whoever is doing the cleaning up will have to go back to the lab, Charlea; you, for instance."

I'd meant it jokingly, but Sepp didn't see the humor.

"Not I. Remember? I have no more laboratory. Not even a nameplate."

"Sepp, I didn't mean it seriously. None of us has worked in the lab for years. But we have several choices. Charlea certainly, and probably also Hiroshi or I, could hire a temporary technician to generate some of the dowry we need for DS. I, for one, could probably smuggle one technician's salary into my current NIH grant."

"And if the experimental input is longer or more complicated, I could persuade a Japanese investigator to take it on," added Hiroshi.

I nodded. "In fact, even Jocelyn could get involved. During this first year, she needs some research experience: learning some of the more specialized techniques; handling some instruments she hasn't used yet."

Charlea hadn't taken her eyes off me. I could see the wheels turning behind them. "I think we'll be able to handle the micro-Skordylis stuff—even with Powers. You're right, Max—it could be a good training phase for her. But if you're taking her on as a Ph.D. student, you're assuming a major responsibility." She waved away the rejoinder, which, for once, I hadn't even thought of making. "Of course, you know all that. But what are you going to do with Jocelyn Powers if we four do *not* come up with a brilliant idea? Or if we bump into some marvelous project that we can handle ourselves; for instance just by computer modeling. What will she do for a thesis project then?"

"In that case, I'll do the same thing I've done for the past thirty-some years: offer Jocelyn a choice from my own grab bag of potential Ph.D. problems. In case any of you had doubts, that bag is by no means empty."

"But what if Jocelyn Powers isn't interested? If she turns you down?" asked Charlea.

I was in no mood to present answers to every hypothetical problem. "She won't," I said. "Period."

Diana had given me a key to her apartment in case our discussion went on too long. I'd barely let myself in when she appeared, still fully dressed. I summarized what had transpired. Her response surprised me.

"You people really know very little about each other. In such an intimate collaboration, shouldn't you know something about each other's personae?"

"Personae?" I cried. "Am I surrounded by closet Jungians?" I was about to say that most scientific collaborations do not require psychological undressing, but instead I told Diana about the conversation I'd had with Sepp in front of the Mark Cross window.

D_3 stroked her chin—a gesture I had not seen before in her. "Perhaps there's hope for Hiroshi's ignorance as well," she said when I was done.

"Hiroshi's ignorance?" I laughed. "Is there such a thing?"

"Everybody is ignorant in something. Hiroshi's weakness is modern Japanese history."

"Let's hear it," I said, preparing myself for something abstruse.

"I wanted to know how Hiroshi's daughters feel about the status of women in Japan. Do you want to know what he told me? That he didn't know. That it was not a topic he discusses with them. Worse, he pleaded total ignorance about the Japanese women's movement, even when I prodded him ever so gently by reminding **115** him that a recent leader of the Social Democrats in Japan was a woman."

"A man cannot know everything."

"True," conceded D₃, "but I'd love to meet his wife and hear her side of the story: life with Hiroshi, and without him." She leaned back into the corner of the sofa. "Did you know one of his daughters is a stewardess for Lufthansa? I'll bet she's the rebel of the family—and Hiroshi doesn't even know it. And his wife paints—did you know that? I wonder if it's an avocation, or an escape?"

"They frequently go hand in hand," I observed. "Or at least one leads to the other. Perhaps he'll bring her along sometime so that you can ask her."

She shook her head. "He won't. I asked him, and he said she spoke no English and was too traditional to be comfortable here."

The idea of having spouses along had never even occurred to me. Did the Bourbakis permit that? Now that Diana had raised the subject, it dawned on me that Hiroshi's wife, whose name I didn't even know, was the only likely candidate.

"He seems so oblivious to women's issues," she mused. "That story about the Emperor's Prize." She mimed a shudder.

"Imperial Prize," I corrected her, "not Emperor's Prize."

"Max, don't act like Sepp." It felt like a quick slap on the hand. "The Imperial Prize, then . . . what's the difference? But take that story and all that Academy phallocentrism."

I pretended to be shocked. "Isn't that a bit strong?"

Diana responded with a dismissive shrug. "Yet otherwise, Hiroshi seems like a very gentle man. He translates Emily Dickinson! Wouldn't you love to learn more about his poetry? Do you think he discusses it with the women of the family?"

"I would think with his wife, yes. But not his daughters. There may be too much of a generation gap."

She looked thoughtful for a moment. "Did you say Sepp has two sons?"

I wondered why my mentioning a "generation gap" had made her think of Sepp.

"I bet they face a giant gap with *Herr* Papa." She stopped short, as if realizing she'd been thinking out loud. "He reminds me of my own father, I suppose," she said offhandedly. "Authoritarian, disciplined—Germanic in a way."

"Sepp is Austrian."

"So?"

I laughed. "Austrians tend to be sensitive about being called German."

"You say that as though you're sensitive about it yourself."

"I suppose it *is* something I have feelings about," I confessed—although I was surprised she had picked up on it. I had thought I was simply lecturing her. "I may have a German name, but my father came to this country as a young man from Hungary, when it was still part of Franz Josef's empire. But what about you, Diana: what about your forebears?"

"Dull Anglo-Saxons; they probably never met a Hungarian in their lives." She laughed and rose from the sofa. "It's been their loss," she said and stretched, smiling sleepily. With a quiet "Good night," she left me sitting on the sofa. I sat there for some time, thinking.

15

"Max, aren't you lonely, living alone?" The question sounded autumnal, even though it was the middle of summer.

Ostensibly, D₃ had come to Princeton for the day to visit her granddaughter, but within minutes after she'd dropped by for tea I became convinced that the primary purpose of the trip was to satisfy her curiosity about my personal abode. She peered at me, as if taking inventory.

"Lonely?" I said. "Not unless I allow myself to think about it."

"That's an odd answer: 'allow myself.' Does that mean you ask yourself permission before you feel something?"

I started to speak, but she continued as if she hadn't expected an answer.

"You haven't told me about your wife." Her eyes remained fixed on the paper napkin next to the tea I had just served her in my living room.

She was right, I realized. Now, why hadn't I?

There had been a time, I knew—and for the life of me I couldn't remember when that time had ended—when I would frequently ask myself what, under this or that circumstance, Nedra would have said or done. But lately, weeks might pass in which I never thought of our life together. Is this why I had never spoken to her about Nedra? Simply because Nedra was turning into history and I am not historically inclined? Then why was I embarrassed at her question?

"No, I haven't," I admitted. "What do you want to know?"

"What was she like?"

"I could show you some photographs . . ." I pointed vaguely in the direction of my study.

"Come now, Max. You know what I mean. I wouldn't mind seeing some pictures—early ones of the two of you—but what was she like as a companion. What did she offer you? What did *you* offer her?"

What did she offer me? Marriage glue, I wanted to say—mostly in the form of ungrudging support, the kind male academics of my generation simply take for granted. And affection. But strangely, little interest in my work. I'd never thought much about it, attributing it, I suppose, to her scientific illiteracy. It's the usual excuse of scientists, I admit, who make little effort to overcome such barriers.

And what did I offer Nedra? Security, I guess. Very conventional security.

"Were you ever tempted by other women?"

I shook my head. What could I say? Of course there were times, even some students, but I'd always kept these feelings to myself.

"None?"

I couldn't tell if she was surprised or disappointed.

118   "I'm really quite conventional," I mumbled. "I married early,"

I added lamely, realizing that D₃ might consider those words a non sequitur rather than an explanation.

"Didn't we all?" she nodded. "That was the convention—then. But what about now? Are you still conventional?"

"I don't know," I said slowly. "What about you?"

I don't think I wanted to know the answer—if I'd thought about it, I doubt I would have dared to ask such a question. But I wasn't thinking—just trying to turn the attention away from me.

"I'm not conventional."

"I don't doubt that," I said, trying to make it a joke. But I knew we were past that already. "And you?" I found myself stammering. "Were you ever tempted?"

"Tempted?" She seemed to be trying the word on her tongue. "Certainly. But you see, Max, on the surface, I always followed social convention. Used to. Now? It's starting to be different. I live alone. I know how fast time passes. I'm intrigued by women who discard convention in their later years. Take Marguerite Duras."

For a change, she wasn't offering the name as a test. "There she is," she went on, "a marvelous writer, pushing eighty and living with someone less than half her age. That's what I most admire about women like her: their ultimate unconventionality, independence at an advanced age. It's unusual in men. In women? Very rare." She shook her head as if she were emerging from a reverie. "I didn't mean to lecture. There are other such women—"

"Charlea Conway," I found myself uttering.

"Charlea?" D₃ frowned for a moment. "Now that I think about it, you're probably right. Isn't it strange? You and I are widowed; Sepp seems to be divorced; and Hiroshi travels alone. If we ever held an affair to which companions were invited, Charlea is likely to be the only one who might bring one along. I wonder what she's like?"

"So do I," I replied, though I wasn't sure whether D₃ had meant Charlea or her companion. "Your tea is cold. Let me make you some more."

She stopped me from rising. "Don't bother, Max. Why don't we go to the movies? We've never done that together."

"Now?"

"Why not? When did you last go to a movie on a weekday afternoon?"

"Never," I broke out laughing. "Or not since high school."

Princeton, of course, is not New York. The only film showing that afternoon was a rerun of *Fatal Attraction*. I remembered having heard something about it, just what I couldn't recall, but as the screen before us flickered into life, Diana turned to whisper, "I'll be interested what you think of the ending. It's weird, but I won't give it away."

"Why didn't you tell me you've already seen this?" I whispered back.

"I don't mind seeing it again: it has its redeeming features." Was it my imagination, or as she whispered had D_3's tongue brushed my ear? I couldn't tell—there was only a fleeting shiver in my skin that could have been anything. With Diana next to me, the nerve endings in my right thigh had transmitted a disturbing sensation of proximity: warmth, or some other signal I could not interpret.

As the two gorgeous lovers on the screen pawed each other in the elevator and then pushed into the woman's apartment, items of clothing dropping left and right, I was grateful for the darkness. I started to blush as Michael Douglas hoisted his lover up onto the kitchen sink, her naked thighs around his waist, the camera focusing on Glenn Close's magnificent derrière hanging over the rim of the kitchen sink, half filled with dirty dishes, one of her hands groping behind her back for the kitchen faucet. When she found it, she turned it on and splashed cooling water on her naked buttocks while her lover coupled with her. That she still had on her blouse gave the scene an even more carnal touch. Such a scene would never have entered my imagination, but now that it had, it was unlikely to be erased. I too felt somewhat naked.

"Well?" Diana asked, after the names of the last gaffer and third electrician had flashed by on the screen. "What do you think of it?"

"Thinking" wasn't exactly how I'd been responding, so I was a little at loss for words.

Diana didn't seem to notice. "Don't you think there was a subliminal message to having the woman reach back to turn on the faucet? It made her seem at least partially in control of the situation." We'd been walking out of the theater, side by side. Now she stopped to face me. "Did you think that was fair—making her the responsible party?"

Good God, I thought to myself, if there was a subliminal message there, I certainly missed it.

I decided to play it safe. "You don't think the Close character, the single woman, was responsible for what happened?"

"Rather than Michael Douglas, the married man, being the villain, because *he* had an affair with her?" Diana took my arm as we reached the sidewalk. "I think the film tries to have it both ways—and that's what's interesting about it. When the single woman gets pregnant, instead of even considering an abortion, all of a sudden she's ready to give up her career to become a mother and wife. In that respect it's about a woman who cracks under the strain: she's sacrificed to her biological clock, while the cheating husband, after apologizing abjectly to his wife, is allowed to get away with infidelity."

I nodded, a student acknowledging a particularly enlightening exposition. "What about the ending?" I asked.

"I suppose I would have changed a few items in the script," she replied good-naturedly. "Most certainly the end. I would have let the woman have her child—on her own without any further contact with the father. And in the end, I would have had the two women—ex-lover and wife—become friends."

I was taken aback. "And the man?"

Diana shrugged her shoulders. "I suppose he'd get his comeuppance."

I regarded her through narrowed eyes. "I wonder if I want to know how."

Diana shrugged again. "I haven't really thought about it. In my version, he's just not that important."

She turned to face me again. "What about your version, Max?"

Like a rabbit caught far from its hole, I froze.

"Mine?" I demanded. Even rabbits fight back when cornered.

"What would you change? Anything?"

I'd heard enough to know that my first impulse—to take the path of least resistance and say I'd leave it as it was—would leave me open to something trenchant, so I did the next best thing.

"I'd have made it much shorter," I said, "and without any message."

"How?"

"By ending it with the kitchen sink scene. Maybe by letting the water run over."

Diana guffawed. "That's not what I expected to hear from you. And what would you call it?"

Near Fatal Attraction Terminated, I was tempted to say; NFAT for short, as always finding solace in my work. But I didn't say it. I doubted that D$_3$ would remember that NFAT is the acronym for my nuclear factor of activated T cells, and if she didn't, a laborious explanation would only have destroyed the effect. Even with D$_3$, I realized, there were limits to what you could take for granted.

We'd just passed the university's bookstore on the way to the train station when Diana returned once more to the subject of movies. "You don't go much to movies, do you Max?"

"Very little. I see them mostly on planes."

"And earlier—when you were still married?"

"More than now. My wife persuaded me from time to time."

"Did you two ever watch X-rated movies?"

I'd never been asked that question, by a man or a woman. Not that Diana asked it with a prurient leer; she just dropped the query in front of me as if it were a matter of simple curiosity.

"Once." I hoped a succinct answer would stop this line of questioning.

I should have known better.

"Do you recall the title?"

"*Deep Throat.*" I was not going to tell her that seeing it had been Nedra's idea.

"You don't think much of sex anymore; or do you?" she asked.

"Not really," I mumbled.

"I do," she said. "You know the saying 'A kissed mouth never grows old'? It doesn't have to be taken literally—even though you scientists have that kind of mind. Sometimes," she stopped and knocked lightly on my forehead, "thinking about kissing can also keep you young—or at least younger. But there are much better adult films than *Deep Throat.*"

The way Diana kept switching back and forth between topics was confusing.

"The trouble with films like *Deep Throat*," she continued matter-of-factly, "is that they were made by men *for* men. The women filmmakers are the ones you want to see."

"Oh," I allowed myself to comment.

"Take Candida Royalle."

"Never heard of her," I said firmly.

She gave me a stern look. "Even the *New York Times* has written about her, Max. They call her films 'quality erotica.'"

I could just see myself spending an afternoon in a small movie house in Princeton, surrounded by stimulated agitated women; finding, after the lights came back on, a couple of our female graduate students staring at me.

"And where do you recommend I do that?" I asked.

"At home, of course. You can rent them all in video stores. One of her early films is called *Femme*—like the French word." She proceeded to spell it, as if I were a total ignoramus. "Promise you'll look at one—you'll then appreciate what Colette once wrote: 'There are fewer ways of making love than they say, and more than one believes.'"

"I promise," I said, mentally crossing my fingers as I uttered the words. But she had aroused my curiosity. "Do you collect erotic films?" I didn't see any hope of changing the subject, but I thought I could at least express it in more academic terms.

Diana shook her head. "Not really. I own a couple of my favorites, but on the whole, I just like to watch them."

"What *do* you collect?" I asked. Again, I was so busy trying to avoid her questions that I didn't stop to consider where this line of inquiry might lead.

I noticed a momentary lift of her eyebrows, as if she'd been taken—pleasantly—by surprise. "Primarily erotic literature," she said coolly. "Early editions. Mostly eighteenth and nineteenth century; French, of course."

"Of course." It seemed the only safe response.

"I'll show you my collection if you'd like. I have some rare volumes that you might find interesting—from a bibliophilic standpoint. For instance, the very first French edition of Casanova's *Memoirs*—the spurious Tournachon-Molin version, an abridged retranslation of the 1822 German Brockhaus volumes, which were based on Casanova's holographic manuscript. Or the twelve volumes of the first complete French version—the one that Laforgue produced during the 1830s for Brockhaus."

I was faintly relieved by Diana's sudden transformation: these were the shining eyes of a scholarly collector, not of a viewer of feminist erotica.

"Is that all you collect?" I couldn't help myself: more than my curiosity was aroused now.

"No . . ." she replied.

"Yes? Go on."

"I have a rather specialized collection of erotic objects—quite small."

I didn't know what that meant: was the collection small or the objects? "What kind of objects?" I asked, simultaneously sensing that I might be trespassing on some private territory.

Diana, who seemed at first to retreat, rallied and smiled alarmingly. "I'll show them to you in New York when you come to see my Casanova first editions."

16

Weeks, then months, passed, and the Skordylis enterprise had started to acquire the character of an extended family, with Diana the matriarchal center. And Jocelyn, even though her initiation into the family started rather slowly, soon took up the role of the surrogate daughter. Throughout the period from June to December, I felt as though events were happening around me with extraordinary speed. Much of the time I found myself in a euphoric frame of mind. Everything seemed to go as on greased rails. And for the first time since Nedra's death, I didn't feel lonely.

Initially, I was Jocelyn's only contact with the group. I began by telling her everything. Otherwise, she would be bound to remain an outsider, and we'd have had to choose our words carefully when she was around. She caught on immediately.

"It makes sense," she said pensively, twisting her hair as if she were continuing the gesture she'd started in my office months earlier. "I can see why Grandma decided to get involved with you. But don't forget that you are offering her something even a MacArthur grant can't buy: the companionship of people she respects. I hope you realize that."

I made standard noises of demurral.

"It's really true," Jocelyn continued, growing animated. "You probably don't see it—I don't think anybody from outside the family does—but behind all that power and energy, the last few years have left her very lonely."

I said only "Oh?" as sympathetically as I could. But the reference to the last few years had caught my attention.

"When I was in my early teens, Grandpa Ditmus was already in his late seventies." Suddenly she stopped. "I'm sorry," she said. "You probably already know all this."

"Not at all," I said quickly. "Please. Go ahead."

"Okay. You should know this. Up until a couple of years be- **125** fore his death, my grandfather was still in great shape, but then he came down with Alzheimer's disease. During his last year, he didn't recognize any of us. That's when Grandma started talking about the dignity of suicide—about ending a life that had been lived to the fullest before it turns into a mere physical shell. Those were her words," she added quickly, as if she were afraid I'd start arguing with her.

Jocelyn had been looking out the window at the leaves swaying in the wind. Finally, she turned back to me. "I think she must have been very lonely these last few years. I bet she scares men: she's too young for men her own age, and too powerful for the younger ones. Having won a MacArthur probably doesn't help."

She gave me an appraising look. "You probably haven't noticed any of that," she said. "That's why you're all such lonely people."

During the first couple of months following our New York meeting, Hiroshi was busy closing up his substantial establishment at the University of Tokyo to move into a couple of labs at a private university. Originally, he had not intended to do even that—after all, why would a poet need a laboratory?—but now he recognized that some experimental facility might prove desirable, especially during the early phases of introducing the Skordylis name to the scientific public.

Sepp was a different case. He had no access to a laboratory at Innsbruck. "There is nothing here in this academic rearwater," he'd told me one morning over the phone. "The closest would be Munich or Vienna."

"It's 'backwater,' " I said mildly.

"What is the difference?" he replied. "In either case, the H_2O hardly moves around Innsbruck."

There was a pause on the line. When Sepp spoke again, his voice had lost some of its asperity. He sounded almost wistful. "That is probably why I got a chair in Innsbruck at so early an age. That was reason enough to stay, for a while. And Innsbruck is a beautiful place," he continued. "My wife—she came from an old Tirolean family." His voice drifted off. I didn't pursue the conversation: a question about his wife was unlikely to fire his scientific synapses.

So I called Sepp from time to time, just to tell him how Charlea and I were progressing. He, in turn, telephoned on a couple of occasions to say that he was getting a "viff" of an idea, which he was following up in the library. "*Gott sei Dank*," he added gruffly, "they're not keeping me out of there." It was too early to talk about the "viff" he was smelling, but if it turned out to be promising, he planned to present it at our next get-together.

Against all odds, then, Charlea and I became the first team to publish under the Skordylis name. Our paper sailed through the refereeing process at *Molecular and Cellular Biochemistry* with hardly a critical comment—rare for a publication by an unknown author. "You see?" Charlea pointed out. "Meritocracy in action."

But what pleased Charlea the most was that in the end I didn't give her a particularly hard time about doing a joint reexamination of my earlier NFAT paper. "For a change, Max, let's not focus on the Himalayas of this problem, but on the foothills." All she wanted, she explained, was to look into the possibility that NFAT induction incorporates two events: translocation of a preexisting component and synthesis of a nuclear component. Thus the first paper published by D. Skordylis (we'd deliberately made the author genderless) was not a correction of my Princeton group's original paper but rather an expansion; and that, I suppose, pleased me as well.

We tested C_3's hypothesis through the use of the immunosuppressant drug cyclosporin, which we expected to interfere with the first step, but not the second. This allowed us not only to test C_3's hunch about NFAT induction but also to try out Jocelyn.

She passed her test, and our hypothesis passed the cyclosporin hurdle—the only difference being that, whereas our ideas saw the light of day (albeit under another name), Jocelyn's work remained completely unacknowledged. Our second article—demonstrating that Fos/Jun proteins are also involved in NFAT complexation—appeared (this time in the *Journal of Molecular Biology*), again with "D. Skordylis" as sole author. Jocelyn didn't mind: she understood that I had to trawl the ponds of my influence in the department before moving to bring her formally under my wing; having her do actual work in my lab before I did so would bolster my claim that I'd long since promised to supervise Jocelyn's thesis work. Her turn would come. .

I did try to be as honest as possible with her. Publishing her eventual thesis work alone would be a marked plus, but there were also minuses to our mode of operation. One of the great strengths of the scientific community is that it actually *is* a community: in addition to the members of one's immediate laboratory circle, one meets constantly with scientists at conferences and other events. Some of that contact would be lost. This isolation would have to extend even to her immediate laboratory colleagues: she would have to keep aloof from the two graduate students still finishing their theses under my direction, and from the three postdoctorate fellows I was still able to support under my NIH grant. True, the graduate students would be gone within a year or two, but I had intended to retain some postdoctorate associates as long as I could keep them funded. And there were other risks, I explained to her, besides isolation. Jocelyn would have to be extremely careful: once her first paper appeared in the literature, collegial jealousy was bound to raise its ugly head. These days, how many graduate students in the biomedical sciences are allowed to publish alone? You can count them on the fingers of an amputated hand!

All I could offer Jocelyn in recompense was an even higher level of intimacy in the most intimate of scientific relationships: that of mentor to trainee. The very fact that I would have to be even more careful—after all, I could run into many more situations where the Skordylis veil might be lifted inadvertently— would mean that I'd particularly value every confidante in my narrow circle. And this confidence would, in turn, expose Jocelyn to three other senior scientists who would themselves be joint mentors for her. There was a joke, I told her, about the importance of a good mentor: the one about a fox interrupting a rabbit typing his Ph.D. dissertation. I looked at her expectantly.

"I haven't heard it," Jocelyn said.

I suspected that she *had* heard it and was simply being a dutiful graduate student, but I went ahead and told it anyway. It's not a bad story, even when I tell it.

"The rabbit is typing up his thesis," I began, "when a fox comes up.

" 'Don't eat me just now,' the rabbit says. 'Let me finish this first.'

" 'What is it?' the fox inquires.

" 'My Ph.D. dissertation,' the rabbit says proudly.

" 'Oh? What's the title?' the fox asks.

" 'How Rabbits Catch Foxes.'

" 'But you've got it all wrong: it's foxes who catch rabbits.'

" 'Here, let me show you,' counters the rabbit, leading the fox into a nearby cave. After a short interval, the rabbit returns alone and resumes his typing. Soon he is interrupted by a wolf, whereupon the conversation with the fox is repeated.

"When the rabbit returns to his typewriter, a woodpecker, who had been observing the scene, approaches. 'What's going on here? What did you show the fox and the wolf?'

" 'Just look in the cave.'

"Peeking cautiously into the entrance, the woodpecker sees a lion finishing the remnants of the fox and the wolf.

" 'You see,' explains the rabbit, 'the title of the dissertation isn't important. It doesn't even matter who writes it. All that counts is your supervisor.' "

I waited for the laugh this story usually gets—especially when told to graduate students—but Jocelyn only smiled, with that easy grace one must be born with to possess, making me feel a bit absurd. "I'd use a different punchline: In the end the rabbit retitles the thesis 'How Rabbits Exploit Lions.' "

"Oh?" I said. Why is it that everyone these days feels they can revise my conclusions?

She shrugged. "Graduate student version, I guess."

By now, I thought I'd encountered most of Charlea's moods, but her voice on the phone this morning was undecipherable. "I was under the impression we had only one predecessor," she said. "Nicolas Bourbaki. You were very persuasive in that regard."

"Hold it a moment, Charlea. Let me put you on the speaker phone." As I stretched out on the sofa—the only luxury furniture I'd been able to squeeze into my new office—I tried to remember which of us had first suggested that we employ the speaker phone during long conversations. I couldn't, but it wasn't important; the speaker had become a habit. It was comfortable for taking notes, wandering around the office, or, as in this instance, listening in a supine position. Invariably, it made you into a better listener.

Get to the point, Charlea, I wanted to say. But I knew that wouldn't get me anywhere. "So?" I said, and waited.

"So I have news for you. You weren't the first in our line of work to borrow the Bourbaki idea. Ever heard of Isadore Nabi?"

"No," I said, and I'm afraid it sounded petulant.

"Ha. I thought so. He—or it, or they—were right here behind my back at Chicago."

"Well, you should have told me, then." I still had no idea what she was talking about, but with Charlea it was never too soon to go on the offensive.

"I only found out yesterday. I had lunch with Leigh Van Valen. He's the editor of *Evolutionary Theory*."

"You mean you told him about us?" I sat straight up on my sofa.

"Don't be silly, Max. *I* told him nothing. *He* told me."

"Go on," I said and lay down again.

"Richard Lewontin, Richard Levins, Robert MacArthur, and Van Valen—all of them Young Turks at Chicago in the middle sixties—were among the first to use rigorous mathematical ecology, and to relate it to population biology. It's not my field, but I'd heard about them when I first came to Chicago. Some of them— especially Levins and Lewontin—had also acquired some political notoriety. Did you know that Levins turned down election to the National Academy of Sciences?"

"I did not." I didn't know anybody ever had.

"Or that in *Who's Who* he still lists his former membership in the Communist party? And that Lewontin *resigned* from the

NAS? Quite a bunch! Anyway, they had little sympathy for the 'soft' population biologists." I could practically see the sneer with which she said "soft." There was little doubt where her sympathies lay.

"They held their own little summer conferences at a place owned by one of their in-laws in Marlboro, Vermont. They knew all about Bourbaki. One day, Lewontin suggested that the four of them pick a name under which to publish." She stopped. I knew she was doing it for effect, but curiosity overruled my pride.

"So? What name did they pick?"

"Nabi. Isadore Nabi."

"Am I supposed to know that name?" I asked, a bit suspiciously. Was this going to become another Charles Denis Sauter Bourbaki story?

"Not unless you're a Hebrew scholar."

"That I'm not," I admitted.

"Nabi is supposed to be the Hebrew word for 'prophet.' A little grandiose, if you ask me. But they were clever. In fact, we could learn a few things from them. They actually managed to get Nabi into *American Men and Women of Science*. I have the volume— number 5—right in front of me. They had him born in Czechoslovakia in 1910, got him to marry at age twenty and father six children—" Charlea's guffaw reverberated in my ear, "with a bachelor's degree that same year from Cochabamba University and an M.D., a few years later, from the National University of Mexico. But then they got a bit more daring. They gave him a Guggenheim at Yeshiva. And they list his current address as— get this—the Biology Department of the University of Chicago. It would be like us having Diana Skordylis publish from the biochemistry lab of Princeton. I'm surprised the editor of *American Men and Women of Science* didn't smell a rat; I mean, some of this is just overkill. For instance, Nabi holds concurrent consultantships with the Standard Oil Company and the Kings County Coroner's Office." She snickered, but I was a little too anxious to appreciate the joke.

"And they published under the name of Isadore Nabi? All four of them?"_

"Don't worry. We didn't get totally scooped. They used Nabi's name for polemics, not for their original research—"

"Aha!" I couldn't suppress my triumph. What young scientist was going to sacrifice his ambition on the altar of anonymity? It takes maturity to do that.

"They put Nabi to a lot of uses we haven't considered. They had him author papers that were caricatures of existing ones they wished to denigrate, or he became their lance in real duels. For instance, after Lewontin moved to Harvard, he used Nabi to attack E. O. Wilson's views on sociobiology—his own colleague, Max. Can you believe it? Or even cuter: as Isadore Nabi, he took apart Richard Dawkins's bestseller, *The Selfish Gene*, in *Nature*, and then continued the argument under his real name in another review."

"Where did you get all this?" I was astounded. Where do these women—D_3 with Bourbaki, and now C_3 with Nabi—dig up all these minutiae?

"It's in Levins and Lewontin's book, *The Dialectical Biologist*. Lewontin faxed me the pages. Just listen to this—it's an absolute gem—and possibly a character model for Skordylis: 'Nabi's retiring and modest nature in a scientific community marked by self-advertisement and intellectual aggressiveness has made him something of an enigma, a kind of intellectual *yeti*, whose footprints are seen everywhere, but of whom no photograph exists.' An intellectual *yeti*," Charlea mused. "Wouldn't you love to have someone say that about Diana Skordylis?"

"They published it? How do they expect to keep Nabi's identity a secret?"

"It's no secret anymore. The editor of *Nature* blew their cover in an editorial in 1981. In fact, we'd better pay attention to the tone of Maddox's editorial. He sounds a bit pissed off: 'First, it is a deception,' he said. 'Second, it allows people with known opinions on important controversial matters to give a false impression that their opinions are more weighty than truth would allow.'"

"But Skordylis is different," I exclaimed, as if I were defending myself in front of the entire *Nature* editorial board. "*She* only

publishes original research, not polemics."

"Max," Charlea purred over the phone, "I love hearing you use the feminine gender. You're improving daily."

17

"Nabi? Yes, of course. Why do you ask?" Diana lowered her lorgnette, through which she'd been studying the exhibition catalog, to inspect me. We were sitting in the cafeteria at the Museum of Modern Art in New York.

"Isadore Nabi—" I started, but she interrupted me.

"Isadore?" she frowned. "I didn't know the Nabis had a *prénom*."

I pinched myself surreptitiously under the table to fight off a swimming sensation. Surely, it wasn't possible that she would produce another Nabi. The odds against it were simply too high. Still . . .

"You know the Nabis?" I asked cautiously.

"Of course." She waved her lorgnette in my direction, a precious, small scythe. "Bonnard, Vuillard, Vallotton—as far as I recall, even Maillot joined the Nabis." She was about to pick up her cup of herb tea, but I stopped her.

"Who," I said distinctly, "are you talking about?"

She stirred her tea, which didn't need stirring because she never used sugar, with an air that struck me suddenly as too casual: was she smiling? She wouldn't look up.

"I don't remember too much about them," she said lightly, "but we can go upstairs and look at some of their paintings. They were influenced by Gauguin, but that didn't last long. By the end of the nineteenth century they had broken up. It was probably too much for their artistic egos." She glanced at me over her lorgnette. "But where does this 'Isadore' business come from, Max?"

As calmly as I could, I repeated Charlea's story. I couldn't tell if she'd heard it all before. For all I knew, she had. Or perhaps **133** she'd been inventing that painterly Nabi. I made a mental note to check upstairs.

"By the way, Max," she said when I was done. "Have you had a chance to look at *Femme*?"

My blank look gave me away.

"The Candida Royalle film I told you about when I visited you in Princeton."

"No," I mumbled, "I've been too busy."

"Don't work all the time," she admonished me. "You need some entertainment. Would you like me to send the video to you?"

"Don't bother," I said quickly. "I'll get it myself in Princeton," I lied, hoping irrationally that would be the end of it.

"All right." She reached below the table for her purse. "I'll be curious to hear what you think about it." She took out her little pocket diary. "Let's make a date at my place, week after next? I have some first editions I'd like to show you."

Like many trivialities, finding *Femme* turned out to be much more of a nuisance than I'd anticipated. This was no *Godfather* or Woody Allen film. The video store in my neighborhood had never heard of it. In the end, I asked Jessica to phone around. I'd only wanted her to find out who carried it so that I could pick it up at my convenience. Instead, the next morning I found a tightly wrapped, unlabeled package on my desk. "Thanks for getting that stuff for me," I said in the most offhand manner I could muster after having opened it—"stuff" being the most neutral term I could think of at the moment. "Dr. Ditmus wanted me to get it." "For her," I wanted to add, but I didn't. I retreated into my office before Jessica's speculative gaze could bring on a full-scale blush.

That evening I popped the cassette into my VCR and sat down in my easy chair, remote control in hand. Half an hour later, I turned the TV off, totally confounded. How could Diana have wanted me to watch such unmitigated pornography? If that was not the ultimate in female exploitation—most of the female characters, in fact, were whores—then I didn't understand the term.

I felt uncomfortable as I sat down, a week or so later, in her living room at the table where we'd had our first dinner together. I spent an uneasy hour not enjoying what she put in front of me, waiting for the preposterous question—"What did you think of *Femme*?"

Diana must have noticed. Over coffee, she touched me lightly with her hand. "Is anything the matter, Max?"

I was inclined to respond with some socially acceptable, hypocritical remark, but what I said instead was, "I looked at your film as I promised you."

"And what did you think of it?" There was nothing salacious in her tone or look, just the barest touch of curiosity. Which confused me most of all.

"I think it is the sort of entertainment I can do without. I didn't finish it."

"Oh?"

Was she disappointed?

"It was . . . what should I say," I started to stutter. "So pornographic as to be without any socially redeeming content." Isn't that the phrase, I thought to myself, that judges use?

"Oh come, Max, you can't be serious. *Femme* pornographic?"

"Yes," I said firmly. "And frankly, Diana, I cannot for the life of me understand why you feel that the director took any woman's viewpoint into consideration. Oral sex may be all right, but *this* takes the cake!" I found some comfort in the force of my righteousness.

"Max," she repeated, a slight flush appearing on her cheeks, "cunnilingus may be illegal in Georgia, but it's done all the time."

"Who's talking about cunnilingus?" I countered primly.

"Don't tell me you've never seen fellatio?"

By now I was getting angry. Was Diana a split personality? Was I talking to a weirdo whose existence I hadn't suspected?

"Diana! What do you take me for: Rip van Winkle? I'm not being a prude."

For a second, I thought that she would laugh, but her hand quickly covered her mouth. "Of course not," she said in a low voice.

"All right, then. Take the hero of the film, if that's how you   **135** would dignify his role. Within the first minutes, he brutally beats up the boyfriend of the woman and then proceeds to rape her. The various whores—admittedly the nicest characters I saw—can't satisfy him, so he proceeds to . . ." I stopped, and finally blushed. What should I call the scene I had seen on my VCR? Until then, I wouldn't have imagined that it was physically possible, even for a contortionist.

Diana looked nonplussed. "I have not the faintest idea what you are talking about."

"Autofellatio," I broke out.

A brief, direct stare, one eyebrow up, faced me. "Wait a moment." She rose abruptly and left the room. A couple of minutes later, she called me from the door.

"Max. Come into my bedroom and sit down. Here, on the foot of the bed, straight up so that you're not too comfortable. We shall watch *Femme* together for ten minutes. That's all. If you succeed in showing me on the screen what you've been raving about, I promise never again to look at a Candida Royalle film. No, I'll go further than that: you can censor every cassette in my apartment."

What could I do? I followed her into her bedroom, my eyes inspecting the ceiling, but not finding a mirror. I proceeded to sit down self-consciously at the foot of her bed, and watched the film logo *Femme* appear in pink script, followed by a woman's voice alluringly intoning the word. A few minutes later, we were both laughing—a little nervously at first, as each of us kept glancing at the other to gauge our reactions. I was wiping the tears off my cheeks when Diana put her arm around my shoulder to give me a squeeze.

"Let's have another movie date," she said. "Just the two of us?"

"Okay," I giggled—from the film or from embarrassment at my earlier tirade, I wasn't sure. What else could I say? Together, we put an explanation together: my faultless Jessica must have picked up the wrong film. Later, when I got home and inspected it, I finally caught the full title: *Femmes de Sade*, by Alex de Renzy, simply labeled "Femmes" on the outside. That one extra letter at the end had made all the difference.

As we returned to the living room, I stopped by the sideboard to pour myself a Diet Coke. "What about the collection you promised to show me?" To my surprise, the real *Femme* had generated in me both interest and a courage I had not experienced in years. Still, I found it difficult to muster an offhand manner: my mouth had turned quite dry.

"Ice?" Diana asked. In my nervous mood, the offer seemed quite daring.

"Why not?" I replied, wondering at my own tone. Clinking the ice in my glass, I followed Diana into a small room that had bookshelves reaching to the ceiling. On one wood-paneled wall, opposite the draped window, stood a tall display case with glass doors. The only items of furniture were two upholstered wing chairs, separated by a dainty oval table bearing a vase filled with silk flowers, and a reading lamp.

Diana turned in the center of the room. "You asked me what I collect: not too much, as you can see."

"Are these *all* first editions?"

"Heavens no," she exclaimed. "Only some. For instance these." Carefully, her fingertips holding it by the edges, she removed one volume from the bookshelf and placed in on the table. *Memoires de J. Casanova de Seingalt, écrits par lui-meme*, it said on the title page. *Edition Originale, Leipsic, F. A. Brockhaus, 1826.* "There are twelve volumes, but only the first four bear Brockhaus's name. And this one," she removed another volume, "is the first English version, published in 1894. This is one of the fifty sets printed on handmade Van Gelder's." She opened it as if it were one of the original Gutenberg Bibles. "You see: *The Memoirs of Jacques Casanova written by himself now for the first time completely and literally translated by Arthur Machen into English in twelve volumes privately printed. H. S. Nichols, 3 Soho Square, London, MDCCCXCIV.*"

What does an ordinary reader say to a bibliophile? "Very interesting," I murmured. "Beautiful binding."

"I also have the 1791 edition of *Justine*." She pointed out for me the spine of the Marquis de Sade's first major work. Beside the volume she indicated were three more, bound in morocco, with the impressive inscription, *INDEX LIBRORUM PROHIBITO-*

RUM, and then six in heavy leather, *Bibliographie des Ouvrages Relatif a L'Amour*, by Jules Gay.

"That's *the* bibliography of French erotica. What's not in there is probably not worth having."

"Have you read all these?"

"What do you think?"

"Frankly, no."

"What makes you say that?" she asked, a faintly coquettish tone in her voice.

"You couldn't possibly have the time. Unless . . ."

"Yes?" she prompted me.

"You started very early in life." I gave a short, sharp bark of laughter.

She gave me a quick laugh back. "Of course you're right."

"So why do you collect these books now? For their rarity? Or their content?"

"Both." She let the word drop neatly between us.

For a moment she eyed me, expecting a response, but I could think of no reply. "If your French were good enough," she continued, "I'd lend you a new one I rather enjoyed: a treatise on eroticism and physical love in seventeenth-century French literature."

I realized that she was translating the title of the book I'd seen by her bedside: *Erotisme et Amour Physique dans la Littérature Française du XVIIᵉ Siècle*, by Roger Bougard. Next to it had been Anaïs Nin's *Delta of Venus*.

"Why would I enjoy reading it?"

"I should hope for the same reasons as I: curiosity. It's intriguing to learn what excited people a few hundred years ago."

"Probably the same as now."

"Between the sheets, yes. But between the covers of a book? I like to read how they expressed themselves then; how open they were; their literary allusions to sex. He has a two-page-long glossary," she grinned.

"What's so interesting about a glossary?"

"I can give you a few examples which don't even require translation: just consider the range from *barricade* or *citadelle* to *palais magnifique* and *remède et poison de l'amour*. In case you don't know, *remède* means 'remedy.' All terms for the sexual parts of a woman, *les parties nobles de la femme*, as Bougard refers to them."

"You don't say," was all I could say. "And what great metaphors did the French produce for the noble parts of the man?" Even as I asked that—a question I'd probably never raised before in my adult life—I thought of Nedra. What would she have said if she'd been present? For once, I couldn't guess.

"Oh, the usual stuff." Diana sounded dismissive. "*Pistolet, serpent, instrument de guerre . . .*"

I frowned. "I get the message. But your Candida Royalle would hardly have approved."

"Let me console you and her," laughed Diana. "There are others; for instance, *instrument consolatif, lance d'amour.*"

"Touché," I laughed back.

"Let me tell you something else unusual about the French language. In French, *vagina* possesses the masculine gender, *le vagin,* whereas *penis* is feminine: *la verge.*"

That's when I recalled something Sepp had said to me some months ago. "Be careful what you say to her," he raised a cautionary finger. "She may be a historian by profession, but I would say she is an etymologist by—what is the word?"

"Avocation?" I offered.

"Exactly! I was telling her about Innsbruck and mentioned one of our most famous former professors, the endocrinologist Ludwig Haberlandt. I thought he would be of interest to a woman. Long before the progestational and estrogenic hormones had been isolated, he had the idea that extracts of the corpus luteum might possibly be useful for contraceptive purposes. I wanted to be sociable, so I asked her whether she knew the origin of the words *estrogen* and *androgen*. By the way Max, do you know?"

"*Estrogen?* No, I'm afraid not."

"It comes from the Latin *oestrus* or the Greek *oistrus*. Both mean the same: 'frenzy' or 'gadfly,' also 'sting.' 'Is that not terrible?' I said, trying to be polite. The word *androgen* means 'to make a male,' so why does the dictionary not have the word *gynogen* for 'to make a female'? I was being gentlemanly, I hoped. But what do you think she said?"

I was thinking what Nedra would have said. Knowing her, instead of wanting to change *estrogen*, she would have come up with a new and witty alternative to *androgen*.

"What?" I asked.

" '*Estrogen* is not all that sinister,' the *Frau Doktor* said. 'Don't the biting flies belong to the insect family *Oestridae?* That word must have been coined long before. And don't male animals go into a frenzy when the female goes into estrus? That must have been known long before the estrogens were isolated and identified.' "

She took me by the arm and led me to the glass case. "I'll show you something else I promised you in Princeton."

She opened the glass door, picked up a small object, and held it under the light. It glinted. "What's this?" she demanded.

"A gold ring." I tried it on my little finger. "But so tiny! Only a little child could wear it."

"Exactly." Diana had moved into her own professorial mode. "The Romans used them as good luck charms around the beginning of the Christian era. Notice anything else about it?"

I held the ring under the lamp. It was so small that my glasses would have helped. "There is some elongated relief with a couple of circles." I looked up at her. "I can't figure out what that is."

"Hm," she murmured in a satisfied tone and placed the ring on the table surface. "What about this?" She removed a small bronze replica of a winged bird from the vitrine.

"A bird, of course." I was surprised at her seemingly simple questions. Why this quiz?

"Anything else?"

"I guess it's an amulet," I concluded. "You could put a chain through the hole in the tail."

"Very good," she said, an ironic smile spreading over her face. "Once more, Max. What about this?" Gingerly, using both hands, she held up a shallow pottery cup until I saw the exquisite face with two huge eyes painted in black.

"Very beautiful," I murmured. "Seems quite old."

"Second half of the sixth century; B.C., that is."

No wonder, she's holding it so carefully, I thought. "Do you notice anything else?" she asked in that same strange, questioning tone, turning the cup slowly upside down.

"You mean this small tripod base?"

She shrugged her shoulders. "You tell me."

I shrugged back. "No."

"I thought so," she said triumphantly. As quickly as care permitted, she added the cup to the other two pieces on the table and reached back into another shelf of the vitrine. The sudden sound of bells startled me.

"A Roman bronze tintinnabulum," she announced proudly. "Without doubt the rarest thing in my collection."

It was the figure of a small, helmeted gladiator, miniature bells attached to his feet and body, attacking with his dagger a ferocious animal that seemed to be his own, monstrously sized, penis. The glans had been transformed by the artist into the head of a beast baring its fangs.

"First century A.D.," she said simply. "You'd hardly call it erotic, would you? Yet it's both humorous and serious. Fighting your fierce phallus is no laughing matter." She gave me an impish look. "It's different with these three." She pointed to the table. "You missed the symbolism in each. In the tiny ring, the incised penis is meant to be a good luck charm."

"Penis?" I picked up the ring again. "I don't see any penis."

"Do you see the two little balls at the base of the relief?"

"Uh-huh," I conceded.

"Well?"

"Are you going to tell me that this cup is also a phallic symbol?" I said testily.

"Of course." I looked from her to the cup, and then back. Some people might have described her expression as triumphant; to me, it seemed smug. "Look at the tripod: two balls and a shaft."

"Well," I muttered, "that's hardly an erect penis."

"I didn't say it was erect, Max. A phallic symbol can come in various shapes and stages of tumescence. But I know what threw you off: the face with the big eyes just above the phallic base. But that's exactly the point: eyes are a charm against the Evil Eye. The phallus was thought by the Greeks to have a special power against the Evil Eye. This cup gave the drinker double protection."

"I see," I said, still somewhat dubious. "And the bird?"

"Elementary," she replied. "A phallus-bird. Just look at his beak."

"I give up. What else do you have in there?"

"More of the same. You get the idea." She put the objects back into the case, only then noticing my curious stare. "Max," she exclaimed, "you're looking at me as if you find all this odd."

What could I say? "What started you on this collection?" I asked. I couldn't think of anywhere else to begin—and I still wasn't sure where all this would end.

"My second husband. He gave me one on each wedding anniversary. After the third, I became a collector on my own." She turned away, closed the case, and led us from the room.

On our way out, I passed a small pen-and-ink drawing that I hadn't noticed before. It showed a buxom, well-proportioned woman, wide-brimmed hat tilted to one side, wearing a high-necked dress covered in embroidery. The artist had drawn her barefoot, stepping into a brook, skirt raised so that it wouldn't get wet. Her bare legs were visible up to her lower thighs. A medieval landscape was the background. I stopped to take a closer look.

"Sixteenth century," she explained. "Swiss—attributed to Urs Graf. Quite rare. The eroticism is in the metaphor: 'stepping in the brook' means losing one's virginity."

"So you also collect drawings?"

"Uh-uh." She shook her head as she headed for the door. "It was an anniversary present from Alex—our fifth. When you marry a second time, you take anniversaries more seriously. You didn't know that, did you Max?"

I didn't. After all, I'd been married only once. But what was this erotica tour all about? Was I simply being quizzed, the way

I'd been examined throughout our relationship? Or was D₃ trying to tell me something about herself? And in preparation for what? I'm sure I must be coming across as something of a prude or sexual simpleton, but at my age, I'm afraid to initiate a sexually charged conversation, because I don't know where it will lead. Was Diana trying to help me?

"What did *you* give your husband?" I finally asked, not knowing how to pose the real question interesting me.

"Affection and TLC."

"I meant for your anniversaries."

"If it had been your anniversary, Max, would you have wished for more?"

18

"I'm coming to New York for the saliva meeting," Hiroshi announced one day over the phone. "Can we all meet then?"

"What saliva meeting?"

"The First International Symposium on Saliva as a Diagnostic Fluid," he replied. "The New York Academy of Sciences is holding it at the Waldorf just before your Thanksgiving holiday. They want me to talk about salivary antibodies: to see whether they could be used for hepatitis diagnosis and surveillance."

It sounded intriguing. "Would it work for HIV?" I asked.

"J. V. Parry from London is supposed to cover that," he said. "Do you think Charlea and Sepp could come to New York? It is time we met again in person."

It was indeed time. For nearly a year we had kept in touch— by fax, E-mail, and Federal Express more than by phone. We had almost given up on conference calls after several of them had nearly broken up in rancor: we interrupted each other too much. "You miss the eye contact," Diana had explained when I told her about the problem. "It's indispensable in love and debate."

"Not much of that, these days," I had grumbled.

"Which?"

"Either. The problem is, it's time for us to get Skordylis on the boards with a major project, but each of us wants to work on a different one. There's no common ground."

"Don't you think it's time you all got together? You can't find common ground when you're not even on the same continent."

"Just look at the other side of the argument."

It seemed so unlike him, to be pleading.

"Damn it, Sepp," Charlea growled, "there are some arguments that don't have another side. The world is *not* flat."

I could see that Sepp was dumbfounded. "Are you joking? What do you mean, 'The world is not flat'?"

"Just that. There are no two sides to that question."

I had appeared too late at Diana's opening soirée to know what they'd been arguing about, but it didn't seem to matter anymore. Charlea, clearly the victor, retired to a corner of the living room. Jocelyn, sitting on a cushion on the floor, glanced uneasily from Sepp to Charlea.

It must have been quite a scene for a beginning graduate student to witness: two scientific lions baring their fangs. There was no blood on the floor, but it was clear that just as much adrenaline must have been secreted as in an arena.

As I settled into a chair—nearer to Jocelyn, in the spectators' seats, I hoped—I wondered why I was so interested in studying our impact on Jocelyn. Was it because she was my graduate student—my last child in a long series of children over a period of decades—or because of her relation to Diana?

"Don't you want to know what Sepp and I were arguing about?" asked C_3.

I had been hoping to avoid the subject completely, but Charlea didn't seem ready to relinquish her laurels just yet.

"Quantum chaos. Sepp says one can't even define quantum chaos; that's why it gives him the shivers. I said, just because you can't define it is no reason to get the shakes."

144   Good God, I thought, what were they doing arguing over *that*?

"*Gnädige Frau Professor*," Sepp bowed with fake formality toward Charlea, his voice full of sarcasm. "What is that the English poet says about running into places where angels do not enter?"

"Never heard of it, *Herr Professor*," Charlea said. She seemed more than ready for a rematch. "But what do poets know about quantum chaos?"

"More than you might think," Hiroshi interjected quietly.

Before Charlea could process that, Diana interposed a reasonable question.

"I have some idea what you mean when you say 'chaos,' Charlea —what I read in the Tuesday *Times*, at least. But what is quantum chaos? And why does it give Sepp the shivers?"

"Because our *Herr Professor* is too organized to accept chaos everywhere."

"All right, Charlea," Sepp jibed. "Define quantum chaos for our hostess, please."

"Friends," I interrupted. "Are you sure you want to spend our precious time on a topic that really has nothing to do with our project?"

"Chaos has nothing to do with us?" Charlea didn't even try to disguise her mocking tone.

"Maybe yes, maybe not," added Sepp. "But I want to see Charlea centimetering her way to an explanation."

"We say 'inching,' Sepp." Charlea turned to address D_3. "If you've been keeping up, you know that *chaos* refers to randomness intrinsic to physical and biological systems, as distinct from any disorder caused by outside interference or noise. It's a randomness so general, in fact, that it seems to be an essential fact of life in our universe. Which suggests that any physical theory ought to be able to account for it. Since quantum mechanics is the current paradigm, 'it better have chaos,' I said to Sepp. Whereupon he got the shivers. A very feminine response," she said with a guffaw. But then C_3 turned back toward Diana.

"In addition to chaos, there is also the problem of complexity—"

From his corner, Sepp muttered something more about angels. **145**

Charlea ignored him. "Here," she continued. "Let me give you an analogy I got from Murray Gell-Mann. He's the man who got the Nobel for the quark," she explained. "Say you want to describe a painting over the telephone, so someone could make a copy."

"That's an odd way of copying a painting," Diana observed.

"Not so odd, really: it's exactly how a fax machine works. What I'm describing here is why you would prefer the original over the fax. And which painting you'd prefer to fax if you had to.

"It has to do with the fact that there are two kinds of complexity: simple and deep. A Jackson Pollock, for instance, looks very messy—all those drips and blobs. But its complexity is actually the kind we call simple: there's a lot going on there, but it's made up of essentially simple forms: drips, blobs, and not much else. Because of that simplicity, it wouldn't be hard to describe a Jackson Pollock over the telephone, going over it systematically, say from left to right: time-consuming, but not much of a challenge. And a reproduction based on that description—a fax, in other words—even if it had a great many dots, blobs, and splashes, would look a great deal like the original. That's because the original, even though it's complex, has the kind of complexity we call simple. To understand the difference between that kind of complexity and *deep* complexity, imagine trying to describe a Breughel."

"Ugh," said Diana.

"Exactly. Much more is lost in the translation. That's what we mean by deep complexity: something that can't be reduced to a rational code. And what's interesting is that even though you can describe a Breughel much more easily than a Pollock—'the Breughel shows a peasant wedding,' for instance—you still can't adequately reproduce the Breughel from the description. And a Pollock, even though it's much harder to describe verbally, is easy to fax."

"Why is that? Why is a verbal description deeper than a digital one?"

"Very good," Charlea beamed. "It has everything to do with the difference between words and numbers. Consider a chessboard with a game in progress. You give it to two persons to memorize. A nonplayer, to whom the board is a meaningless puzzle, will take a long time. To a chess master, on the other hand, the board is made up of familiar patterns—'chunks' the theorists call them, or words, you might say; part of the vocabulary of chess. By breaking down the board into those chunks, the chess master can memorize and reproduce the pattern almost instantaneously. They even have verbal descriptions for many of them: 'the Sicilian Defense,' or 'the Allgaier Variation of the King's Gambit.' Unless, of course, the pieces have been placed on the chessboard at random. In such a case, even the master will have difficulty."

"But isn't it time to focus on our own chunks?" I felt that I had to get C_3 off her chaos complexity kick. "And make sure that those chunks actually constitute a winning gambit?"

That same evening, Hiroshi had told Jocelyn that he had come upon a paper of his that deserved a major revision. Some experimental checks would be required before the revision would be suitable for publication under the Skordylis name. He told Jocelyn but not any of the rest of us. We didn't hear about it for several days. When we finally did learn about it, as Hiroshi repeated the story, Jocelyn broke in.

"Hiroshi says he wouldn't mind if I did the experiments for him. From what he told me earlier, they don't sound too difficult. I could easily do them in Professor Weiss's lab back at Princeton."

So he's "Hiroshi," but I'm "Professor Weiss"? Before I had time to reflect on that, I received another jolt.

"If any problems arise that aren't faxable, I can always fly over to Tokyo for a few days and check them out with you in person."

So this is my last graduate student? She's so goddamned affluent that she thinks nothing of flitting back and forth between continents.

Watch it, I admonished myself. The essence of the Skordylis experiment is communality: shouldn't that also apply to one's assistants? And affluence? Only then did it occur to me that perhaps Hiroshi had offered to pay for the trip.

For the rest of the evening, I kept an uncharacteristic silence. **147**

Hiroshi, equally uncharacteristically, was loquacious: birds and dolphins, fish, and whatever else I didn't follow, noticing only that Jocelyn was an enthusiastic audience. But then, everyone was.

The meal that night was fish. Diana had hardly lifted her fork when she addressed Hiroshi. "What did you mean, Hiroshi, about Japanese playing Russian roulette with fish?"

Hiroshi smiled. "Not all fish." He lifted a bite to his mouth. "But there is a Japanese saying: 'Last night, the four of us ate fugu. Tonight, three of us carry his coffin.' Fugu is our greatest fish delicacy, a species of what you call puffer fish. We slice it into paper-thin pieces and then arrange them in beautiful designs, like cranes or chrysanthemum blooms. Fugu is delicious, but some of its organs—especially the liver—can be so poisonous as to kill you. The responsible agent, tetrodotoxin, has been isolated and even synthesized. It is used in neurological research because essentially it shuts down the whole nervous system: it is several hundred times more toxic than cyanide."

"You don't say." Even though Diana's remark was addressed to Hiroshi, she sent a meaningful glance in my direction. I had a feeling I would be getting a request for a supply of tetrodotoxin the next time we were alone. "So why do you Japanese take the chance? Or is it only for potential suicides?"

Hiroshi shrugged. "Why do the Russians go mushroom hunting? I imagine more people die from mushroom poisoning than from eating fugu. I love fugu. A few years ago, a friend invited me to go with him to Shimonoseki to witness a fugu auction." A reminiscent smile passed over his face. "At a fugu auction, the auctioneer has a long, wide, black sleeve covering his right hand. In order to bid, the buyers have to push their hands inside that sleeve to give the auctioneer a secret hand signal. While this is going on, the auctioneer chants some gibberish—much as your tobacco auctioneers do. He keeps all the bids in his head until the time is up. Then he announces the winner." He looked around at us. "Does that explain how we feel about fugu?"

Sepp shook his head; Charlea laughed out loud. "Not really," she said. "It just sounds crazy."

Hiroshi shrugged again and lifted another forkful of fish. "What can I say?" He looked at Charlea under heavy lids. "No one can understand another person's—what?—craziness? Is that what you call it?"

"I thought you called it love," Diana said.

"Ah," Hiroshi grunted. "No difference."

We had reserved four days before the start of the saliva meeting for Skordylis, alternating between the Century Club and Diana's apartment, with our focus on broader topics that might generate the project that would put DS firmly on the scientific map. We still didn't know what that project would be, but Sepp had started to argue that we should concentrate on methodology.

"If we want to make a big splash, an important new technique is the way to go—something everyone will be using inside of a year. Remember, Skordylis does not have too much time to make its reputation."

"Her," Charlea corrected him. "But you're right. She better start earning her keep."

Without giving Sepp a chance to expand on his comment on methodological advances, Charlea turned from Sepp to the rest of us. "So let me put something on the table. Have Skordylis come up with a general theory of epigenetics. Since Waddington coined the term back in fifty-three, it has acquired a slightly derogatory connotation," she curled her lip in mock disgust. "Primarily out of ignorance. If you can't explain the activity or inactivity of a given gene during the developmental process by mutation or some other conventional mechanism—"

"Such as control by a repressor," Hiroshi interjected.

Charlea gave him a sharp look. "Of course. But suppose it's not that. Suppose the mechanism is not known. That's when people call it an 'epigenetic' mechanism. What they mean is that it's unknown." She gave us a lecturer's pause, during which, presumably, we were supposed to be scribbling down notes.

When she resumed with, "In point of fact," I had to repress a smile. We all say that when we lecture, I thought, and wag our fingers the way Charlea had just started to do. "There are some principles of epigenetics that are now starting to be accepted— rules that apply to the temporal control of gene activity, to the seg- regation of such activity during somatic cell division, and even to the inheritability of active states.

"I'll stop here. I know none of us is a gene jock, but not having preconceived notions may be an advantage."

I could see from Sepp's expression that he was not ready to jump on the epigenetics train. "I disagree," he said firmly. "Most of the time, preconceived notions are exactly what one needs. I wish we had some now."

"I have spent the evening thinking," Hiroshi said after we'd reconvened the following day.

"And?" Charlea asked.

"You want us to agree to work on epigenetics, which we will then take home for deeper thought."

I glanced at Charlea. We could all hear a "but" coming. She made no response, except for a perceptible narrowing of her eyes. "But I have a feeling that epigenetics is not for us. Not that it is not an important problem. I just think it is too tough for us. It will take too much experimental support. We cannot do it with Jocelyn and my Japanese colleague, who speaks such terrible English." He smiled briefly at her.

"Go on," she said calmly.

He nodded. "There is another venture we might consider. One that would not require some of us to enter a totally new area."

I kept waiting for Charlea to explode, but for all I could tell, she hadn't taken in a word Hiroshi had said. Charlea, I realized, had basically an unreadable face.

But Hiroshi was obviously aware of the risk he was running. "Take your knowledge and experience in computer modeling," he said to C_3. "That beautiful paper you published in *PNAS* on the active site of . . ."

I was startled by the transformation in Charlea's expression: unreadability had turned into transparency. I had never realized how susceptible she was to flattery—or how good Hiroshi was at it. "Your knowledge of binding-pocket chemistry of enzymes," he nodded at Sepp, who straightened and preened as visibly as Charlea. "And . . ." he turned to me, but I stopped him.

"Never mind, Hiroshi. Just go on." He didn't need to get me on his side, and there was no reason to dilute Charlea's and Sepp's enjoyment.

"So let me mention a very different topic we might want to pursue—one that takes advantage of our considerable strengths. You, Charlea, were talking about the aristocracy: the genes, DNA. I want to talk about the proletariat: the enzymes. Specifically, a very sophisticated proletariat: catalytic antibodies. I realize 'sophisticated proletariat' sounds like a contradiction in terms. But think for a moment why our car and electronics industries have done so well. Japanese workers have become more sophisticated."

Compared with whom? I nearly asked.

His words started to speed up. He'd given us the title. Now he wanted to present the text, and he started by focusing on the most general reader: D_3, who by default had acquired the combined role of popular audience and potential referee.

"Enzymes are the catalysts that cause all our body chemistry to proceed rapidly at body temperature. To do that, an enzyme must bind to the substrate that is to be altered chemically. The active sites of the enzymes—really only a small part of those big protein molecules—are the key. Charlea and Sepp have done a lot of work in that field. But in addition to enzymes, we have another class of proteins that bind selectively: the antibodies."

I was getting a bit impatient. Hiroshi was shifting back and forth between flattery, exciting hints of things to come, and elementary exposition. But then he caught all of our attention by the simple device of using a metaphor none of us had ever heard.

"I call it the myopic versus the blind watchmaker." It worked. I could see it in all the faces around, and I certainly felt it myself. Is it the poet in him that generates these phrases?

"The blind watchmaker is evolution. Even epigenetically

speaking," he chuckled. "It took millions of years to develop the optimum binding sites in the thousands of enzymes that constitute our body's workforce."

"And the myopic one?"

I couldn't titrate the nuance in Charlea's question. Was it sarcasm or curiosity? A mixture of both, I concluded.

"The immune system," he said flatly. "And us. That is, if the three of you agree."

"Get to the point, Hiroshi," Charlea said.

"I will. But let me do it in my own way by telling you how the idea first came to me." He turned again to D_3. "The fundamental concept behind catalytic antibodies is simple enough. The antibodies are our body's natural defenses; they bind selectively to invading molecular entities. Our immune system is probably capable of producing a billion *different* antibodies to cope with most potential invaders. But in addition . . ." Hiroshi stopped for effect, "the antibody can fine-tune its active site by a process called express mutagenesis. The process takes no more than six weeks, which is certainly express compared with the million years of ordinary evolution by which enzymes learned to bind selectively with the compounds they manipulate in our body chemistry. Moreover, this process is not blind. During mutagenesis, the antibody binding site reaches the optimum shape and structure as if the greatest biophysicist," he nodded toward C_3, "were sitting in front of her computer terminal designing a molecule with the highest binding energy. Express mutagenesis is very good. But we"—he nodded at the rest of us—"are even better. There are people like Sepp, for instance, who know how to carry out *synthetic* modifications of active sites."

I had to admire Hiroshi's skill, the way he was using Diana as the vehicle for offering tribute to Charlea and Sepp.

"In spite of their use as therapeutic vehicles, as diagnostic agents, as special probes in all kinds of recent biological research, we have so far tapped only an insignificantly small portion of the billion different possible forms of antibodies."

Hiroshi was leaning forward over the table, his words almost stumbling over each other. "We can now generate, with hybridoma techniques, antibodies against just about any molecule of interest. Why not think of some way to introduce catalytic activity into antibody-combining sites? This would yield *new enzymes with absolutely tailored specificity.* We could do reactions that evolution—the blind watchmaker—has not even thought of! For instance, we could attach a cofactor binding site or an appropriately positioned catalytic amino acid to see whether we could increase the speed of a reaction."

"Or overcome the entropy requirements involved in orienting the reaction partners." Charlea had overcome her initial suspicion. She seemed to have forgotten it entirely.

"Or insert a catalytic group directly into the combining site of the antibody by chemical modification," Sepp added.

"Or do it by site-specific mutagenesis," I stated in the most offhand tone I could muster.

Charlea got up. She walked over to Hiroshi and removed his glasses. "You don't need them anymore. Who said you're myopic? Let's drop epigenetics."

Hiroshi just sat there, his hands spread open, palms facing upward, a contented Buddha without his spectacles. He'd made his point.

19

I was still in bed, though not asleep. I had just passed through that heavenly state of semiconsciousness after a dreamless sleep, musing how lucky I was to find myself in Diana's apartment without feeling an iota of guilt, when I heard a persistent knocking on my door. It was Diana telling me through the closed door to pick up the telephone.

"Max," Sepp's voice reverberated over the phone. "I have it."

Not knowing Sepp had been missing anything, I'm afraid my reply was ungracious.

"Saliva, Max!" He cried, oblivious to any lack of enthusiasm for the subject on my end of the line.

About then I realized that something else was bothering me besides the interruption of my morning lassitude. I'd never mentioned to anybody, not even Jessica, that I'd been using Diana's apartment this week as a pied-à-terre. It would've been a pain to commute every day from Princeton.

"How did you know I was here?" I grumbled.

"There was no answer at Princeton."

Does that mean I'm staying with Diana? I wanted to ask, but then thought, what's the point? What am I trying to hide?

But Sepp was much too interested in his saliva to pay any further attention. "I've got to see you," he said. "Right away. Either I am overlooking something absolutely obvious or this is the greatest idea of my life."

"Tell me over the phone," I compromised.

I could hear the intake of a deep breath. "All right," he said. "Remember what Hiroshi was saying after the morning session on salivary monitoring in diseases? 'We need a better way of fishing the right antibody out of this teeming sea of saliva.' He would also need it for his catalytic antibody project. Here is a candidate: in vitro amplification of targeted DNA sequences."

"That's easily said. How are you going to do it?"

"Let us denature a double-stranded target DNA, anneal synthetic primers to the terminal sequences flanking the target DNA sequence of each strand, and add some DNA polymerase."

"Let's," I said, getting impatient. After all, what was new about that?

"A new DNA strand will be produced, beginning at the primer terminus, and extending across the entire target sequence."

"Yes, Sepp. So you get a copy. Big deal."

"Aha," he cried triumphantly, "but if you do this n times, you get 2^n times as much target."

"And?"

"Twenty repetitions will produce one million copies. You may not be able to find one antibody molecule in the saliva specimen, but one million?"

"But Sepp," I said, "that's too simple. There must be something wrong or others would have discovered that long ago."

"I know," he replied. "That is why I am calling you. Tell me: what have I overlooked?"

That morning, the four of us spent hours hashing and rehashing every detail of Sepp's concept; setting up and demolishing one straw man after another. For once, the physical environment had become unimportant. We might as well have been in a windowless basement.

Diana joined us for lunch, but after a couple of attempts at entering our conversation, she gave up.

"You people have turned into the most consumingly focused bunch I have ever encountered," she said admiringly. "I can hardly wait to have you translate what this is all about."

"Only if we can figure it out ourselves," Charlea responded, distracted by a diagram she was sketching on a notepad. "At this stage, it only seems that Sepp has discovered a new fishhook. We're all searching frantically for the appropriate line to attach it to."

This was not going to be easy, I realized. The difficulty wasn't a scientific one—I had every confidence that, in time, the appropriate line would be found. But what about finding the appropriate line for Skordylis? I hadn't forgotten Diana's point: if I couldn't explain it to her, it probably wasn't the earthshaking idea that would make Skordylis a star. But then, who would have guessed that on the very first day after its birth, I would be asked to give a popular description of PCR—an invention that eventually would turn out to be one of the great coups of contemporary biology?

"What's PCR?" asked Diana, pencil poised in midair.

"Be patient," I admonished her. "We only coined the term a few hours ago. First, we have to deal with another acronym: DNA."

"Nucleic acid," Diana interrupted. "Don't talk down to me, Max. Everyone knows that."

"*Deoxyribo*nucleic acid," I corrected, trying to hide my annoyance. "The essence of all genetic material—of the thousands of genes that are responsible for our uniqueness and, in a way, our immortality." Now what had made me add that? I wondered—I, the last branch of my family tree.

"I wish we had at least a strand of colored beads," I said, actually standing up and turning around, as if somewhere in Diana's living room I might find a supply of such beads, conveniently labeled "guanine," "thymine," "cytosine," and "adenine." If I were in my office, I was thinking irritably . . .

"Would crayons do, Max?" Diana offered. Taking me gently by the hand, she made me sit back down. "I'll be right back," she said. At the time, I didn't understand why she was smiling that way.

God only knew why Diana had them, but when she returned she had thirty-six of them, in colors with names I had never heard of, like dusky plum, and alizarin crimson. But they had an instantly calming effect.

"When discussing DNA," I explained, taking alizarin in hand, "it's convenient to use a simple shorthand. It has four terms— four letters, or four colors—standing for the four compounds that make up DNA."

Diana looked reassured.

"It's a miraculous fact," I continued, "that the entire genetic library of this world—" I waved a hand in a gesture that embraced all five of us in the room, "—the structure of every living thing, is reducible, ultimately, to four chemical compounds: adenine, thymine, guanine, and cytosine.

"Never mind the names," I added. "That's why God invented crayons."

I wrote the letters A, G, and C, in black, green, and red, sketching an open box—white—for T.

"Why those colors?"

"No reason," I replied airily. "Just as the chemical nature of these compounds—bases, we call them—is irrelevant to what I have to tell you today. All that matters is how they fit together— how they function, you might say, in a code.

"Imagine an enormously long strand consisting of thousands of these four bases, strung together like colored beads; here:

I'll illustrate a segment of that chain by writing TCCAGTTGTC: white, red, red, black, green, white, white, green, white, and red." I drew the letters on a sheet of legal-sized paper and held it up for my audience.

"Is there any reason for that particular sequence?"

"No reason," I said, my impatience returning swiftly. "It's just an example. It could just as easily be CGGTAACGG or some other combination."

"That's only nine," Diana noted judiciously, "but I see your point."

"Good," I said, somewhat more patronizingly than I intended, and tried to recall where I was. "Human DNA consists of two such strands—each some three billion beads, or bases, long."

I paused a moment while the number sank in. "In other words, if the entire chain were made up of bases as large as the squares I've drawn on this sheet, a strand of human DNA would be nearly fifty thousand miles long." I looked at Diana and was pleased to see her straighten slightly. "That's roughly twice the circumference of the earth."

"So we are talking about a very simple code, but an enormously long message: very great complexity generated by almost endless variation on a simple theme." That's when C_3's lecture on complexity flashed across my mental screen. "Remember Charlea's Pollock painting?"

I could tell I had her. Now it was time to expand the picture. "But of course it's a little more complicated than that—it always is, isn't it?" I added with my most disarming smile. "And the thing that complicates it is coupling."

This is a standard line I have been using in lectures for years, and I always follow it up with another general smile. This time, however, I noticed Diana smiling back at me and almost forgot the thread of my argument. I took refuge in a fact.

"The human genome is not, you may recall, a single strand, but two strands, coupled together in parallel, base to base, in a double spiral."

"The double helix," Diana murmured.

"Precisely," I said. "And that is where it gets complicated. **157**

Only a little," I added hastily, "because the linking of the two strands follows a very straightforward set of rules.

"The two strands don't link haphazardly: each chemical base can link with only one other base—what we call its complement."

While I was speaking I had drawn a strand of ten colored boxes, each of them labeled A, C, G, or T. I suddenly realized how extremely difficult it is to describe even relatively simple chemical concepts without recourse to at least paper and pencil.

"Fortunately, there are only two rules to remember," I said encouragingly: "white (T) goes with black (A), and green (G) with red (C); the other combinations, for instance white pairing with red (T-C), don't occur. Following those rules, you should now be able to draw the unique strand that would couple with the ten-letter chain I've drawn here." I handed the crayons to Diana. "Go ahead: just draw the order of the new chain yourself."

With a wry glance at her audience, Diana took the proffered crayons and quickly sketched in the correct sequence: AGGTCAACAG.

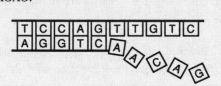

"Fine," I said as soon as she had finished. "Just one more point, which you may immediately forget, because it is of no relevance to what I want to explain to you. I didn't tell you the complete truth: earlier on, when I referred to the four letters as the chemist's shorthand for four bases, I really meant that they are abbreviations for four units called nucleotides, which are combinations of such bases with a simple sugar, called deoxyribose, and phosphoric acid. This sugar is responsible for the *D* in the acronym DNA. I am only telling this to you so that my colleagues won't accuse me of oversimplification." I gestured at the three pairs of eyes aimed at me. Since I hadn't intended to fully obey Albert Einstein's proscription for oversimplification, I felt that I should at least pay some lip service to it.

"Now we are in business: since you have learned how to write correctly a ten-base sequence based on complementarity with a given template, you can write one with thousands of bases. Indeed, if you were given one strand of the entire human nucleic acid sequence consisting of some three billion bases, you could generate the entire complementary strand by just following the simple rule that only T and A or G and C bind to each other—except that, working day and night, it would take you about ninety years to finish the job. Still, you have just discovered how natural replication occurs: a single double helix uncoils into two separate strands, with each strand then picking up individual bases from its cellular environment."

"Okay," Diana nodded. "But one question: when the strands separate, how are the bases added? Do they just clump on at random until the strand is full, or is there some system to the way they latch on? Is it like a zipper? And what zips it up? And just what makes them join on in the first place?"

"I thought you said *one* question."

"Well, I think what I'm asking is, How does it work?"

That's the problem with giving simple explanations to an intelligent audience: even if they don't know much about science, they can ask questions that get complicated very quickly. I found myself looking beseechingly at Charlea—our guru of complexity—but her gaze remained opaque.

"Could we not go into that today?" I pleaded. "But part of your 'one question' is very much to the point. What makes them join is an enzyme called DNA polymerase. As you'll see, this is one of the key components of Sepp's idea and of a very clever modification Hiroshi has come up with this morning. But there is something else you must understand about the DNA chain first. Information about the many thousands of genetic traits is encoded in segments of the chain, the genes—each of which can include as many as 100,000 base pairs. To work with an individual gene—to isolate the parts of the DNA responsible for any genetic trait, whether it's blue eyes or a killer disease—one needs to locate the section that contains that particular gene's sequence of pairs and cut them out from the strand."

"Cut them?" Diana asked. "With scissors?"

"In a sense. Only our scissors is a series of enzymes, restriction endonucleases."

"I'll assume you know how to make scissors out of enzymes. But how do you know where to cut?"

"Ah," I said, "that's where it gets tricky. The enzymes know: they rupture the chain wherever they recognize a specific group of bases, generally a particular sequence of eight. The longer the DNA, the more often such a sequence of bases will appear. And that's where the real challenge lies. The DNA in an *E. coli* bacterium, for instance, will be cut around 70 times, which is not very much; sifting through those 70 snippets for the one you want isn't that hard. In yeast, you'll be left with nearly 230 pieces, which is still not bad. But in the human DNA, after the cutting is done you're faced with perhaps 50,000 fragments. If you're only interested in one of those pieces, you soon realize that cutting the strand isn't the real challenge: it's sorting through the debris. You're looking for a needle in a haystack; or, more precisely, a particular straw in that stack."

For the last few minutes I had been addressing my words to Diana alone. Now I leaned back, so as to include the rest of my colleagues. "Fortunately, we now have automatic sequencing machines, which can read the codes of individual fragments; there are separation methods that can fish out the desired piece from the rest of the molecular garbage, even when it exists in only a minute amount; and, finally, we have learned to increase the quantity of a particular segment by cloning it. Cloning," I added, not quite directly to Diana, "is not a trivial operation. A small piece of the desired fragment of DNA is incorporated into a microorganism, usually a bacterium, which, in a fermentation culture, becomes a sort of chemical factory producing identical copies of the DNA segment that we want, until we have sufficient quantities to work with. Which is fine, but it's a very cumbersome process. The point I wanted to make is that by the middle 1980s we had reached the point where all these processes could be accomplished, albeit slowly and laboriously. Got it?"

"Got it," she said. "When you say 'we,' do you mean that the four of you have worked all this out yourselves?"

"Good God no!" I exclaimed. " 'We' means many molecular biologists and biochemists, including probably a dozen or more who won Nobel Prizes along the way." Did I see a twitch in my colleagues' eyes when I said "Nobel," or was it my own unconscious response?

"Does that mean Sepp will win a Nobel for his brainstorm?" Diana grinned.

I shook my head. "That's part of the price we all agreed to pay in forming this group. It's like celibacy when you join a monastery."

"Surely not celibacy," she protested, throwing up her hands in mock horror.

"I mean anonymity," I said, self-consciously patting Diana's hand—a gesture I'd picked up from her.

"To understand Sepp's PCR—which stands for polymerase chain reaction—let's assume these two parallel lines represent all the DNA in a cell. For simplicity, let's also assume that this genome is only two hundred bases long. Somewhere within it lies a sequence of, say, fifty base pairs we want to work with. This, of course, is much too simple to be exciting in practice, but for today, it will do."

Between the two parallel lines I drew crossbars, representing the binding of the two strands through the individual base pairs— the A-T or T-A, and the C-G or G-C combinations. "We now heat this material, which causes the bonds to break, thus leaving us with two separated single strands. Call the first bead on the left end of each strand 'number 1,' and the last bead on the right 'number 200.'

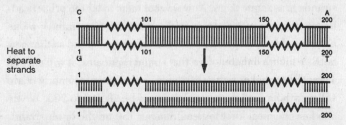

Heat to separate strands

"Now I'll come to the crux of Sepp's idea. Let's say that the needle we want to work with in this haystack is the fifty-base sequence from numbers 101 to 150. How do we make copies of it other than resorting to the cumbersome process of cloning? This is where Sepp has had a stroke of genius: rather than searching through a huge haystack for a single needle, he has conceived of a way of quickly and simply multiplying the needle hidden there, making so many copies that you can't possibly miss them.

"That conceptual switch is the heart of his idea, but the beauty of it is in the technique. You may find this heavy going, but bear with us: we're so excited by this concept that I can't resist going over the details again. And it may help us see if there's something we've overlooked. Okay?"

"Will there be a quiz?" she asked primly.

"No," I laughed. "Not for you, anyway." I looked at my colleagues, who didn't seem so amused. "It's the rest of us who are going to have to make sense of it. But here's what we have so far. First, by means of a sequencing machine, one determines the exact sequence of the entire chain. Then, using an instrument called a DNA synthesizer, one synthesizes two primers."

Like a good teacher, I wrote down the word *primer* and underlined it. "A primer is a small, unique sequence of bases—for instance the eight-base series that the enzymatic scissors recognize—that marks one end of the desired piece of DNA material by binding to it. In a two-hundred-base-long strand like the one I drew, such an eight-base order is almost certainly going to appear only once; but to be safe, we make two primers: one, with complementary bases corresponding to the sequence 101 to 108 of the top strand, and the other with eight bases matching the string 143 to 150 on the bottom strand. Remember, we've heated the strands to separate them. Now we cool them to let the primers adhere to the respective places in these two discrete strands; we tie a chemical knot on primer bead 101 on the top strand so that new beads can't bind there; when that strand replicates, it will only do so by adding beads on the 108 side, so its complementary chain will only be a partial one, consisting of beads 101 to 200. We tie another chemical knot to bead number 150 on the lower strand, so that this chain can only replicate toward the lower numbers.

162 When each chain forms its complementary strand in the presence

of our bead stringer, the DNA polymerase enzyme, the complement will be partial, but the partial strands will overlap in the sequence 101 to 150 we're interested in.

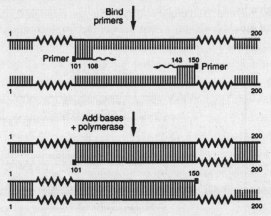

"From this point, the rest is straightforward. Each chain replicates itself as much as it can, extending forward or backward from its primer, in a matter of minutes. Then you heat the mixture to disengage the new double strands, and now you have four single ones." I drew four lines: the two original long ones, numbered 1 to 200, and two shorter ones, numbered 101 to 200, and 150 to 1. "Note," I added, "we have yet to produce any 101 to 150 pieces, which are the ones we're after.

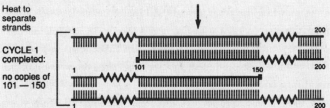

"This is where Sepp's proposal comes in. Rather than stopping here, we repeat the process: add the primers again, cool the mixture to anneal them to the four single strands from the first round, add some more enzyme and lots of extra bases, and again let the polymerase enzyme do its stitching work. When the products from this second cycle are heated, we end up with *eight* individual strands." I quickly sketched and numbered the eight components of the four newly produced double helices. "Now we've got the two original 1 to 200 parents, two daughters of 1 to 150 length, and two covering the range 101 to 200. *But,*" I tapped the table for emphasis, "*we now also have two copies of our 'needle': the 101 to 150 combination.* You might call them the granddaughters, which are derived from the single 101 to 200 and 1 to 150 progenitors generated in the first cycle."

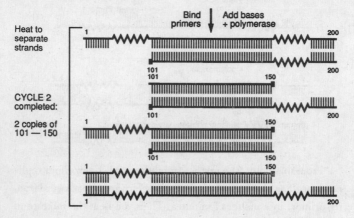

"You probably think I'm not following this," Diana said dryly. "But I notice that you've still got a ratio of three to one. How are you going to separate what you want from what you don't?"

"Aha," I cried. "That is the genius of Sepp's idea. From now on, the two granddaughter strands will multiply in exponential progression while the other strands will increase much more slowly, in arithmetic order. Go on," I urged Diana, "work out the next cycle on your own right here on the paper. Take these eight strands that we have just produced and see what the composition of the resulting sixteen will be."

It may have taken her five minutes, while she carefully drew her primers on the 101 and 150 positions of each strand, counted each product, and checked once more. "*Eight,*" she said in amazement.

"And now we're in clover," I chuckled. "It takes only *thirty* cooling and heating cycles to produce *1 billion* copies of our 101 to 150 sequence. Actually, Charlea calculates the precise number as 1,073,741,824. That's quite a stack of identical needles com-

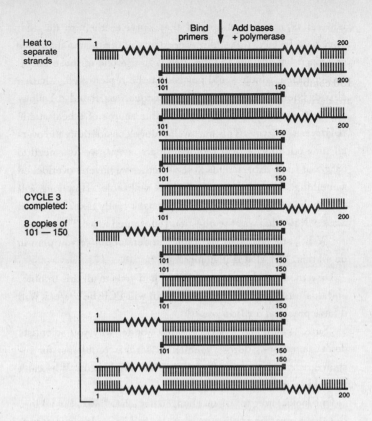

Bind primers
Add bases + polymerase

Heat to separate strands

1   200

101
101   150

101
101   150

101   150
101   150

CYCLE 3 completed:

101   150

8 copies of 101 — 150

1   150

101   150
101   150

101   150

1   150

101   150
150

1   150

1   200

pared with the piddling number of 1–150 and 101–200 strands that are generated at the same time. Sepp predicts that this process should only take a couple of hours. If it works, it would be an enormous achievement."

"There is a question I would like to ask you, Max," said Diana, "or perhaps Sepp—"

"Before you do," I interrupted, "just let me tell you one more thing. Sepp's concept, though brilliant in its simplicity, is still laborious, because it envisages adding new DNA polymerase after each heating cycle. We have to do this, you see, because heating denatures—inactivates—the enzyme. This is where Hiroshi comes in. He reminded us that natural thermal springs and volcanic environments contain bacteria that survive—indeed flourish—at high temperatures. If they survive, then so do their enzymes. In fact, we're all descendants of organisms that once colonized hot springs. So the idea is to use one of those bacterial enzymes, which would not need to be replenished. Charlea already knew of a bacterium, *Thermus aquaticus*, found at Yellowstone; it seems to be a readily available source of a heat-stable polymerase enzyme. This may well reduce considerably the overall time our process will require. In any event, we now need to carry out some experiments to see whether we haven't overlooked something. Are all these predictions realizable? How long will the whole process from needle to haystack really take?" I leaned back. "Now what was the question you wanted to ask?"

"Well," she hesitated, "I *think* I understand *how* you plan to do all this. But what is it all *for?*"

For a moment, I was speechless. I had gone to all this trouble, and this was what I heard? "You mean will PCR be *useful?* Will it have practical *applications?*"

"Sure," continued Diana. "I often wonder why you scientists don't sometimes address yourself to serious problems: for instance, why can't we smell garlic on our own breath? Why can't we tickle ourselves?"

One look at my expression changed her tone. "Max, I'm joking. But there must be applications *we, the public* could understand. Otherwise, who'll care?"

Applications: I wondered for a moment what Diana would say if I asked her what applications she could come up with for a Bach fugue. Nothing makes a research scientist more defensive than talk of application. "Give us a chance," I said. "We've been at this for less than two days. At this stage, we're talking solely about the *theoretical* aspects of a methodology that still needs to be checked out experimentally. We aren't even sure yet *which* experiments to do. Any talk about applications would be premature."

"Do you mean that you won't even think about practical applications until you've decided if it'll work?"

"Why does that bother you?" Charlea grumbled. "*Applications,*" she snarled, putting all the spin on that word a theorist can apply—which is considerable. "It's hard enough to figure out if it's going to work; why should we have to figure out what it might be good for?"

"For one thing," Diana said in an even tone. "There's the question of what it might be bad for."

"Bad for?" echoed C₃. She threw her hands into the air. "What on earth could this be bad for?"

20

Within weeks of the saliva meeting, Jocelyn had started work in the lab. Charlca had also moved into high gear. A culture of *Thermus aquaticus* arrived in Princeton by overnight mail, together with a precise description of its optimal growth medium. We expected the usual problems of start-up experiments: one step backward for every two forward. But the weeks passed and no unforeseen difficulties rose in our path. And as the experiments advanced, the telephone calls and faxes passing among the members of our group began to carry a rising tension. I found myself stopping by the lab two, three times a day, until the remaining members of my lab group began to wonder. Jocelyn, imperturbable as ever, seemed oblivious to my increasingly intrusive interruptions. Within days, she was handling the DNA synthesizer with the calm efficiency of someone who'd played with it since childhood.

The other confrères were not so calm. Sepp, especially, kept the wires busy, calling me at hours that indicated he had either forgotten about time zones or simply didn't care. Finally, he couldn't take it any longer.

"Sepp is coming over," Diana informed me one day over the phone. "I think he's turned superstitious: he's worried that something may go wrong at the last moment. 'I want to be there when it happens,' he said. I didn't ask him whether he meant the triumph or the debacle—I just made a reservation for him at the Empire Hotel, across from Lincoln Center. There's enough in Manhattan to distract him—at least until Jocelyn's done."

I was flabbergasted. Why had he called D_3 rather than me? Had he expected she'd put him up at her place?

Perhaps it was something in my tone, but Diana sounded defensive. "I didn't think it would be a good idea for Sepp to stay too close to Princeton," she explained—although I had not asked for an explanation. "If he hangs around too much in the lab, what will the other people think?"

But D_3 and I had both overlooked one thing: Sepp's impatience.

We weren't given the chance to overlook it for very long. The day of Sepp's arrival in mid-March I had popped into the lab around four in the afternoon, as usual, to check with Jocelyn about her progress. All I found was a note: *Professor Krzilska asked me to join him for dinner in Manhattan to bring him up-to-date. Jocelyn.*"

During the next couple of weeks Sepp called Jocelyn almost daily. I found out about these calls only because, on my late afternoon visits to the lab, more and more often I arrived only to find Jocelyn's station unoccupied. Jocelyn barely alluded to her abbreviated lab days. I was starting to worry about her losing momentum, yet I felt uncomfortable bringing it up. Jocelyn was not just my graduate student; as Skordylis's silent partner, her time was as much Sepp's as mine. And it was Sepp's idea that we were now pursuing—a point he'd started to make with increasing frequency every time we met in New York, which must have been every second or third day. Yet, despite the frequency of our own meetings, the announcement of his departure also reached me secondhand.

"Sepp is leaving the day after tomorrow," Jocelyn told me one morning. "It's got something to do with his divorce. He says it's been a long, messy business, but it seems that it's almost over."

So Sepp had confided to Jocelyn about his divorce? And he's "Sepp" to her while I'm still "Professor Weiss"? I suddenly wanted very much to hear her call me Max, as Diana did. But how could

I tell her to do that in the lab, where all the others still call me, at least, Prof? How could I possibly have my *last* and youngest graduate student be the *first* to "Max" me? As is so typical of me—at least, so Nedra used to say—when I encounter something unpleasant, I have a tendency to put it into a mental drawer. This time, I closed it firmly.

" 'Sailing to Capri.' Just the title for a poem about us."

I couldn't help but classify the accompanying grin as undisciplined. Usually, Hiroshi retained merriment for his private consumption, not to be dispensed freely to an audience; now it was displayed all over his face.

"This *is* a country for old men." Hiroshi sounded pleased as we gazed over the hydrofoil's rail at the receding coastline of the Bay of Naples. Sepp glanced quizzically at me, but I gave nothing back. I hadn't a clue what Hiroshi was talking about, but I wasn't going to admit it.

"Doesn't Yeats start with something like 'This is *no* country for old men'?" Diana faltered.

"Yes," Hiroshi admitted, and then grinned sheepishly. "But I was quoting Skordylis, forecasting his own fate."

"*Her*, not *his*." Charlea poked him with her index finger for emphasis. "You and Sepp are having trouble keeping our author's gender straight."

"I beg your pardon," he replied without a hint of irony. "It is the Japanese in me: we have no gender-specific pronouns in our language."

Charlea grunted skeptically and turned to gaze at the sea. "Maybe we're making a mistake," she said a minute later, "using just her initial. I say we use 'Diana Skordylis' for the PCR manuscript."

"I disagree," said Sepp and walked away.

"Why not call it 'Sailing to Malaparte'?" I asked Hiroshi, trying to restore the conversation to its pleasant beginning. "It sounds more mysterious."

"I disagree," he said, sounding like Sepp. " 'Capri' has a better ring."

"That's putting it mildly," chimed in Diana. "I'm still amazed you people are not superstitious about having picked such a place. 'Malaparte' . . . 'bad side.'" She mimed a shiver. Or perhaps it was genuine: the sun was high overhead, but the October breeze off the sea was chill. I moved closer to her, until we stood side by side at the railing.

This had been Sepp's idea. Not the trip itself: we had all agreed that we needed a change of scene while we wrote up the results of the PCR experiments. The destination—the Villa Malaparte on the Island of Capri—had been Sepp's suggestion. So far, he'd pointed out, he had always come to our side of the Atlantic. Wasn't it time to reverse directions? What had clinched it, though, were Sepp's and Hiroshi's invitations to a NATO workshop at the *Stazione Zoologica* in Naples. Charlea had her NIH grant pay for most of her Capri trip by combining it with attendance at a European Biophysical Society meeting in Heidelberg. That left only me. Usually, my trips abroad were like pizzas, based on scientific dough, that were free. I only had to pay for the extra toppings: the touristic anchovies or the entertainment pepperoni. For the first time in many years, I found myself paying for a European plane fare out of my own pocket.

Sepp had been as excited about our arrival as I'd ever seen him—buoyant and boyishly happy. "Wait until you see the Villa Malaparte," he had announced proudly. "The location is unbelievable, *fantastisch*." Years earlier, he'd seen it from a boat during a vacation in Capri; its perch atop a rugged promontory —accessible, essentially, only by boat—within sight of Capri's Faraglione Rocks, had made an indelible impression on him. Recently he had learned that it had been taken over by a foundation that put on seminars for architects, and on occasion also offered it as a retreat to artists and scholars. Without telling any of us, he'd managed to persuade the Fondazione Giorgio Ronchi to house and feed us for a week.

In the end, our fifth colleague in Capri was not Jocelyn, who couldn't miss an obligatory graduate course at Princeton, but Diana. The Fondazione Giorgio Ronchi had meant nothing to her, but the Italian writer Curzio Malaparte had—indeed, sufficiently so that she had invited herself to our retreat. "Why not?" said Sepp, "there are six bedrooms."

We were panting after we had climbed the steep, rocky path from the minute dock to the Pompeian red stucco and brick edifice atop a rocky spur on Point Massullo. Wedge-shaped steps extending along the entire rhomboid side of the two-story structure led to the terrace roof: they reminded me of the approach to a Mayan temple. As we assaulted this final obstacle I couldn't help but think that it would have violated every American building code. No rail, no parapet whatsoever on the remaining three sides, prevented a visitor from crashing a hundred or more feet down onto the rocks by the sea. We were careful not to approach the edge of the terrace. Huddling near its center, we seemed to be floating high above the Tyrrhenian Sea, with Capri's dramatic south shore on both sides and behind us.

Once we had settled into our rooms, Diana produced an unexpected nugget of historical lore, one that it was obvious she had been hoarding for our arrival. "Did you know that Malaparte's original name was Kurt Erich Suckert?"

Sepp looked startled, as if he'd just been accused of keeping a dark Germanic secret from us. But Diana had been looking past him, at the fissured surface of the rocks framed by the salon's picture window. Against the hallucinatory blue of the Tyrrhenian sky, the view reminded me of an enlarged electron micrograph of a frozen cell slice.

"He changed his name in the early twenties," she said, "when so many people under Mussolini Italianized their names. He was first a fascist"—I suddenly thought I understood Sepp's discomfort, which was growing visibly as she went on—"but then he turned into an equally fierce antifascist. And shortly before his death in 1957 he converted to Catholicism and left the villa to Chairman Mao!"

"Come now, Diana," I started to remonstrate, "you aren't telling us that we are in a Chinese villa in Capri."

"It's a fact," she said complacently. "Luckily for us, the Chinese and Italians had no diplomatic relations in the late fifties. Malaparte's testamentary wish was not implemented." She looked at us and broke out laughing. "I thought I'd better do some home-work before joining you."

Was this just a historian's nervous tic, or was D₃ telling us something? "Do you know that his most famous book is called *Kaputt?*" She shook her head. "'Malaparte' . . . 'kaputt' . . . are you sure you aren't going to jinx Skordylis's masterpiece? Of course, the site *is* spectacular." She turned and whispered to me. "Max, you've got to come to my room—I don't think you've seen anything quite like it."

My bedroom had surprised me, too, but not in any way that would have prompted me to show it to others. Hiroshi, Sepp, and I occupied three of the four bedrooms on the ground floor: small, dark, almost bare quarters resembling monastic cells. Only when the wooden shutters were opened did the light and the view re-lieve the cloistered atmosphere. Charlea and Diana occupied the two upstairs bedrooms, accessible only through the salon. Were they so different?

"This is where Malaparte put up his mistress," D₃ explained as she opened the door. Though larger than mine and containing two beds, there was nothing distinctive about her chamber except for the flowered floor tiles and the extraordinary tile fireplace, which rose like a slender pyramid all the way to the ceiling in the corner. Not bad, compared with my room, I thought, but hardly meriting a private invitation.

As if she'd read my mind, Diana whispered, "Not that," and led me into the connecting bathroom. "This."

Facing the entrance was a luxurious sunken tub—really a small pool—lined on three sides with vertical gray-and-white-striped tiles. The stone floor looked like alabaster or marble. "Not bad," I murmured.

"Look at the view."

"The Faraglione di Matromania." I pronounced the words care-fully, wanting to demonstrate that I'd read the guidebook too. "Spectacular."

"Not that view—this one here."

My expression must have been something to behold, because D₃ almost doubled over with laughter. Eventually I joined her, after I had taken it all in: the tall mirror, virtually from floor to ceiling, with a bidet centered in front of it, faced the window through which I had admired the dazzling scenery. Diana, fully clothed, was sitting on it—I guess to illustrate what didn't need any illustration. If used by a woman—as a bidet is meant to be used—a spectator would see the woman's naked buttocks framed by the Faraglione Rocks, with the sky and clouds above her.

"Don't you wonder what Malaparte must have been like?" I finally said.

Diana rose from the bidet. "It could have been the mistress's idea."

The following morning, the four of us arranged ourselves on two sides of the salon's massive wooden table. Diana deliberately separated herself, moving to the only sofa in front of one of the four picture windows. The absence of art and bookshelves— unexpected in the home of a writer—was surprisingly effective in this sparsely furnished, whitewashed, stone-flagged salon: the emphasis was on the spectacular vistas. Even the lower back of the fireplace was glass. I was speculating what the sea must look like through the flames.

Small stacks of white bond paper had been left at each place; there was also a supply of ballpoint pens, pencils, erasers, and glue sticks. I had just distributed to each a copy of Jocelyn's manuscript: "Specific DNA Amplification: Use of DNA Polymerase from the Extreme Thermophile *Thermus aquaticus*," by Jocelyn P. Powers.

"And what is *this?*" Sepp grumbled.

I threw a glance at Charlea, but she seemed suddenly transfixed by the view. "It's Jocelyn's manuscript," I explained.

"I can see that."

"In that case, what's your question?"

"I thought the purpose of this trip," he tapped the table firmly, "was for *us* to prepare the first announcement."

So that's what's bugging Sepp, I realized; but I was not prepared to help him. If he's bothered, I decided, he'll have to say so openly.

"Should Jocelyn not have waited until she saw what *we* have written? And why have we not seen this before?" He didn't look at me, but it was obvious to whom the last question was addressed.

"Because I only got it three days ago," I replied calmly. "I didn't see any purpose in faxing it all over the world when we'd meet here so soon."

"So nobody has seen it before?" He glanced suspiciously at the rest of us.

"I have, of course." Now I was getting irritated. "Jocelyn works practically next door to my office. And she didn't write this in a vacuum." I was not going to tell Sepp that most of what he saw in front of him had actually been composed by me. Jocelyn had never written a scientific paper before; and even if she had, this was too important to leave up to her.

"Oh, calm down, Sepp," Charlea said caustically. "It's only a draft. Jocelyn can't scoop us, anyway. She can't publish without the theoretical paper, which we haven't written. But remember, that won't be worth much without Jocelyn's contribution." Her voice softened slightly, but the rancor from the day before remained. "Let's not waste any more time nitpicking. This is going to be hard enough."

Charlea was right. Writing Skordylis's first three papers had been relatively trivial because not much was at stake. The first two were composed largely by Charlea and me, the third by Hiroshi. Before I sent them off under D. Skordylis's name, we had gone over the draft as a group, massaging the contents a bit. None of us got very excited, because we didn't expect much attention to be paid to these first articles by an unknown author.

Unexpectedly, the NFAT paper had raised a slight problem— amusing, to be sure, but nevertheless it struck me at the time as a warning of unlooked-for complications to come. A group at Scripps in California had organized a symposium entitled "T Cells and the Immune System" for early December in La Jolla—a favorite spot for scientists from the wintry East Coast. Of course, I'd been invited, because my group had been active in the T cell field for years. But shortly after D. Skordylis's expansion of our original NFAT research had appeared, the symposium organizer had sent an invitation to our New York post office box. *"Dear Dr. Skordylis,"* the note had read, *"We invite you to comment on your recent NFAT work from the Renga Institute after the main paper by Professor Max Weiss of Princeton."* Of course, Dr. Skordylis had turned the invitation down, pleading a prior commitment. We had all gotten a good laugh out of it when I told the others over the phone. Still, it had served as a warning of what might transpire if she published something hot.

Composing a short scientific paper on a truly hot subject does not have to take long, but this one did. Back in Princeton, when I'd sat down with Jocelyn, it had been easy. We just focused on a description of her experimental work—assuming that everything else would be in the yet-to-be-written Skordylis paper; furthermore, with Jocelyn I had been free to arrange things exactly as I wished: her part in the actual writing process had been more amanuensis than collaborator.

But here we had four prima donnas who seemed, for a time, unable to agree on anything, much less concede a contested point. It seemed that as each of us assumed the persona of Diana Skordylis, we got greedy.

I was glad that Jocelyn was not present. How would she have responded to seeing us debating whether this sentence belonged to Skordylis or to Powers? I saw how useful it was to have the draft of her paper in front of us as a silent referee, reminding us that this was experimental material belonging to Ms. Powers rather than to Dr. Skordylis. It may not have kept us from squabbling, but at least it defined some limit to our imperial pretensions. I felt almost virtuous, reminding myself that at Princeton I'd had very little difficulty in being fair to Jocelyn: when all was said and done, it was her name on the paper; that far, at least, I'd been selfless. Why, then, was I down in the theoretical mud with Sepp, Hiroshi, and Charlea, grappling and gouging for control on this one? Was it because, unlike Jocelyn Powers, a real person, Diana Skordylis was a power vacuum?

It took us the better part of the day to come up with a rough outline of the Skordylis paper. In the end, we resisted most attempts at cannibalizing Jocelyn's manuscript, using it instead as **175** a reference. The draft composed at Princeton became, with trivial alterations, the final version of the Powers article. And I reflected on that with some private pride, reminding myself how much of it was really mine.

At teatime we decided that we'd been together long enough; we needed a break for individual reflection. On the following day, each of us would work alone on the draft of the Skordylis paper; we would reconvene the day after and work from the four revisions to produce the final text. The process was hardly economical; but it seemed to be the price of peace.

"You people look rather grumpy," observed Diana, who was the only one of us who'd gone exploring. Although all supplies had to be brought to the villa by sea, there was a narrow footpath leading up the steep incline, past two locked gates, that eventually joined a wider public trail. Within half an hour of the Villa Malaparte, Diana reported, one could explore the streets of old Capri, barely wide enough for two to walk abreast. She warned us about an unexpected hazard presented by the island's dog population: on the narrow paths of Capri, you could enjoy the view *or* shitless footgear, but not both.

"I would have thought you'd be celebrating your success. Didn't you say, Max, that it all happened remarkably quickly?" She glanced around our conference table, which had now been set for dinner, looking for a cheerful response.

"Pleasure goes in waves," observed Hiroshi.

"Even in science?"

"Especially in science. And today, we are in a trough."

Diana's eyebrows displayed a mocking lift. "Since I seem to be the only one on the crest of a wave, why don't you enlighten me, Hiroshi?"

I'd been playing, almost morosely, with my soupspoon. Was that a strand of hair I saw floating around in the consommé?

"First you are on the top," Hiroshi was saying. "You are enjoying your success. But writing up your results: that is less pleasant. You are happy when you finish the paper; worried whether it will be accepted; euphoric when it finally appears in print;

but then you brood: will anyone find something wrong with your work? Or even worse, nobody writes or calls about it; then you are depressed. There you have the wave."

Suddenly, I found myself being lifted from the trough of Hiroshi's wave. "Hiroshi," I said loudly. It was the first word I'd said that evening. I lowered my voice and leaned closer to him. "Look at the liquid in my spoon."

"Yes?" he said, a blank expression in his eyes.

"What's floating there?"

"A hair."

"Are you sure?"

A shadow of concern passed over his face. "You have nothing to worry about, Max—it's just a small hair."

I became impatient. "I'm not worried. But suppose it were important to find out if it *is* a strand of hair, and if so, whose?"

"Are you serious?" He had lowered his voice.

"Serious."

"Analyze it. The amino acid composition alone will tell you whether it is human hair—"

"Okay," I stopped him. "But whose?"

Hiroshi started to perk up. "DNA analysis—"

"Precisely! Listen, people," I called out to the group, "Hiroshi and I have just been discussing something interesting. Suppose there was a hair in this soupdish," I waved my spoon until liquid fell in bright beads.

"Max," Diana exclaimed, "hair in *this* clear consommé?"

"One strand only. And very tiny. That's exactly what I want. Now," I looked at Sepp and Charlea, "how could you tell whose hair it was?"

"You mean differentiate between a rat's hair and a human's?"

"Charlea!" Diana looked shocked. "Rat hair in *this* soup?"

"No," I intervened, not wanting us to get off on a tangent, nor wishing to imply that rodents were running around in the Villa Malaparte's kitchen. "Human hair. How could we identify the owner?"

"Owner? A funny word." Charlea chuckled. "I suppose by DNA fingerprinting." Ever the pedagogue, she turned to Diana. **177**

"The way they determine the origin of semen samples in rape cases—comparing a suspect's genetic makeup with DNA from semen found on the victim."

"Right," I said quickly. "But would there be enough in a single strand of hair?"

"Ah!" Now Sepp, too, was interested. "With PCR there almost certainly would be!"

"If the root is still intact."

We all looked at Charlea. "Hair roots contain enough nuclear DNA for fingerprinting. But suppose it's just a hair shaft. I'm sure that's mostly dried protein."

"Wrong!" Sepp said it so bluntly that we were all taken aback. "I am certain the shaft contains some mitochondrial DNA."

"Maybe," she said reluctantly.

"If it does, that would simplify things," I said.

"How?" asked Diana.

"Mitochondrial DNA is more stable than DNA from cell nuclei. If the hair were old, we might be better off with the mitochondrial material."

"How old?"

I was getting slightly irritated by Diana's questions. "A couple of thousand years," I replied, trying to be funny.

"Jesus, Max!" Charlea cried out as if someone had dropped an ice cube down her back. "Do you think PCR could be used even in archaeology?" She asked excitedly.

The idea took me a long moment to absorb. "Too bad we're not in Pompeii," I said slowly.

Then the entire group exploded in a babble of suggestions, C3's full-throated voice riding over the hubbub. "I know somebody who could get me some mummy tissue," she cried.

The rest of us fell silent at that.

"Let us first do the proper experiments with fresh hair," Hiroshi said at last. "With and without roots; determine the limits of sensitivity; decide what we are going to focus on when we have amplified enough of the DNA. Are we just going to stick to restriction fragment length polymorphism?"

"What terrible gobbledygook are you speaking, Hiroshi?"

"That's not important for the moment." I wanted to stop Diana from interrupting. "It's a method for establishing a type of super-market bar code."

"There is a problem with mitochondrial DNA," Hiroshi went on. "Max is right: it is more stable. But in contrast to nuclear DNA, the mitochondrial is only inherited from the mother."

"So?" Charlea demanded. "I don't see a problem."

"How do you differentiate among siblings from the same mother?"

"Who *cares* about that, Hiroshi? Surely there are a lot of situations where narrowing a sample down to a single family would be enormously useful."

"Hmph." Diana's monosyllabic interruption was audible across the room. "Back in New York, when I asked you to tell me what PCR might be good for, you almost jumped on me. But the minute one of *you* suggests a *practical* application"—she put enough emphasis on the word to make me wince—"the rest of you can't contain yourselves. But I still don't think you're really address-ing the issue: what if you succeed with all this PCR reading of hairy texts?"

Hiroshi shook his head. "It is too early for such a question. There is a Japanese saying, or maybe you also have it in English: 'When all you have is a hammer, everything looks like a nail.' PCR is quite a hammer—I am convinced of that. But when you first pick up a hammer, you must be careful not to hit your finger." He glanced around the table, traces of a smile playing around his lips. "Maybe Diana Skordylis is lucky that there are four people behind her. Before we decide which nail to hit, the finger is out of the way."

"When you first pick up a hammer," I echoed. "Quite a starting line for a Malaparte *renga*."

"Ah," Hiroshi said, a sharp bark of pleasure. "Who wants to be next?"

"Look also for the pliers."

Charlea said it so quickly that no one else had a chance.

"No." Sepp shook his head vigorously. "It must be something like 'then collect all the nails.'"

"You can't change the rules, Sepp." Hiroshi wagged his finger. "You have to follow Charlea. She was second."

"I have no use for pliers."

"Is that your new line, Sepp?"

"No." He glowered at Charlea. "This is my opinion. Not if the hammer is PCR."

"And do not lose your temper."

"That is not fair." Sepp looked hurt.

"That is my *renga* line." Hiroshi's face was a mask. "You need not take it personally. So what is your line?"

Sepp shook his head angrily. "None. There are times when the *renga* form does not work—in poetry or science. This is one of them."

So instead of hammer, pliers, or nails, we spent the following day with scissors, tape, and paper clips. But before I could use the Villa Malaparte's word processor to fuse the mangled structure that emerged from our efforts into something like a final form, we had to agree on a journal.

"*PNAS?*" On the face of it, Sepp's choice—the *Proceedings of the National Academy of Sciences*—was eminently reasonable. In our field, it was arguably also the most prestigious journal.

"Out of the question!" Charlea didn't even glance at Sepp. "Three of us," she pointed at Hiroshi and me, "are members of the Academy."

She was right, of course. Although anyone can (in theory, at least) publish in *PNAS*, contributions by authors who are not Academy members must be submitted by someone who is. Charlea, Hiroshi, and I were the only ones who could conceivably sponsor a manuscript by the unknown D. Skordylis—after all, as a nonperson, she didn't have any old boy (or old girl) network to help her out. But as hidden authors, we couldn't possibly take the risk of being implicated in her manuscript's submission. Charlea was right, but she could have been more diplomatic about Sepp not being a member. He looked grim.

"*Science* is the obvious choice," she continued. "Unless we get some jerk for a referee, this paper is bound to breeze through. And everybody reads *Science*."

"There's *Nature*," Sepp retorted. "I prefer *Nature*."

Charlea looked as if she were about to argue the point, but then she seemed to change her mind. "Let's vote and get it over with."

To my surprise, we split evenly, and on quasi-nationalistic grounds. Charlea and I chose *Science*—its editorial office is in Washington, and we'd published many of our most important articles in that journal. Sepp argued forcefully for the British journal *Nature*, claiming that not everything in science—money, postdocs, Nobel Prizes—had to end up in America. To my amazement, Hiroshi backed him.

"What the hell," grumbled Charlea. "Since Sepp had the first brainstorm, let's send it to *Nature*." The following day, crisp, laser-printed copies of "The Polymerase Chain Reaction: A New DNA Amplification Technique," by Diana Skordylis of the Renga Institute, and Jocelyn's paper, both assembled in *Nature*'s style, were stacked around the table waiting to receive our final blessing.

We spent the rest of the week in a kind of weary relief familiar to anyone who has finally consigned a manuscript to the mail, except that in this instance the envelope was still unstamped. We were not going to trust the Italian mail out of Capri. I promised to send it to London by Federal Express the day I got back to Princeton.

For the most part, we played tourist, taking numerous excursions, including the obligatory boat ride to the Blue Grotto and the hike to the Villa Jovis on Mount Tiberius on the eastern edge of the island. We visited Anacapri to look at the residence of the other famous local author, Axel Munthe, who had written his *Story of San Michele* there. Munthe's villa was jammed with tourists, and I suddenly felt supercilious, reflecting on the fiercely guarded privacy of our Villa Malaparte. Yet while we relaxed, the implications of PCR continued to grow. Every time one of us threw a new pebble into the pond, the ripples spread with alarming speed. The widest-reaching ones occurred when we took up the possibility of using PCR as a tool for detecting viruses that cause serious diseases.

"Hepatitis," one of us said.

"Herpes detection is more important."

"Epstein-Barr syndrome, cytomegalovirus, human papilloma in cervical carcinoma—"

"Stop," warned Hiroshi, "or we will get nowhere. I know how Sepp feels, but it is impossible to hammer down every nail. Or even just a few. There are hundreds of diseases for which PCR could be a diagnostic tool. Let us concentrate on one: if we can do something with just the AIDS virus, we will have hit a very big nail."

"Agreed." Charlea didn't even look around for confirmation. "HIV may well be the most dramatic example. But who is *us*, Hiroshi? Jocelyn can't do everything. I don't think she can even do all the work on the hair in Max's soup."

"Now that we have two manuscripts," Hiroshi offered, "we could send preprints to some people, enlist their participation. Whenever one develops a new technique, it needs to pass through some shakedown cruises in different labs. I know someone in Nagoya who could do a first-class job—"

"And how would we get Skordylis's name on that Japanese paper?" broke in Sepp.

"We would not," Hiroshi replied. "It would be like with Jocelyn. She is publishing alone—with an acknowledgment to Diana Skordylis for providing a preprint of her work."

"Jocelyn is different."

"How?" I couldn't help asking. Did it have anything to do with the fact that Sepp had been sharing his personal troubles with Jocelyn?

"She is Diana's granddaughter. She is one of us. Except . . ." Sepp didn't finish the sentence. He just threw up his hands.

"But once Diana Skordylis's paper appears in *Nature*," Charlea said, "the genie will be out of the bottle. PCR will be fair game for everybody. It's not like the good old days in prewar Germany, when the *Herr Professors* used to write: 'I reserve this field for myself.'"

"What war are you talking about?" Sepp asked suspiciously.

"You pick the war," Charlea snapped back, "it makes no difference. Those days are gone forever."

"Sepp," Hiroshi tried to intervene. "Forget for a moment *who* will work on HIV. Let us concentrate on *what* should be done. One of the most important diagnostic contributions to the AIDS problem could be the analysis of the genetic diversity and evolution of HIV in infected individuals. PCR could be ideal for that."

"What about false positives?"

"Exactly," Hiroshi responded. "That is why more people should work on this problem. Sepp, if we have learned one thing, it is that there are already too many nails."

Breakfast at the Villa was a buffet spread in the small, wood-paneled room adjacent to the kitchen. This morning, having lain sleepless until well past midnight, I was the last to arrive. I was just putting honey on my roll when Diana walked up to whisper in my ear. "Tell the rest not to meet until ten. I've got to talk with Sepp."

Her voice held such a note of urgency that I turned around, but she was already on the way out. Later, as I got up to leave, through the door I saw Diana and Sepp on the small outdoor patio. The sun shone brightly, but for once D_3, in T-shirt and slacks, stood with her bare arms and unshaded face exposed to the ultraviolet rays. The two of them were too far away for me to hear their voices, but I could see Diana's hands grasping Sepp's stiffly held arms. Her back was toward me; my view of Sepp's face was occluded. But he was shaking his head.

We were all scheduled to depart on the late afternoon hydrofoil for the mainland. Before our departure, one final meeting was scheduled. Because this was to deal primarily with organizational matters, Diana joined us in the conference room. Sepp sat across from me at the table. His expression was grim.

"Sepp has something to say to you," Diana said in a strained voice. Her eyes were fixed on the manuscript in front of me as if she were attempting to burn holes in the paper.

Hiroshi, Charlea, and I exchanged glances. It was obvious that neither of them had had any advance warning.

"I have changed my mind," announced Sepp, lifting some pages into the air. "This cannot be published under the Skordylis **183** name. PCR is too good for that. I have never before had such an important idea, and I never will again. I want my name on it." Only now did he raise his eyes to gaze around the table. He must have seen the shock in our faces, because he continued quickly. "I do not mean alone. Hiroshi came up with the thermophilic bacterial DNA polymerase idea; and you Charlea, and Max . . ." he waved his hand in a manner that could be interpreted as dismissive or all-encompassing, depending on the observer's mood. "All four of us should be authors. But my name comes first." When I looked across the table, I saw that Sepp's fists were clenched and his lips a thin line. If it hadn't been for his deep suntan, his face might well have been the color of litmus when touched by acid.

I do not know how long the silence lasted—probably only seconds—but it seemed hours until I heard Hiroshi's voice. Had he not been sitting next to me, I wouldn't have recognized it. It was filled with cold anger.

"You are again changing the rules, Sepp. But this is not a *renga*. The Diana Skordylis authorship is the rule of the Renga Institute. We all agreed on that before we joined."

Charlea rose from her chair. "If any man ever has the gall to talk in my presence about raging hormones in women, I'll tell him what happened in Capri." She glanced back at Hiroshi before stepping out of the salon. " 'Kaputt at Malaparte'—that's what you can call your poem about old men."

21

In the semidarkness I couldn't tell who'd tapped me on the shoulder to give me the message. I held the slip of paper up to the wash of light from the slide projector: "*Call Jocelyn Powers,*" it said. "*Very urgent.*" Ducking my head to avoid the slide projector beam, I made my way to the pay phone in the foyer. It was 9:30 A.M. in La Jolla, halfway through the first morning talk of the T cell symposium.

She picked up on the first ring. "Have you heard from Professor Krzilska?" she asked. No preliminaries. She sounded anxious.

"I spoke to him briefly a week or two ago—" I started.

"No," she cut me off. "Has he called you today, or yesterday?"

"Why should he have called?" I was worried. After the Capri debacle we had agreed to a cooling-off period, and there were still five days of it remaining.

"I was just wondering." I decided Jocelyn sounded more unhappy than scared. "I'm really calling about something else."

"Let's hear it," I said, steeling myself for the worst.

"Have you seen the latest issue of *Nature?*"

"I don't know which one you mean." I was getting impatient.

"The one with the PCR papers," she said miserably.

"PCR?" I felt a constriction in my chest. "You mean somebody scooped us?"

"No. The one with the articles by Diana Skordylis and me."

It was one of those simple statements that refuses to register. "I don't get it," I said.

"I sent them to *Nature,*" she confessed. "After you returned from Italy."

"You?"

"My grandmother convinced me. She said as long as one of the papers was mine . . ."

"But—"

185

"You had all agreed on the final versions."

"Yes, yes," I said helplessly. "But what about Sepp? Did you check it out with him?" I could imagine Sepp's reaction. Ever since Capri I had been worrying about how to keep Sepp from bolting the group, how to keep my Bourbaki idea from vanishing just as it seemed within my grasp. And now this? I could imagine his reaction. I just couldn't imagine being the one to tell him. "Did he okay it?" I asked, knowing the answer already.

"No," she said. "But I consulted a psychoanalyst. Gran said I should."

The pay phone was in an open cubicle, only partly shielded from the sounds around the hall. Was there a hum in my head or was it the background noise from the people who'd just come out for the first break? "He's a Jungian," I heard her say.

"Goddamn it, Jocelyn," I snapped. "I don't care if he's a raving Reichian. How did a shrink get into the act? What's he got to do with PCR?"

"The shrink is Jakob Krzilska." Jocelyn's voice had turned severe. "Professor Krzilska's son. His *adopted* son." She said this as though it was supposed to mean something to me. All I knew was that I had a sudden urge to lie down. The crowd released from the symposium was surging around me now, and several of the closest seemed to be staring.

"I'll call you back from my hotel room," I said weakly. "After the morning session."

I don't remember the subjects of the other papers I heard that morning. All I know is that I was lucky that my own talk wasn't scheduled until the following day.

I called Jocelyn during lunch, and she told me the entire story. As I listened, silent as an analyst, recumbent as an analysand, I began to realize that she had known much more about Sepp than I'd ever suspected. Not only what had transpired in Capri— I wasn't surprised that D_3 had provided her with a synopsis—but about aspects of his personal life that I had only wondered about, idly, without ever bothering to investigate seriously. I remember noting blankly that the story cleared up the discrepancy between

Sepp's marriage date and his eldest son's age; amid a sea of uncertainties, it was a small island of comfort. But only a small one. The bottom line was that I had failed to understand what motivated Sepp. If only I had tried a little harder, perhaps I could have prevented the Capri disaster.

"How did you find all this out?" I finally managed to ask.

"Sepp told me."

"But how?" I asked, finding myself getting angry. "This isn't exactly a standard topic for after-dinner discourse."

"He wanted to talk."

What Sepp had wanted to talk about, it seemed, was his adopted son, Jakob. But the story hadn't ended there: her conversations with Sepp had been only the beginning. Jakob had called her, at his father's instigation, while attending a Jungian conference in Boston. They met in New York, and a month or two later, Jocelyn decided to spend a holiday in Austria. Their relationship had blossomed into something sufficiently close that even her grandmother knew about it. Why had D_3 not mentioned it to me? Was it only discretion, or did she suspect that I would have been bothered by Jocelyn's pipeline into the Krzilska family? I had known I was jealous about Jocelyn and Sepp—but had my jealousy been that obvious to others?

In any event, Jocelyn had telephoned Jakob as soon as she'd learned from D_3 about his father's sudden betrayal of our group enterprise at the Villa Malaparte. Jakob hadn't considered it strange; he had never thought that a serious scientist would be capable of launching a new ship under anything but the original banner. He recommended that Sepp—indeed, all four of us—be faced with a fait accompli. And Diana had concurred. So, without telling any of us, Jocelyn had sent the two manuscripts off to *Nature*.

"But I never thought that they would come out so soon," Jocelyn cried. "I just wanted to get the earliest possible receipt date in *Nature*—so we wouldn't get scooped," she added lamely.

So the priority virus has infected even this young graduate student, I thought with grim satisfaction. I suppose Jakob had been right. Faced with the accomplished fact, I saw no reason to complain. Indeed, expedited publication by *Nature*'s editor seemed to me the ultimate validation of PCR's importance.

"There were no comments by the referees," she continued. "Nothing: just a note from London that the manuscripts were accepted. I hadn't expected that. I thought there'd be the usual requests for revisions, that there'd be plenty of time for the four of you to discuss it. That it would help you come to an agreement."

"And your paper?" I said, because despite my pleasure with the result, I realized that I disapproved of the independence she'd shown. "If we hadn't agreed, what would you have done about that?"

There was a long pause. "I can't say."

Of course, Sepp's betrayal could not be undone. In one sense, Jocelyn's intervention had saved the Skordylis idea. Yet in another all was lost: the trust that such a project had required—the shared sacrifice of individual credit for the common good—was destroyed. No wonder the original Bourbakis had kept their personal research contributions to themselves, making Nicolas Bourbaki primarily an interpreter or teacher of mathematics rather than an inventor. Or, like Isadore Nabi, published solely as a contentious critic. It was in the act of creation that the ego found its raison d'être: it was *that* the self couldn't let go of.

The invented Diana lingered on. PCR not only kept Skordylis alive, it made her a spectacular success. Everybody seemed to come up with new applications, sometimes prompted just by a catchword. "How is the supermarket bar code business?" D_3 asked me one day.

For a moment, I drew a blank. "Bar code business?"

"Your hair research," she laughed. "At least that's how you described it in Capri."

"Jocelyn is working on it," I started. "She's doing fine." Then I stopped, because the term *bar code* had triggered a new chain of thought: Why not use PCR as a general bar code? Not in the supermarket. That would be technological overkill, but . . . "I've got to hang up now," I said abruptly. "I've got an urgent interruption."

How about DNA-laced ink to make important signatures unforgeable? I wondered. Or an industrial bar code to trace the origin of a product? Charlea had already pointed out the stunning information-carrying capacity of DNA sequences: a hundred base pairs could give rise to billions of different sequences. Now that we had established the power of PCR, amplifying a hundred-base sequence was a cinch. How about labeling oil, explosives, industrial wastes—even money—with a tag of a double-stranded nucleic acid segment which could carry information on the producer, lot number, date of manufacture, and who knows what else in DNA language? Suppose oil were so labeled before a tanker was loaded? With PCR, it would be easy to identify the source of an oil spill by amplifying the DNA tag and reading the code.

I blush to admit that for once, I didn't share this idea with anyone. Theoretically, I saw no reason why the idea shouldn't work. Practically, I realized that we still had a multitude of smaller experimental hurdles to overcome. Even our hair project had not yet been finished. I decided to file this idea away until the time was right. Initially, I rationalized my decision by telling myself that right now there were too many immediate problems to be solved; why complicate life by bringing up another? Moments later, I realized that I had been infected by the same virus as Sepp. I wanted this idea for my own.

It didn't take us long to discover the difficulties of coping with the avalanche of attention that rained down on Diana Skordylis via the Renga Institute's post office box. The next few months became an extended marionette play, with several pairs of hidden hands required to keep the act going.

The only *real* character in this drama was Jocelyn Powers. We had to be so careful to screen Diana Skordylis from the public that some of her reflected glory was bound to shine on Jocelyn. Most phone calls, as well as all correspondence, went straight through to her. The whole affair could easily have gone to her head, but she handled it admirably. Indeed, there were times when I felt she overdid the modesty: "*Miz* Powers," she insisted each time someone "Doctored" her. When her callers discovered that they were speaking to a second-year graduate student, Jocelyn acquired even more notoriety. I didn't even want to guess how she coped with the jealousy of her coworkers in the lab or the other students in the program. Finally, the attentions became so many, so distracting, I had to have a talk with her.

"You have to make yourself less available," I told her. "Answer queries on experimental procedures by mail—you can ask Jessica for help—but otherwise claim you're too busy working on your thesis. If you allow this much contact, sooner or later someone is going to catch on. We don't want the Skordylis identity known too soon."

"Why?"

"Well, you know . . ." My explanation started to peter out. I could have made up some reason about wanting to do more under the Skordylis name before the secret was out. But I didn't feel comfortable saying that. It would have felt like a lie. I doubt I would have been aware even of this much of my feelings were it not for something Diana had said to me a few days earlier. "You're going to have to talk about it sometime, you know." I had looked at her blankly, not really feigning my ignorance of what she was talking about. "The four of you," she explained, knowing that on some level I understood, but willing to explain it to me anyway. "You've never discussed what happened. By doing nothing, you're acting as though nothing happened. Like a married couple that refuses to face the impending breakup of the marriage, all the while keeping up a good front for their friends. I have no intention of acting as a marriage counselor," she'd added. At the time, I hadn't known what to say. Only when confronted with Jocelyn's question, and my own unwillingness to keep up the lie in front of her, did I start to realize that Diana was right. We *were* going to have to talk about it, sometime. Still, for the moment, things seemed to be going so well. As long as we didn't have to speak to each other, and Skordylis's fame continued to grow, it was possible to pretend D. Skordylis was still alive. It was so much easier than organizing the funeral.

But Diana wouldn't let it rest. One day she asked, "Aren't you mad at Sepp?"

I shrugged. "Back in Capri, I suppose I was, yes. Damned mad. But now?" I didn't know how to finish.

"What's different now?" Diana persisted.

"What's the point?"

"You mean, you don't see any point in stirring Sepp up again? You hope he's gotten over it?"

I won't say she made the question sound scornful. Only that, hearing it put that way, I could no longer keep up the pretense, even with myself.

"No," I said. "I mean we might as well accept an irreparable fact: Diana Skordylis is mortally wounded." And even as I put it into words, I was sure that unconsciously, Charlea, Hiroshi, and especially Sepp must feel the same way. "Under the circumstances, I suppose what we have to do is let the patient die with the least amount of pain. And make plans about the funeral."

Diana had moved closer to me on the couch. "At some stage, you would have had to do this anyway," she observed. "Even if nothing had happened in Italy, sooner or later you would have had to kill Diana Skordylis in order to reveal your identity."

I nodded, but there was no pleasure in acknowledging the fact. "That's true. But still," I said, looking up from my lap, "it would be nice to have a big funeral, wouldn't it?"

"The biggest possible. Viking style: flames and all."

I didn't laugh. "Then we've got to keep DS alive a bit longer," I said. "The longer we wait, the more evident it will be that PCR is a sensational invention. Only then should we undress Skordylis." Somehow, I felt that *undress* was more delicate than D₃'s *kill*. "And being mad at Sepp won't accomplish that."

Fortunately, the very nature of PCR helped draw immediate attention. In principle, not only the concept but the procedure as well were so simple that biomedical laboratories all over the world were able to utilize the technique almost overnight to solve a breathtaking range of problems. The two potential bottlenecks—an adequate supply of the DNA polymerase enzyme from *Thermus aquaticus* and the somewhat tedious but crucially important steps of template denaturation and primer annealing—were quickly broken by some industrial entrepreneurs. Seemingly overnight, advertisements appeared in the biomedical literature announcing the commercial availability of both the bacterial DNA polymerase and an instrument that did all the denaturing and annealing cycles automatically.

The most convincing evidence for the rapid acceptance of the PCR technique was not the number of reprint requests—you never know whether people just file them for future reference—but the number and diversity, geographic as well as topical, of *pre*prints of other people's papers dealing with applications of the PCR technique that came pouring into the Renga post office box. The mailing of preprints is almost always a compliment: an invitation to join an invisible, collegial circle of scientists. By sending preprints to two such obscure authors as Skordylis and Powers, the authors were bestowing the ultimate compliment: a disinterested one.

It was Charlea who urged that Sepp be kept informed of every significant piece of mail addressed to the Renga Institute.

"Primus inter pares—that's how we should treat Sepp," she advised. "If for nothing else than out of gratitude."

"Gratitude?" I brayed. "For heavens sake, for what?"

"He could have made asses out of all of us by complaining to *Nature*. But he didn't even complain to me. Did he call you?"

"No," I said, not wanting to disclose to her what I'd heard from Jocelyn: that Jakob had managed to convince his father that nothing would be gained by accusing any of us of having caused Diana Skordylis's meteoric appearance in the pages of *Nature*. To this day, I'm not certain whether Sepp accepted Jocelyn's sole responsibility for crushing his dreams of immortality.

Despite all our efforts, within three months, Diana Skordylis's correspondence had become so voluminous, and the number of

excuses sufficiently repetitive, that we decided on a drastic step:

on March 29, we planned to have Diana Skordylis enter an unnamed hospital for cancer treatment.

As I focused on the illness and eventual demise of Diana Skordylis, I realized that I was becoming progressively more interested in the living Diana. D_3 and I had made it a habit to meet at least once a week in New York for evenings, which frequently extended into overnight stays at her place, and even weekends. Thus it was only natural that I'd keep her up-to-date on some of the applications of PCR that were popping up all over the world.

I resisted the temptation to explain two clever extensions of our original approach that had been developed elsewhere: inverse PCR, in which the DNA amplification occurs outside, rather than within, the two primer sites; and anchored PCR, for studying genes that encode proteins for which partial sequences are already known. Instead, I stuck to some of the medical applications that had started to appear over the horizon: an exceedingly simple diagnosis for sickle-cell anemia and the rather startling results in the HIV area. According to a group from Northwestern University, the presence of the AIDS virus had been detected by means of PCR in high-risk individuals at least six months prior to a positive antibody test. But that was only the beginning.

"In AIDS patients, the immune system collapses even though some infected persons have only minute amounts of HIV in their blood—on the order of one in ten thousand blood cells," I related. "This has puzzled investigators, some of whom even argue that AIDS is not caused by the human immunodeficiency virus. But now," my index finger rose triumphantly skyward, propelled by vicarious authorial pride, "the Northwestern group, using PCR in conjunction with a fluorescent probe, has detected HIV genetic material in as many as one in ten blood cells. Another nail in the coffin of the HIV disbelievers."

"What a metaphor! And that's supposed to be good news?" She arched an eyebrow.

I was silent a moment, rearranging priorities. "We get carried away," I said. "No, it's never good news for the patient, I suppose. But isn't life itself a terminal disease, sexually transmitted?" Before she could critique that metaphor—for me a truism—I quickly added, "at the very least, such sensitive methods might lead to better screening of the blood supply. And even more important for the long run, investigators have now demonstrated by means of PCR that the HIV virus continues to replicate in the lymph nodes. Another—" I was about to say "nail" but caught myself "—missing piece in the AIDS puzzle that we need to solve before a logical therapeutic approach can be proposed."

"What about cancer? Any progress there?"

"That's almost certainly next. But there are so many different kinds . . ."

Another silence built between us. What was going on with her today? I had arrived so full of good news, and she wasn't having any of it. I felt like a foolishly cheerful comforter at a wake.

"But isn't it better to know?" I said finally. "At least then you can make plans . . ." I trailed off again, suddenly remembering that this might bring us back to the subject of our first conversation on Virgin Gorda. She sipped her tea, gave a slight shrug, and spread her fingertips, smoothing the tablecloth.

"So what else have your clever colleagues been doing with Diana's work?"

I started to regale her with an esoteric application that I'd just heard about, one that might appeal to Diana's sense of humor and her interest in erotica.

"Until quite recently, it was believed that well over 90 percent of all bird species are monogamous," I announced.

"You don't say."

"PCR looks like an extraordinarily sensitive and accurate method of establishing paternity."

"And?"

"And when this method was applied to fledgling birds still in their nests, it was discovered that at least 30 percent of them had a different father than the resident male. In other words, there is plenty of adultery—in fact, cuckoldry—among supposedly faithful, monogamous birds. And this is just the beginning; scientists are now starting to look at the question of true paternity in one species after another. Even providing unequivocal evidence for cleptogamy."

"Are historians supposed to know that word?"

"Maybe not French ones. A British biologist, John Maynard Smith, studying the sexual behavior of subdominant baboons came up with a polite word for 'sneaky fucking.'"

"Well, well," an approving wink sailed toward me, "even the prudish Princeton professor resorts to earthy language. Now enlighten me about 'sneaky fucking' . . . in baboons."

For once I didn't blush. Was that a sign that exposure to antique phallic objects had started to raise my sexual consciousness, which had been so dormant in recent years?

"Easy," I said. "The dominant baboon is so busy fighting all the time, that some of the subordinate males sneak in and quickly fuck a female." My goodness, I thought, Max Weiss is really proceeding down the slippery slope of four-letter terminology. "And now, we can prove all this with PCR."

"Good heavens!" she cried, pretending dismay. "Are you sure this research should be continued? Think of all the illusions it would destroy."

I decided to play along with her mockery. "Not all of them," I continued. "Let me tell you about a piece of cetological research by a British-Swiss team I just heard about."

"Cetological? Another four-letter derivative?"

"Five letters, and very respectable ones: from *cetus*, the whale." I was fully aware that I had moved into my lecturing mode, but this was too good to be missed. Besides, what's wrong with presenting some esoteric PCR tidbits that at the same time stop us from talking about Capri?

"Bill Amos from Cambridge just sent me a preprint about some fascinating PCR applications to the social structure of pilot whales, who swim in large groups, or pods, frequently exceeding one hundred individuals. A key aspect of their social organization is the cohesiveness of such pods, which can lead to mass strandings. Fishermen used to take advantage of this follow-the-leader behavior to herd such whales with boats. They still do this in the Faeroe Islands, and Amos and his Swiss colleagues got hold of skin and kidney tissues from many members of a pod and determined their genetic relatedness."

"And put a new lead in their pencil."

Was Diana mocking me? "What are you talking about?"

"PCR, of course."

"Of course," I echoed. "PCR analysis of those tissues showed that pod members form a single extended family."

"Does that surprise you? I would have expected it."

"Maybe so." She was interrupting me too much. "But what about their reproductive behavior? What would you expect?"

She barely hesitated. "Lots of inbreeding."

"That's where you're wrong. PCR analysis showed that the mature males in a pod were not the fathers of *any* of the fetuses found in the female whales! Apparently, these males mate when two or more pods meet or when they pay short visits to other pods—something that would be extremely difficult to prove by just simple observation."

"I *am* impressed." Diana sounded as if she meant it.

Why not go on? I thought. "And then take bear shit," I said, mustering all of the offhandedness in my professorial repertoire.

"I beg your pardon?"

Gotcha, I triumphed silently. "Bear droppings. Of brown bears in northern Italy."

Diana's facial expression seemed to imply "go on," but she didn't say it.

"The European brown bears of northern Italy, like their Pyrenean cousins, are on the decline, and the Italians are think-ing of introducing some of the more common Balkan bears." Like any honest scientist, I cited my sources; I didn't want her to think I was bragging about cetan or ursine esoterica: "A group of zoolo-gists from Munich reported that they used PCR analysis of bear droppings to study the genetic variation of this dwindling bear species without having to catch or even disturb the animals."

This seemed to do it. D_3 raised a policeman's palm to stop any further PCR verbal traffic. "Enough for today about PCR. Let's talk about something else."

"All right," I said, and my voice revealed a frustration I hadn't known I was feeling. "What *should* I talk about."

She gave me a look I realized I'd been getting from her lately:

a little sad, a little—disappointed? I couldn't read it. "What do you think?" she said.

"I think you mean Skordylis," I said. She nodded.

"All right. We're removing her from circulation."

Why had I put it so bluntly? I didn't know; but if I had expected her to be shocked, it was I who was surprised. She only nodded, this time with simple approval, as if I had suggested we turn on the lamp. The room was growing dim.

"We can't keep inventing excuses," I said, sounding as though I was inventing excuses. "We need something unambiguous."

"Such as?"

"Cancer," I said.

"Max!" She exclaimed, and now I did seem to have upset her. "Why does she have to get cancer? Why not shingles, a heart bypass, a serious traffic accident—"

"Stop, Diana," I calmed her. "Her cancer doesn't necessarily have to be fatal. Just extensive chemotherapy or radiation. Enough to take her out of circulation. She doesn't have to die."

When I finished, she put both hands on mine and held them there. "It's not her dying that I mind, Max, or that eventually you'll be killing her—even though you named her after me. I've known it was necessary even longer than you." She stopped and looked away, into the dim recesses of the room. "It's not the death I mind. It's how it's done."

She was still for another moment, and then, with a visible straightening of her spine, she recovered herself.

"The idea," she said at last, "was what really attracted me. *She* was amusing, but less important." Her eyes rose to meet mine. "Have you and Sepp ever discussed what transpired at Capri?"

"Not really," I replied. "Authorship, meaning credit, is probably the most difficult subject to discuss in science—at least among equals."

"Strange," she murmured partly to herself. "I understand Sepp least. I suppose he craved personal recognition more than any of you, having worked all his life in an academic backwater. Hiroshi already had his emperor's vase, so he seemed to be taken more by indulging in a form of scientific Kabuki."

"And Charlea?" I ventured.

"Ah, Charlea," she continued in the same murmur, "the most complicated of all of you. I think she more than any of you really wanted to test the limits of scientific collaboration." But then she continued in a louder voice. "Let me confess something, Max. On more than one occasion I wanted to tell you that I didn't think the Skordylis idea would make it. Now don't say anything," her hand moved back to cover mine, warmly and protectively, "just listen. The idea of offering your most precious asset, your brain, to a collective seemed to me touchingly important. But each of you had a secondary motive. You were honest about yours: revenge."

"True," I admitted, "but it had started to change."

"Perhaps," Diana conceded, "but even so, as I got to know the four of you, I was struck that competitiveness was always the undercurrent, even when you were most collegial. I am beginning to think that this is the nature of the scientific animus. Actually, I found it fascinating to watch you four: you never bored me, and I learned a great deal."

"In your own way, Diana, you're also quite a teacher." I suddenly had the feeling that we were saying good-bye to each other. I didn't like it.

"I'm not so sure whether your colleagues feel that way. But then, I knew you first. The others I always saw in relation to Diana Skordylis."

I started to say something; she rode over it. "But deep down, Max, I never thought that it would work."

"And why didn't *you* tell me that earlier?"

"Because I didn't want to discourage you. And I didn't believe it would end so soon—perhaps I didn't imagine you people would come up with such an important project so quickly. I thought great science takes much longer."

"It almost always does; or else somebody beats you to it."

"Ah, you see: it's your competitive streak again." This time, her laugh was unclouded.

I shook my head. "I didn't mean it that way. There are cocks who think that if they didn't crow, the sun wouldn't rise. Most scientific cocks know that the sun will rise; that the discovery will be made. If not by them, then by others.

"But how did you think *it* would end?" I started to feel that we were using this impersonal two-letter word the way shy people do when they talk about sex.

Diana glanced at me out of the corner of her eye. "I imagined that once you had made your great discovery, published it under your secret name, and saw your peers rave about the work—more or less the way people seem to be doing now—you'd pick some big public event and explode the myth."

"And how did you think we would set off the explosion?" I couldn't help but grimace at that metaphor, thinking about what Sepp had done at the Villa Malaparte.

"You tell me."

In the end, nobody had to decide on Diana Skordylis's fate. PCR did it for us. Fate made its appearance on September 2 in the form of a slightly peeved telephone call to Jocelyn, who had just returned from another holiday in Austria. She told me later that she had barely glanced at the pile of accumulated correspondence, let alone opened it, when the telephone rang in the lab.

"Dr. Powers," a voice said, not even giving Jocelyn the opportunity for her usual "Miz Powers" correction, "we have had no response from you or Dr. Skordylis to our letters of two weeks ago. Does that mean you are not accepting the Levenson Prize?"

"The Levenson Prize?" Jocelyn had never heard of it. Fortunately, the question was received at the other end of the telephone line as a sign of pleased surprise rather than of total ignorance. "What letter?" Jocelyn continued, "I've just come back from vacation."

"I see." The irritation level had dropped noticeably. "But Dr. Skordylis? We have written to her at the Renga Institute—"

"I believe she's been in the hospital." By now, Jocelyn had become an expert at providing alibis for DS's unavailability. "Could you tell me what was in the letter?" Jocelyn had been shuffling through the mail with one hand; she'd found the envelope from the Levenson Foundation and managed to tear it open without dropping the receiver. She read the letter while hearing a more flowery version over the phone.

No one would have had to explain to me what the Levenson Prize stood for. But while I have received my share of awards over the years, the Levenson has never been one of them. It doesn't carry a lot of money—even less than the miserly Japan Academy Prize. Nor is the medal solid gold; but its prestige is very much worth its weight in gold—like the Pulitzer Prizes, which are also given by Columbia University. The Levenson is supposed to recognize the past year's most important achievement in the biomedical sciences. Rather than taking the easy way out—anointing a widely recognized scientific coup, already slick with the oil of earlier blessings—the Levenson board takes pride in searching for the newest work. At times, this leads to recognizing scientific fireworks: spectacular flashes followed by total oblivion. But such fiascoes are easily forgotten. Remembered are the Levenson triumphs, by now quite a number, when the Foundation was first to publicly honor a new piece of research that subsequently garnered most of the famous prizes, all the way to the Nobel itself.

The Foundation never solicits nominations. Rather, to operate with the least delay, a large, anonymous panel meets in mid-August for two days in plush secrecy on the Levenson estate in Westchester County to pick the winner and an alternate. I would love to have been a fly on the wall of their meeting room to learn who'd first brought up PCR.

After Diana and I had congratulated ourselves over the phone, she was silent for a moment. When she spoke again, it sounded as though the subject had changed. "Can you have dinner with me this evening, maybe even stay overnight? I have a plan."

The plan, I learned that evening, was the answer to our question about immolating Skordylis. The Levenson Prize, Diana felt, offered an opportunity—and an ethical imperative.

"You people can't turn the Levenson down, because Jocelyn would then also have to refuse it. Or do you think she doesn't deserve it? That she is too young?"

"No, no," I assured her. "She certainly deserves it. Besides, the way she's handled herself so far suggests that she won't be spoiled by it." I wish somebody had spoiled me that way in my twenties, I wanted to add, but didn't.

"I am delighted to hear you say so. Because I'm sure Harold doesn't realize that Jocelyn is my granddaughter."

"Harold?"

"Harold Levenson, the chairman of their board, a Columbia Law School alumnus and former senior partner in my husband Alex's law firm. Max, I don't know how you want to handle this affair, but you four can't possibly show up at the award dinner in November and claim you're Diana Skordylis. *That* simply won't do."

"Of course not," I answered automatically. But deep down I asked myself: Why not? Still, I had no idea what the other three actually wanted to do. Faxes had gone out earlier in the day to Hiroshi, Sepp, and Charlea. C₃ had already left a pithy message on my answering machine: "That ought to be fun." I had no idea what "that" she had in mind, but my own thoughts had already been running in several interesting directions.

"Here is *my* proposal," Diana said in a tone to which I had learned to pay attention. I had a feeling that this was the manner in which she might have introduced a major faculty reorganization at NYU. "Have Jessica write an acceptance letter on behalf of Diana Skordylis, who is still convalescing from her cancer surgery. Jessica will be faintly optimistic that DS will be well enough to attend, but if doctors should advise against it, a surrogate will appear to accept the award for her. Jocelyn, of course, will write that she will be there in person. Needless to say, on the day of the dinner, Dr. Skordylis will still be too weak to attend. Her surrogate will say a few words on her behalf, perhaps even make

201

a short speech." A contented smile shone at me. "What do you think of my suggestion?"

"Sounds reasonable. But who should that *one* surrogate be?"

"Don't you think it should be a woman?"

"Probably," I agreed, although I didn't really know why the surrogate ought to be a woman. "You mean Charlea?"

Diana shook her head. "Impossible. If she didn't admit on the spot that the whole thing was a hoax, she'd be guilty of bad faith, at least."

"Who, then?"

Diana curled her lip—faintly, but nevertheless recognizably. "Considering that half the award should really be credited to a 250-year old woman, shouldn't it be someone fairly mature?"

I clapped myself on the head. "My God," I blurted, pointing at her, "I'm an idiot. Of course you're right. Who else?"

She made a modest bow. "But it would be tragic—no, I would say criminal," I reminded her, "if we four couldn't attend the award ceremony. And those events aren't exactly open houses."

She raised a beneficent hand. "I've been working on that. It won't be easy. But Jocelyn's already found out that the formal dinner will be at the Plaza. Aside from Columbia people and family, I understand they invite mostly scientific big shots from around New York. 'Maybe as far north as Yale, and down to Princeton, or perhaps Penn,' Jocelyn said. She thinks that might be extended to include you—"

I didn't rise to the bait. "Jocelyn could always bring me as a guest—after all I'm her professor. Maybe even Charlea—as a friend from Chicago. But how many guests can she bring?" I worried. "They'd probably wonder. Especially when they saw Hiroshi, whom many would recognize. I'm afraid somebody might figure it out."

"I hadn't thought of that," she said. "I'd been thinking we'd get half of you in as Skordylis's guests, half as Jocelyn's." She lapsed into thought for a moment, then brightened. "I know," she said happily. "We'll have somebody videotape the proceedings, ostensibly for Diana Skordylis. Afterward, we'll all meet at my apartment and watch it on my VCR." She gave me a preposterously salacious nudge. "Tape's almost as good as the real thing, Max."

"Why Diana!" Was I blushing? From the way she laughed, I suppose I must have been. And after that, there was no way I could suggest an alternate plan. A recording it would have to be. Still, I was reassured to think there would be a small crowd gathered in front of the TV.

In the end, though, only four of us watched the proceedings on the TV screen: Charlea and I, Jocelyn, and D_3. Hiroshi had sent his regrets: he had a previous engagement, speaking to a binational poetry conference at the East-West Center in Honolulu.

"I can see where your priorities are moving to, Hiroshi," I had kidded him. Actually, I understood: this was his first professional appearance as a poet before a new species of academic peers—a group of American and Japanese literati. Watching a recording of yet another scientific award ceremony, only one-fourth of which was meant for him, and that anonymously, was no real competition for his first appearance on the academic poetry circuit. He could always enjoy his portion of the Levenson Prize at home on videotape.

Sepp's absence was another matter. He hadn't been to the States since the Capri affair, and all our communications since then had been limited almost painfully to technical matters associated with PCR. The Levenson celebration could have been the right opportunity to clear the air, to convert Malaparte into Bonaparte. I don't know whether I would have confessed it openly, or even to myself, but I was beginning to feel more and more sympathy with Sepp. During the past few weeks I had been pursuing with increasing excitement the possibility of industrial bar coding with PCR—a development of such potential that for the time being I was not prepared to share the idea with anyone else.

But Sepp had turned us down—in a letter mailed to D_3.

"Most scientific discoveries eventually turn either into the permanent brick and mortar of an ever-expanding edifice, or they become rubble. But every once in a while, the scientific building is not just

an accumulation of bricks, but features some distinctive, separate component: functional as well as beautiful, like a great column. My past work has mostly been scientific brick and mortar—very little rubble. But late in my life, I came up with a radically new concept, PCR—a column that someday will sustain a great edifice. I do not want to be a participant at a public homage to this breakthrough, with the originator present and yet unrecognized. I want to be honest with you: it hurts too much."

"Max, you've got to talk to Sepp," Diana had said after she'd read the letter to me over the phone. "In person. He was the first to join your group, and when it comes to PCR, he . . ."

She didn't have to finish the sentence; I could have finished it for her. Five days later, I rang the bell at Aspernbrückengasse No. 5, a turn-of-the-century apartment building at the foot of the Aspernbrücke—the bridge crossing the Danube Canal at the juncture of the fashionable First District and the Second District, in pre-Anschluss days the predominantly Jewish quarter of Vienna. Dr. Jakob Krzilska, whose combined office and personal residence were located on the first floor, offered these and other historical facts (Sigmund Freud had attended the neighborhood Gymnasium; Elias Canetti had lived around the corner on Ferdinandstrasse); the list went on as we made small talk while waiting for his father, because Sepp had insisted on meeting me in Vienna. "Not in Innsbruck," he'd said when I telephoned that I was coming to complete an unfinished conversation.

I didn't have to explain. "Such conversations are best held in a *Klapsdoktor*'s place, especially if he is your son and already knows most of the facts. Remember? I told you in New York that a *Klapsdoktor* is what you call a shrink. Besides, I have to show you something fantastic"—he pronounced the word as if it ended in three *k*'s. "You can only see it in Vienna. If I am lucky, this may be the most sensational application of PCR."

The use of the first-person singular didn't escape me, but this time I didn't mind. I understood, and I had come to Vienna to say that to Sepp. And this time we didn't stall by dancing a conversational minuet. The moment we sat down in an alcove of the high-ceilinged living room—Sepp with his back to the window so that I could look past him across the Aspernbrücke to the curve of the Ring, Vienna's most famous street—he started.

"My son tells me that people are most credulous when they are happy. If that is true, Max, you agree the reverse must also be true?"

I grunted an affirmative, which seemed sufficient fuel for Sepp to proceed. "So you do understand how suspicious I was when the two papers appeared in *Nature*?"

"Sure," I said. "You have no idea how surprised *I* was when I first heard about it from Jocelyn."

"Tell me." He leaned forward. "You knew really nothing about it?"

"Nothing. Zero. Null." I even managed to make the word sound German, "nooll." "Given your apparent intimacy with Jocelyn, I am surprised you hadn't found out about it before me."

Sepp didn't seem to have noted the innuendo. "Jakob told me that it was his idea, but . . ."

"Sepp." I touched his hand in the Diana manner, something I'd never done with him before. "Let's forget *Nature*. Let's talk about Capri. About our last day at the Villa Malaparte. I've been thinking—"

"So have I, Max," he interrupted. "And I thank you for coming here so we can speak." It was one of the warmest looks I'd ever seen on Sepp's face. It made me feel good that I'd followed Diana's advice to see him without further delay. "You were the common denominator in the Bourbaki-Skordylis equation. Let me talk about one of the numerators." He tapped his chest with his pointed index finger.

"But Sepp," I said, "when it comes to PCR, surely you're the denominator."

"Who knew that?" He almost growled. "You—with your National Medal of Science? Hiroshi—with his Imperial Prize? Who else? This was my last chance."

"What about Charlea?"

"Women are different." It sounded like an experimental observation, a non sequitur, really, rather than a response to my question.

"You mean women don't deserve major recognition?"

"No . . ." he wavered. "They do not crave it as much."

In mixed company, and especially if Charlea had been present, I might have demurred. But this was different. By remaining mute I acknowledged that my craving was just as fierce.

"Sepp." Again I found myself touching his hand, this time almost ethereally. "I understand. But think about it: The public doesn't know it yet, but Diana Skordylis is dead. If you hadn't killed her in the Villa Malaparte, another one of us would have done so eventually."

"Meaning you?"

I nodded. "Doing science solely for science's sake is the ideal. But if you use the overworked analogy to mountain climbing, how many first-time climbers of an Everest or an Annapurna— claiming they are heading for the top solely because it's there— are willing to descend quietly, without leaving a flag behind or announcing their success to the world?"

"And what about doing science for the sake of revenge?"

I was taken aback by how this one question had suddenly reversed our respective roles. Subconsciously, I found myself moving forward in my seat, my weight on my toes as if I were poised for flight. "It doesn't work, does it? One's ego gets in the way."

"That is what Jakob said after Jocelyn talked to him. '*Renga*-style research doesn't suit big egos.' Yet he thought that the intrinsic idea of another Bourbaki-style enterprise was so attractive— on the face of it, so idealistic—that the bubble should not be punctured just as it was ready to float into the air." With one palm open, Sepp gingerly launched an imaginary balloon. "That's why he told Jocelyn to send it off quickly."

"How did you respond when you learned about your son's advice? Or did you consider it treachery?" I had been curious to know ever since Jocelyn had told me about Jakob's role.

"I was furious, but eventually Jakob calmed me down. It's useful to have a *Klapsdoktor* in the house." Sepp had risen and walked over to the window, as if he wanted to check whether the Danube was still flowing. "You know what he told me?" His back was still turned toward me. "That four scientific egos won't be able to keep such a secret for long. But that considering what had happened in Capri, I should not be the one to break that secret in public."

"Nobody has disclosed Skordylis's identity so far," I said quickly.

"I told this to my son when I heard you were coming to Vienna." Sepp turned around. "You know what he said? 'Be patient, Papa. Sei geduldig.'"

"And?"

Sepp stood in front of me, looking down. "I shall wait."

"My father often seems to argue like a person who takes a plane apart and after pointing to each component as being heavier than air, asks you to rationalize how it could possibly fly. After you hem and haw for a while, he then explains why planes fly, and in such detail that you beg him for just the nuts and bolts without getting the thread's diameter to the fourth decimal place."

I looked quickly at Sepp, but he just laughed. "Just look at the *Herr Doktor*. No respect for his father. It was different when he was younger. When both of us were younger." He played with the last dollop of whipped cream that remained from his dessert, moving it with his fork from one side of the plate to the other. "But there are advantages to having a *Herr Doktor* in the family." He tapped his head. "I can tell him my troubles. When you are alone after so many years of marriage, a good *Mann-zu-Mann* talk is excellent medicine. I recommend it for melancholy, loneliness, even boredom. What about you, Max?" He pointed the cream-smeared fork at me. "You are living alone. Any *Mann-zu-Mann*—"

"Not really," I said quickly. "At least not of this sort."

Across the table from me, Jakob Krzilska had been slouching in silence for the past few minutes, his head moving in unison with our verbal Ping-Pong. "What about *Mann-zu-Frau*— man-to-woman?" As he spoke, he gradually straightened as if he wanted to reduce the distance between us. Now he was almost **207** leaning toward me. "Jocelyn tells me you are seeing quite a bit of her grandmother."

So they'd been talking about me! Jocelyn and Jakob. Jakob and Sepp. Or maybe all three? "A bit," I said.

"She admires you," Jakob continued.

"Diana?" I asked, sensing my damned blush.

"Perhaps she does," laughed Jakob. "But I meant the grand-daughter. Jocelyn thinks you are good for her grandmother. What about the other way around? What does Dr. Doyle-Ditmus mean to you?"

Wait a minute, I wanted to say. What's going on here? Is this the shrink taking over? Or Jocelyn's boyfriend? Or does one call a man who is almost twenty years older a paramour?

The mind doctor must have been a mind reader. "You may wonder what right I have to ask such a question. In spite of what my father says about me," he pointed to Sepp, "I don't always act like a psychoanalyst. In some way, Jocelyn's current relation-ship with her grandmother is not unlike that of us here." Again he gestured toward his father. "I meant your relationship with Dr. Doyle-Ditmus. It started with a scientific venture, but this is rapidly coming to a close. What now?" His eyes remained fixed on mine. "I have met Jocelyn's grandmother only once [*now when was that?*], but I feel that through Jocelyn I have come to understand her fairly well. She sees much more in you than just a scientist."

I knew exactly what was coming next: What did I see in D₃? But Jakob Krzilska, the Jungian psychoanalyst, surprised me.

"What do *you* see in yourself?"

It's a question no one had ever asked me in so many words. How come even I have not asked myself that? What insight does Diana have into a Max Weiss I do not know? Why am I so reluc-tant to ask such questions? Am I a typical workaholic scientist, unable to peel away any but the outermost layer of his onion? Or am I afraid that, like an onion, if I continue peeling, nothing will be left?

I pushed my chair back from the table. "It's too late to answer such a complicated question." Was I referring to the time of day
or life?

Jakob rose and patted his father on the shoulder. "I will drive Professor Weiss to his hotel."

Sepp raised his hand. "Wait, Max. Just one more question. The one Jakob asked me when he heard you were coming. The one I thought Jakob meant when he asked about the conclusion."

Jakob moved back toward his chair, but instead of sitting down, he remained standing, his hands on the chair's back. Like a preacher. Or was it a judge?

"Your initial meeting with Dr. Doyle-Ditmus started everything: your noble Skordylis experiment [*did I hear him pronounce the word as Nobel?*], my father's PCR idea [*the loyal son speaking!*], my connection with Jocelyn [*connection? What an all-encompassing diplomatic term!*]. But what now?"

"You mean the Renga Institute?" I shrugged my shoulders. "That dies with Skordylis."

"I did not mean your scientific collaboration. Your purpose all along was to explode the Skordylis myth in public, once a great discovery was made. My father just lit the fuse prematurely."

"And Jocelyn?" I couldn't help asking.

"She delayed the major explosion by setting off a smaller bomb."

"And when will the big one go off?" Sepp, his expression suddenly unreadable, had addressed the question to his son.

"That was the question I was addressing to Professor Weiss."

I was struck by Jakob Krzilska's mixture of formality and intrusive intimacy. Asking *Professor Weiss* about his feelings for *Dr. Doyle-Ditmus*. "Certainly not at the Levenson shindig," I replied.

"I am glad to hear you say that." Suddenly, he sounded like Sepp's son rather than the professional analyst.

"Oh?"

"I would not like Jocelyn's recognition to be too diluted."

"Don't worry. Jocelyn's grandmother seems to have everything under control."

"And what about the next award?"

"What next award?" I asked.

"If PCR is as important as I hear from my father; and especially if his latest idea—"

"Jakob!" Sepp's voice was loud, rather than angry. "I have not yet told Max—"

"*Entschuldigung*, Papa. Please go ahead."

"Tomorrow," said Sepp. "It is getting late for Max's physiological clock."

"Of course," said Jakob. "I just meant that Diana Skordylis, alone or with Jocelyn, will surely receive some other public recognitions. What then?"

I felt relief at the direction the conversation was turning. "Frankly, we have been so busy keeping Diana Skordylis incommunicado that we haven't given that topic any thought."

"Really?" Jakob's eyebrows had risen. "I am surprised."

Of course *I* had fantasized about the topic. In fact, I'd hate to admit how often and how grandiosely. But these were private fantasies, and I was not Dr. Krzilska's analysand. "As a group, we haven't. Not so far, anyway."

"In that case, you and my father have another good subject for tomorrow: speculate about the right award for the big bomb."

It had been a lousy night. Was it the lumpy mattress of the Hotel Wandl—a marvelously situated but otherwise fairly crummy small establishment in the center of the First District, just off the Graben—or was it last night's inquisition? By contrast, Sepp was all cheer when he arrived to pick me up.

"*Wien im Herbst*—Vienna in the autumn. You picked the best time, Max. And this hotel has quite a history."

And so does my mattress, I wanted to add. But it would have been churlish to say so. "They have great coffee for breakfast," I volunteered instead.

"So do most Viennese hotels. But do you know who used *this* hotel? Arthur Schnitzler and Hugo von Hofmannsthal put up their guests here." Sepp looked positively beatific as he pronounced the names of these Viennese fin de siècle luminaries.

"You don't say. Do I even deserve to stay at the Wandl?"

"Who knows? If the big PCR bomb goes off, they may even cite you as one of their former guests. But enough of this banter." He put his arm momentarily around my shoulder—another gesture of intimacy I'd never before experienced from Sepp. "I have a surprise for you. Come, we shall walk there. Good exercise." He patted his firm belly. "And you can use some, Max." He threw an accusatory glance at my minute paunch, which produced my usual reflex: I drew in my stomach.

I rather enjoyed the stroll, and especially Sepp's pride in his role as Viennese tourist guide. For the first time in our long acquaintance we were on his home territory. Coming out of the hotel, we passed the Peterskirche on the way to the Graben. "See this monument?" Sepp remarked. "The Pestsäule, commemorating Vienna's deliverance from the plague in the Middle Ages. Everything bad eventually passes—even our psychic plagues." We turned left on the Kohlmarkt until we reached the Hofburg, the Imperial Palace. As we entered the covered entrance off the lovely Michaelerplatz and proceeded through one courtyard after another, Sepp gave me a running architectural-historical commentary on the Austro-Hungarian Empire. This prompted me to tell him of my Hungarian Jewish ancestry—a topic we'd never broached before.

"So we have something else in common," said Sepp. "Products of Franz Josef's empire."

I dismissed the emperor with some snide remark about a historical dinosaur, but the words propelled us into the present.

"Dinosaurs! I might as well tell you where we are going. No sense in being mysterious about it. As soon as we get to the other side of the palace and through the Heldenplatz, we shall be on the Burg Ring. Once we cross it, you will see another relic of our dinosaurian past: the statue of Empress Maria Theresa, flanked by our two biggest museums. Most tourists head for the one on the left with all the art. I am taking you to the Museum of Natural History."

"To show me the local dinosaurs."

My banter elicited an unexpected surprise. "In a way, yes. Just wait and see."

We headed up the stairs through the main entrance and then down into the basement. Looking at the low ceiling and the narrow corridor, I wondered which dinosaurs we'd be examining, and why. Sepp pointed to a closed door, labeled simply *Privatdozent Dr. Ignaz Bär.*

"One of my former students from Innsbruck, now head of the small paleoentomology laboratory in the museum." His hand rested on the doorknob. "And as of three weeks ago, the owner of the most precious piece of amber imaginable."

I waited for more, but that was it, until I found myself sitting at a small table, a bright light shining at a few pieces of amber— each in its own Plexiglas container.

"Bär is out of town," said Sepp, "which is just as well, because I wanted to tell you this story personally. These pieces were found in a Tyrolean deposit from the Mesozoic era."

He eyed me as if he were expecting some comment, but what could I say? "Interesting"? What little I'd learned about paleontology in college had fallen between the dimmest cracks of my memory. I didn't even remember what periods the Mesozoic era encompassed. Besides, to me the pieces of amber looked fairly pedestrian; they were not even completely clear. I doubted whether any jeweler would have bothered mounting any of them. I kept staring at them, saying nothing.

"You know, of course, that the Mesozoic blankets the Cretaceous and Jurassic periods."

I nodded noncommittally, which kept me from being a liar or a paleontological nincompoop.

"That makes these pieces rare, but certainly not unique. These here, however," Sepp made an all-inclusive gesture, "are over 150 *million* years old, which places them right in the Jurassic period."

"Dinosaurs," I said. Sepp ignored my interruption. He was speaking faster now. I could see that something else was coming.

"These specimens were sent here because microscopic studies in a broken one indicated that some insects are embedded in them. Bär concluded tentatively that they are mosquitoes, but he wanted to characterize them taxonomically. Electron microscopy suggested the presence of intact mitochondria."

A slight blip appeared on my personal radar. "Go on," I said, thinking of the hair in my soup.

"Bär has forgotten most of the biochemistry he learned from me, because years ago he moved into entomology. But he knows whom to call for information." Sepp grinned with evident satisfaction. " 'Professor Krzilska,' he said, 'entomologically speaking, these are the rarest pieces of amber in existence.' 'Of course,' I replied, 'after all they come from Tyrol.' He did not even smile. 'If we destroy the amber and remove the insect—an act for which I would probably be crucified by most paleontologists—could we get enough undecomposed DNA to carry out some genetic analysis to determine this specimen's relation to contemporary mosquitoes?' "

By now I realized what Sepp was driving at, but I couldn't halt his nonstop verbal train. "I told him what you and I know perfectly well: that mitochondrial DNA is more stable and that it is propagated through the maternal line; and that I had heard of a method that might aid in the generation of enough DNA for genetic studies, provided even a trace of undecomposed DNA is present. In other words, I told him to take a hammer and crack open the pieces of amber." He chuckled. "I am sorry I lost my temper over Hiroshi's hammer *renga*. It would have made a good line."

"Are you the same Malaparte Krzilska from last year?" I asked. "You certainly are in a different mood."

"The same and not the same. Ask Jakob. But to continue: You know I have no more laboratory in Innsbruck. But when Jocelyn was here in Vienna—to see Jakob, not me—I asked whether she would give me a few hours of her precious time."

I looked away from Sepp at the small piece of amber, the one he had moved forward, the one containing a Jurassic mosquito. Jealousy is first reflected in one's eyes, and if it was about to break out, I didn't want Sepp to notice.

"I conceived PCR, but I have never done a PCR amplification with my own hands. I had to go to our disciple, Jocelyn, for practical guidance. I took her to the Biochemistry Institute of the

University of Vienna, where another of my former students had agreed to collaborate with me and Bär on what I described as just a little problem. Jocelyn gave him a crash course in practical PCR. He is now examining ordinary mosquito DNA, but as soon as he is sure of his technique, Bär will crack open this amber jewel in front of us. This may test the limits of PCR, but—"

I cut him short. "Did you tell anyone what you were going to do?"

"Only Jakob." Sepp's glance shifted from my eyes to the amber piece.

"Not even Jocelyn?"

"No."

"Why?"

"Because there is something else I want to try."

Only then did his look depart from his amber jewel. He scrutinized me with crafty innocence. I was dying to know, and I could tell that he wanted me to ask. But I wanted him to volunteer the information without my prompting. It was my turn to stare at the amber.

I don't know how much time elapsed. Probably only seconds. "Mosquitoes feed on blood," he said slowly. "If PCR picks up a few molecules of undecomposed DNA from a Jurassic mosquito and manages to amplify them for appropriate sequencing, why—"

"Shouldn't this work also on the DNA from the blood of the animal bitten by the mosquito?" I finished the sentence for him. "And then?"

"Publish it in *Nature*. I have already picked the title: 'PCR Amplification and Sequencing of DNA from a 150-Million-Year-Old Dinosaur.' You do understand, Max, don't you?"

I was about to answer, but I'd waited too long. Sepp was too agitated.

"There have already been dozens of papers on PCR. And we all know that a flood is about to come out during the next few months. What is the difference if *my* name appears on one of them?"

I pointed to the amber in front of us. In my mind, the image of the embedded mosquito had become so magnified that I seemed to see every morphological detail with my naked eye, even the drop of blood . . . "If it's dinosaur blood, it would create quite a sensation. Some crackpot might even suggest that on the basis of such DNA sequencing results, one of these days cloning of dinosaurs would become possible. Even make a movie about it."

He dismissed my comment, admittedly a gratuitously silly one, with a wave of his hand. "Surely you do not expect me to deal with such science fiction. But you do understand now why I have told only Jakob about this idea? Do you, Max?"

I didn't want him to plead for understanding. Not to me, of all people. "Yes, Sepp. I do understand." And then I proceeded to tell him about the possibility of PCR bar codes for explosives and other industrial commodities. "I haven't told this to anyone, Sepp," I concluded, "not even Diana."

"I understand, Max."

23

The evening of the ceremony, Charlea and I waited and waited for the others to return. Charlea read quietly in a corner; to me, each minute had acquired extra seconds, each hour extra minutes. I spent most of the interminable time pacing up and down Diana's living room. Finally Charlea told me to relax. "You're acting like this is your first award," she said caustically.

My mood had ripened into irritability. "I hope you don't mind my being sensitive—"

"Sensitive? You're touchy and a pain."

"I can't understand what's keeping them," I said, trying to settle myself into an easy chair.

"You know exactly what's keeping them. Jocelyn's staying to get the last possible bit of praise. God knows what Diana's up to." She looked nervously at the television set, as though it were somehow tuned in to the Plaza. "I suppose she's waiting for Jocelyn. But for heaven's sake, stop that pacing! It's been well demonstrated that subjective time increases for everyone within ten meters of a pacer."

"Really?" I said.

"You can look it up," she sniffed and returned to her book.

I spent an immeasurable period after that wondering how the control group in that study must have felt.

The two women finally arrived, at least an hour later than I'd expected them. Diana was wearing a high-necked black silk gown, whose severe lines set off her slender figure. She seemed to be in a mischievously mysterious mood.

"First, we need to open a bottle of champagne to toast my granddaughter," she hugged Jocelyn, "and only then will I let you and Charlea watch."

We had barely clinked our glasses when Charlea pointed to the screen with the remote control. The television sprang to life. "Quick, Diana: the tape. If Max doesn't see it soon, he's going to explode."

Diana produced the cassette and slid it into the machine; there was a tedious moment before the screen solidified, showing us a static view of a dais carrying the usual freight of seated dignitaries.

Harold Levenson was a distinguished, elderly gentleman, tall, white-maned—the Hollywood image of a judge. D_3 was sitting on his right, Jocelyn on his left. He stood at a lectern set up in the middle of the table, where he had apparently just finished introducing the other board members of the Levenson Foundation as well as a dismal of Columbia deans and provosts. Reading from notes obviously prepared for him by someone else, he gave a brief account of the importance of Jocelyn's work, ending with a nod at Jocelyn, who rose and accepted the chairman's outstretched hand, the diploma, and the medal. The two posed until the flashes stopped strobing. Jocelyn looked handsome and composed in a green satin pantsuit, the mannish jacket, worn without a blouse, providing more than a hint of décolleté. I thought I noted the wit of her grandmother in this outfit. "Green looks great on you, Joss," Charlea said. "You ought to wear it more often."

Suddenly, I remembered something Sepp had said to me in Vienna, claiming I didn't pay any attention to women: "I suppose you have never even noticed Jocelyn's buzzem."

"Not only green," I said now, "but also this jacket." Should I write Sepp that I had finally noticed Jocelyn's bosom?

Jocelyn, seated beside us in the same outfit, said a demure thank you. She seemed to have trouble taking her eyes from the screen.

So did I.

After a gently humorous introduction, focused primarily on the observation that Jocelyn was their first prizewinner without a doctorate, a condition that would be remedied in the near future, Levenson offered the microphone to Jocelyn. She spoke without notes.

"I have been warned by my colleagues at Princeton that your recognition of my work is likely to spoil me; that successful research usually takes much longer and proceeds along circuitous paths; and that luck, though helpful, does not strike that often. Nevertheless, I have decided to take my chances and to accept the Levenson Prize with deep gratitude and all the modesty I can presently muster." With a disarming smile, she bowed to the audience and sat down.

"Well done, don't you think?" I remarked without taking my eyes off the screen.

"She could have thanked her Ph.D. adviser."

I turned to look at Charlea. Was that a joke, or was she testing me? "That would have been unfair to the rest of you," I said. "I think Jocelyn handled it just right."

"Spoken like a true Skordylis," Diana said.

"Hush." Charlea raised a finger to her lips. "I want to hear what you had to say."

Harold Levenson took more time for the second part of the citation reading. "The Levenson Foundation has a tradition of recognizing and honoring seminal contributions—"

"Before the semen has even dried," guffawed Charlea.

Since DS's professional c.v. was remarkably meager, Levenson focused on the reasons for her absence. "However," his voice boomed over the loudspeaker, "I am particularly pleased that Dr. Diana Doyle-Ditmus, a distinguished former dean of humanities and sciences at New York University, is here to accept the award on behalf of Dr. Skordylis, because Dr. Ditmus is also the grandmother of our other awardee." Judging from the murmurs passing through the audience, it was clear that most had not known of that familial connection. "Diana," he bowed to D_3, "the floor is yours."

"Thank you, Harold," she replied crisply. "Ladies and gentlemen."

"Good for you, Diana," whispered Charlea.

"She hasn't said anything yet," I whispered back.

Charlea laughed. "You just don't get it, Max," she explained. "Calling a mature woman by her first name under such circumstances is patronizing. Calling him 'Harold' puts him in his place."

On the screen, Diana had started to speak. "I understand that most scientists are incapable of giving a talk without visual aids. Since I am here on behalf of Diana Skordylis, let me use at least one slide. In view of Dr. Skordylis's absence, and her relative obscurity up to now, it seemed to me appropriate to show you whom you are honoring tonight. Would you dim the lights, please?" As the lights went down, behind Diana a huge, blank screen grew bright.

"What on earth is going on here?" I turned toward Diana. "What is there to show?" She had a faintly smug smile on her face.

"My God!" exclaimed Charlea.

I looked back at the TV to see the screen filled by an extraordinary human image: a composite, a multiracial hermaphrodite. I had barely had time to gasp when Charlea's laugh exploded.

"Hiroshi Krzilska! Or is it Sepp Nishimura? And look at my legs!"

Charlea's chortles could barely be heard over the swelling cacophony rising out of the console speakers. It was a complicated sound, composed of laughter, catcalls, clapping, and unrecognizable words. At the head table, outrage had taken over. Diana acted as if she were oblivious of the commotion her slide had caused, until she looked down at Harold Levenson's scandalized expression. Her hand rose to signal silence.

"May I have the lights again?" For another second or two the Skordylis image loomed over the scene, then the lights came on and attention reverted to the dais.

As the image lingered on my retina I tried to understand just what Diana had done. She had somehow gotten hold of full-length photographs of Charlea, Sepp, Hiroshi, and me. Each had been cut into quarters: the left upper quadrant of Sepp's body and Hiroshi's right side; Charlea's and (I supposed) my legs. The resulting Eurasian face was virtually unrecognizable. I had never seen such frivolous height in C_3's shoes, nor had I ever noticed that her ankles—at least her right one—were so shapely. Even though Charlea's face had been discarded, her quarter gave the image a strangely hermaphroditic character. Was there any deeper meaning to the fact that I—the original "head" of the Skordylis idea—had now been relegated to the foot? I wondered if I would ever have the courage to confront Diana about such a seemingly trivial detail.

"I can see from our chairman's expression," for an instant D_3 touched Harold Levenson on his shoulder in a calming, almost ethereal gesture, "that he thinks I have just made a joke in questionable taste." Once more she glanced at him, but his grim face stared straight ahead into the audience. "Harold," she said more forcefully, waiting until he finally looked up at her, "you are mistaken on both counts." She waited for the collective murmur to subside. "There is no proper way to reproduce Diana Skordylis visually without showing four individual photographs. Yet these would be ill-suited, because they would not do justice to the mind behind the invention of PCR. A mind, I want to say first, that is over 250 years old." She paused again; I heard the murmur behind her fall away, then start to rise again.

She cut it off. "The four brains behind this figure called 'Diana Skordylis' belong to one woman and three men—each beyond the age of sixty, and all but one virtually retired because of their institution's regulations.

"Believing that they still had much to offer to a scientific world that was starting to reject their gifts, they decided to work collectively—*and anonymously*—under the name of Diana Skordylis. The intended lesson—at least as I understand it," and here she looked into the camera, addressing the four absent honorees, "was to demonstrate that the individual is *not* what matters: it is the *work*, not the character, shape, gender, or physiognomy, of the scientist. In science—true science, that is—the pursuit of truth is what matters. And so it should be in the institutions that exist, finally, to serve science: in our research academies and in the foundations that support and honor scientific research. If it is otherwise, then you do no honor to the person or your Foundation. I conclude by pointing out that this year's prize has given you an opportunity to do both: to focus solely on the work by offering half the award to Diana Skordylis, who has chosen to remain anonymous; and to recognize a scientist in person, by including my granddaughter." Diana gave an intimation of a bow, as if she were finished. The initial applause demonstrated that Diana had carried the evening. But then she raised her hand once more. She was not finished.

"Harold," she said to the chairman, who had risen uncertainly during the first scattering of applause. "May I request your indulgence for a few more minutes?" She waited for him to sit before continuing.

"Please do not misunderstand." Again she stopped, this time looking first at Harold Levenson and then at the rest of the Levenson board on either side of her. "This is not to upstage or in any way criticize your program. There is a foundation—specifically the John D. and Catherine T. MacArthur Foundation—that makes special grants to older creative persons, frequently above the age of seventy, to indicate its confidence that persons in that age group—like the Skordylis four—are still full of creative power. But these, like all other prizes, recognize creativity by focusing on the individual rather than on the work. Tonight,

I would like to express the wish that on occasion the situation might be reversed. I am not certain whether such an ideal is truly realizable among a group of scientists, for whom individual recognition generally counts for so much. After all, even the Levenson Foundation has, until today, contributed—at least indirectly—to such personal ambition. Let us hope that on some future occasion, another Skordylis might win a Levenson Prize. I thank you for your attention."

Charlea pressed the button on the remote control.

"Wait!" I exclaimed. "They aren't finished yet."

"They are as far as Diana Skordylis is concerned." C3 turned to me, eyes slightly narrowed, an unreadable expression on her face. "Some woman—that Diana of yours."

24

"Don't feel too bad, Max," Diana said to me a couple of days after the Levenson dinner. "Skordylis has been as successful as you had wished; even more so. No one but the insiders know what didn't work. And if nothing else, there's always PCR. Didn't you tell me it'll change biomedical research for years to come?"

"That's fine," I said distractedly. "I'm thinking more personally than that, I'm afraid: I don't know what *I'm* going to do next."

That's what it was. Diana Skordylis had been the answer to that question ever since, ages ago, it seemed, I had broached my plan to Diana. Skordylis had been a shield for me, I realized, something I'd held up between me and the deans of the world, an identity I had far preferred to "Senior Research Biochemist" or even to "Emeritus Professor." Now that shield was gone. "I simply don't know what to do," I said.

"Is that all?" she asked.

No, that wasn't all. And it wasn't the future that worried me either, I realized. With a cold brush on my spine I realized that the time had come to admit to her that I understood some of what Sepp had done.

"God help me, Diana," I said. "I want some of the credit."

"For?"

"PCR. I didn't come up with the initial idea, but some of the work was mine. Just think of some of the applications . . ." I smiled ironically. Not so long ago, I had resented Diana's question, "Is it useful?" And now I was keeping some of the most useful applications to myself. "It was a wonderful project, an important one, and, I'm afraid . . ." I trailed off.

"It will be your last?" Diana touched the back of my hand. "Wait a year or two, Max. You have time." She smiled gently. "Believe me. There will be more ideas. And in the meantime, the four of you can take out an ad in *Nature* or *Science*. Let the world know the identity of the brains behind Diana Skordylis."

I laughed. "I like the idea. It would be funny. Or maybe tragicomic. But that's not exactly how public relations works in science."

"Why?"

"Because, among many other reasons, it would be too late. By the time such an ad could run, hundreds of papers will have carried references to the two original articles in *Nature*—by Skordylis and Powers. 'Skordylis, D.' cannot now be excised from the scientific literature. And even if we did claim credit in this novel way, it would be a futile gesture—PCR's no road to immortality. New techniques aren't like new theories: a theory is often named after its originator, but when a technique becomes a standard tool in a scientist's kit, it soon becomes public domain, even though the creator may win an award or two." Or more, I added silently. "Nobody knows who invented the hammer. And nobody bothers to recall who came up with HPLC. Or TLC. Even ESR—"

"Whoa, Max! HPLC?"

"High performance liquid chromatography, thin-layer chromatography, electron spin resonance. I myself don't remember the names of any of the people behind these discoveries. Nobody refers to them anymore. Yet all these discoveries were made during my professional lifetime. TLC and HPLC are used routinely in my lab—probably right now, today. So we might as well let Diana Skordylis keep her laurels—before they wilt." I held my hands out, palms up, fingers spread: how things slip through one's grasp.

She took my hand and clasped them in hers—a gesture I was now accustomed to, and welcomed. It was usually a preamble to something reassuring. "Max, I have two proposals."

"Yes?"

"How about forming another Skordylis?"

That wasn't what I had expected. Emphatically, I shook my head. "You know it won't work. You said it yourself. It was a noble experiment, but I'm now convinced it isn't doable in science. Maybe because 'noble' is usually spelled 'Nobel.' What's the other proposal?"

"Are you lonely, Max?"

"That's a question, not a proposal."

"I know that. One thing at a time. First a question, then the second proposal. Are you lonely?"

"You asked me that once before," I reminded her.

"Do you remember what you answered, back in Princeton?"

"That I only felt lonely when I permitted myself to think about it."

She gave me a searching look. "Well then: will you permit yourself?"

"I suppose I can, when I'm not busy working, but—"

"Max," she interrupted, plainly impatient with me now. "I'm suggesting we get married."

I'm sure my face turned crimson. From a distance, I heard myself say, first "We?" then "Why?" and finally, simply, "When?"

"New Year's Eve. And if the next question is 'Where?' the answer is 'right here.' But you must wear your galoshes, Max. You can't get married in wet feet." She reached over and tousled my hair.

I was regaining my senses. "We can't get married. You're—"

Diana did not let me continue. One of her hands was clapped tightly around my mouth, while the other cupped my chin. It's **223** lucky she did that, because I wouldn't have known how to continue. "Too old?" In many respects Diana was at least a decade younger than I—maybe more. Is that why she'd told me about Diane de Poitiers and Marguerite Duras?

"Don't be a fool, Max. Neither one of us has an unlimited amount of time." Had she been reading my mind? "Historians are storytellers, which makes them good conversationalists. Scientists are mostly lecturers: they instruct, analyze, argue, and even turn into preachers. You are a bit of an exception."

To my amazement, I found that even at such an intimate moment my mind could operate on two simultaneous tracks. While wondering how I should respond—no one had ever before proposed to me, and surely no one ever would do so again—I remembered Jakob Krzilska's question: "What do you think of yourself?" I must ask Diana for help, I thought. To tell me why I am an exception. But this was not the moment, not with her hand on my mouth.

"Let us enjoy what's left in company and in style," she said. "You aren't a pauper. You may not be drinking Pètrus every day, but I don't see you sipping jug wine. Your clothes are not threadbare—though rather conservative, I'll admit. You have been known to winter in one of the fanciest resorts in the Caribbean . . ." She released my mouth and stepped back, a marvelously warm look in her eyes. "Max, what we both need is TLC. Not your type, but the real stuff."

That's when we kissed.

We didn't send announcements to many people, and those we sent stipulated no wedding presents. Only two chose to disobey. The first was Hiroshi, who sent an exquisite brush painting made by his wife. The calligraphy, of course, meant nothing to us until Diana opened the accompanying envelope. The card read only: *"My wife's painting illustrates a Moritake haikai of the 16th century. I thought of it when I learned of your marriage: 'A fallen blossom / returning to the bough, I thought— / but no, a butterfly.'"*

I was the other exception. It took me a long time to come up with the right gift. I browsed in numerous midtown Manhattan establishments until I found precisely what I wanted: a small eighteenth-century wooden box, the grain like that of a Stradivarius violin, exquisitely finished and lined in red velvet. It was in mint condition and also cost a mint, but I hardly noticed: it was, after all, only the container of my real gift.

"Do you have any antique phials?" I asked the owner. "To fit into this box. Two matched ones." It was important that they be antique.

"For perfume?"

I shook my head. "No, no liquids."

He had nothing suitable, but at another dealer's, down in the Village, I found two just the right size. He guaranteed to have them inscribed in time for the wedding.

I am not a good wrapper of gifts. Besides, I didn't want this box wrapped in paper. Red velvet occurred to me, a rich, deep red to match the lining of the box. The dealer promised to come up with a small velvet sack with a plush drawstring.

The ceremony was arranged for late afternoon of December 31, in Diana's living room, in front of the fireplace, not too far from where I'd unthawed my frozen feet four years earlier. It was the smallest wedding possible: a judge and two witnesses, Charlea and Jocelyn. The latter had flown in only the day before from Vienna, where she'd spent Christmas with Jakob Krzilska. The judge, a comparatively young man in his early fifties, seemed taken aback when Diana announced, "Max is bound to be my last husband. For once I am marrying a younger man."

Diana's winter-white gabardine pantsuit, with wide trouser legs just breaking over her champagne-colored boots and a fingertip-length jacket—a rather androgynous ensemble—elegantly delineated her slim body. This afternoon, her dyed black hair was pulled back tightly into a bun, which made her look even younger since it called attention to the smooth skin of her face. A brown, black, and chartreuse scarf was tied loosely around her neck. Her neck, I realized, seemed always to be covered: on the beach, in a dinner dress, in this wedding suit. Did that serve to hide some of the years?

That's when it dawned on me that I still didn't know my bride's precise age. The occasional hints ("you don't mind, Max, that I've dyed my hair for years, do you?"); the allusion to a French plastic surgeon; my sporadic calculations (based, for instance, on Jocelyn's age—a fixed point of reference—and then working backward through plausible intervals between mother and grandmother); all these loose pieces of evidence pointed toward the early seventies. Or more? I concluded that at my age, such subtleties were not important. Besides, I couldn't possibly ask just a few minutes before our wedding, "By the way Diana, how old are you precisely?" I decided it could wait.

After the ceremony and the toasts, the judge departed and the four of us went out to a private wedding supper at an Italian place, the Ristorante Serbelloni, in homage to our Italian sojourn. We had never gone to Italian restaurants on the occasions we had dined out in Manhattan. So I wanted to be different, yet also appealing. Like a new, third husband.

The entire evening resembled the lemon soufflé we had as a coda to our feast—a delicate marriage of the sweet and tart.

Sipping her espresso, Charlea paid me a typically tart Conway compliment.

"Diana, when I first met Max in Washington, I couldn't possibly see how one could live with him. Work with him? Yes. But live?" She grinned affectionately at my wife. "But you brought something out in him that's made me change my mind."

"Someday, I'd like to meet your companion," responded D₃.

"You will. She's curious about you. And even you, Max," she winked.

We raised our glasses. "To Diana Skordylis," toasted Diana, "who brought us together. And without whom Joss would never have met Jakob Krzilska. Shall we tell them, Joss?"

"You tell them," Jocelyn said. It was the first time I'd seen her blush.

"Couples don't seem to get engaged anymore, it seems," said D₃, "at least not in this country. But apparently they do in Vienna."

Before I could even toast her, Jocelyn motioned with her glass toward me. "What do I call you now, 'Grandpa Max'?"

"Just call me Max," I said and clinked her glass.

We were back in "our" apartment—at least that's what Diana called it as the two of us, finally alone, stood by the window staring out at the skyline beyond the dark foreground of Central Park. Diana's pearl, a full moon, hung in the sky. It dawned on me that this was a true *blue* moon: the *second* full moon of this month. I thought it was time to present my gift. "Here," I said, opening the drawer of the side table where I'd secreted the small velvet bag, "this gift is for my wife."

"Max," Diana exclaimed, shaking her index finger, "we'd agreed there would be no presents. They're too possessive. It's how we keep a hold on other people."

"You're right," I said, "but this, my dear, is special. Why don't you look at it?"

We sat down on chairs next to a table lamp. Diana was like a little girl, feeling the velvet bag without opening it, to prolong the pleasure of the surprise. "A small box?"

"You're getting warm."

She pulled the drawstring apart and removed the box. Under the lamp, the polished wood gave back the light, every detail of the grain clearly visible. "How do you open it?" she asked, finding it locked.

"There are two keys in the bag, one for each of us."

"Here," she exclaimed as she felt inside the bag. And then she opened the box.

I saw her frown, not angrily, but with puzzlement. She picked up one of the small crystal phials, filled to the brim with a white powder. It was the one marked "HIS." For an instant, she studied the word as if it were a sentence in some foreign tongue.

She picked up "HERS," and held it to the light. The crystal flashed once, brightly. "Max, my love . . ." Diana started, and then stopped. "Is it really cyanide?"

I placed my hand over hers, simultaneously covering the two

containers. "Read this," I whispered and lifted the small card from the bottom of the box.

> *But suicides have a special language.*
> *Like carpenters they want to know* which tools.
> *They never ask* why build.

She looked up, tears filling her eyes. "My love, I would never have thought that someone would have the courage to give such a gift."

"My dear," I replied. "It's a gift for both of us—or perhaps just a placebo. Now put it back and lock the box. And remember: I have the only other key."

It was after midnight—a new day, a new year. I don't know how long I'd been standing there, thinking of all that had happened during the past four years, when I heard Diana's voice in the background.

"Why, Max," she sang out, "you're still there, fully dressed. Aren't you coming to bed?"

I turned to see Diana by the door, in a white silk peignoir that reached down to her ankles. Her feet were bare. Standing by the window I had forgotten that I was a new groom on my wedding night. Suddenly I panicked. I'd been celibate for years. I had never been to bed with any woman but Nedra. And now I was expected by one, older than I—how many years older I didn't even know.

Diana walked toward me. She was only a foot or two away when she caught my expression. She reached out to take my hand. "Come, my love. You needn't be afraid."

New Year's morning, Diana woke up sometime before me. A gentle touch to my cheeks made me open my eyes. It was my wife, wide awake, in another peignoir—this one a light peach, her favorite color—sitting on my side of the bed.

"Maxi," she said, using a name I'd never heard before we'd gone to bed last night, "do you want breakfast in bed or in the living room by the window?"

228 "Over there," I replied after kissing her, "but what's the hurry?"

"Your new wife wants to spoil you. Just tell me what you want."

"I'll help," I offered.

"Stay in bed until I call you. Besides, I've already got most of it under way. And I want us to eat our first connubial breakfast in style. So what will you have?"

I was tempted to ask for eggs Benedict and a double cappuccino in honor of the occasion, but out of spousal loyalty I proposed half a grapefruit, one toasted English muffin with margarine, orange marmalade, and black coffee. It was the sort of breakfast I'd seen Diana have on numerous occasions, except that she seemed to prefer toast.

I must have dozed off again, because a second "Maxi" rang in my ears. "It's time for nourishment."

I put on the new silk robe I'd found last night next to my silk pajamas. "Don't be silly, Max," she'd said when I'd reminded her about "no gifts." This was before I'd turned into Maxi. "These don't count as *gifts*. These are *necessities*—like your phials and keys."

Diana had set a spectacularly formal table with an overabundance of silver accoutrements. Considering the rather ascetic breakfast I'd ordered, I took it as homage to the occasion. I was pleased to see that I'd guessed right: two silver bowls, filled with ice—each containing half a segmented grapefruit in a glass dish—were waiting for us.

"Shall we start with the grapefruit or have it later?" she asked as she destroyed the origami construction of her starched napkin by covering her lap.

"Later, I guess." I'd been admiring the two large silver domes covering what I presumed to be my English muffin and Diana's toast. In spite of the heavy silver, I suspected that my muffin would have been cold by the time I'd finished with the grapefruit. But I was certainly not going to gobble it down in haste on the morning after my wedding night.

"Fine," she replied and moved the two covered dishes in front of us. I poured the coffee.

"And now Maxi," she reached over to squeeze my hand, "we'll have our first married breakfast, just *entre nous*."

I was about to lift my silver dome when I realized that Diana's was almost twice the size of mine. Was she having a double order of toast? "Let me help you, my dear," I said, grasping the knob and lifting her cover. I nearly dropped it when I saw Diana's plate: a small steak, covered by a lightly fried egg, hash browns, and two broiled tomatoes.

My wife must have missed the expression on my face, because she'd been reaching over to the serving cart. Lifting a smaller dome, she took a brioche and proceeded to butter it. I was certain it was butter because my small margarine balls lacked the swirly curls I saw on her dish.

In every corner of the world, on every subject under the sun, Penguin represents quality and variety—the very best in publishing today.

For complete information about books available from Penguin—including Puffins, Penguin Classics, and Arkana—and how to order them, write to us at the appropriate address below. Please note that for copyright reasons the selection of books varies from country to country.

In the United Kingdom: Please write to *Dept. JC, Penguin Books Ltd, FREEPOST, West Drayton, Middlesex UB7 0BR.*

If you have any difficulty in obtaining a title, please send your order with the correct money, plus ten percent for postage and packaging, to *P.O. Box No. 11, West Drayton, Middlesex UB7 0BR*

In the United States: Please write to *Consumer Sales, Penguin USA, P.O. Box 999, Dept. 17109, Bergenfield, New Jersey 07621-0120.* VISA and MasterCard holders call 1-800-253-6476 to order all Penguin titles

In Canada: Please write to *Penguin Books Canada Ltd, 10 Alcorn Avenue, Suite 300, Toronto, Ontario M4V 3B2*

In Australia: Please write to *Penguin Books Australia Ltd, P.O. Box 257, Ringwood, Victoria 3134*

In New Zealand: Please write to *Penguin Books (NZ) Ltd, Private Bag 102902, North Shore Mail Centre, Auckland 10*

In India: Please write to *Penguin Books India Pvt Ltd, 706 Eros Apartments, 56 Nehru Place, New Delhi 110 019*

In the Netherlands: Please write to *Penguin Books Netherlands bv, Postbus 3507, NL-1001 AH Amsterdam*

In Germany: Please write to *Penguin Books Deutschland GmbH, Metzlerstrasse 26, 60594 Frankfurt am Main*

In Spain: Please write to *Penguin Books S. A., Bravo Murillo 19, 1° B, 28015 Madrid*

In Italy: Please write to *Penguin Italia s.r.l., Via Felice Casati 20, I-20124 Milano*

In France: Please write to *Penguin France S. A., 17 rue Lejeune, F-31000 Toulouse*

In Japan: Please write to *Penguin Books Japan, Ishikiribashi Building, 2-5-4, Suido, Bunkyo-ku, Tokyo 112*

In Greece: Please write to *Penguin Hellas Ltd, Dimocritou 3, GR-106 71 Athens*

In South Africa: Please write to *Longman Penguin Southern Africa (Pty) Ltd, Private Bag X08, Bertsham 2013*